THE
FRACTURED
WOMAN

THE
FRACTURED
WOMAN

NATALIE LAHARNAR

BOUNTY
AT PLAY

First published in Australia in 2026

This is a work of fiction. All characters are fictional. Liberties have been
taken with some actual places.

Self-published by Natalie Laharnar operating as Bounty at Play
ABN 52 231 824 224

 A catalogue record for this
book is available from the
NATIONAL
LIBRARY
OF AUSTRALIA National Library of Australia

ISBN 978-1-7641522-1-1 (paperback)
ISBN 978-1-7641522-0-4 (ebook)

Cover design by Claire Smith, BookSmith Design
Bounty at Play logo design by Stuart Hipwell
Author photograph by David Madden Photography
Text design by Simon Paterson, Bookhouse
Typeset in 11/16 pt Minion Pro by Bookhouse, Sydney

Connect with the author on LinkedIn
linkedin.com/in/natalielaharnar

TO BOUNTY

who lives on in our memories
and in some small part through the character of Hercules

Black clouds hang low over the menacing sea as a vein of silver light pierces the dark afternoon. The sea heaves in anger. It is answered by a deafening thunder crack, its fury disturbing the residents of the grave site on the cliff. Five wispy spirits whoosh around headstones in figures of eight. As the wind howls through the stone-lined corridors, someone watches from the ghostly sandstone mansion on the hill that is shrouded in an eerie brown light.

৹৵৹

Chapter 1

Edith is agitated as her young housemate gazes out the window. Jaclyn has been nothing but trouble since she moved in with a battered suitcase and a bossy attitude. The incessant Sunday dinners she hosts with guests dressing up in silly colonial outfits are the final straw.

And what is she staring at while these strangers are left unattended?

I've had it with her. She can't impose these people on me. This is my house.

Without warning, Jaclyn pulls the floor-length red velvet curtains together, blocking out any of the natural light, though it is already dimming from the time of day and the approaching storm. Edith feels her annoyance rise as Jaclyn fusses around the long wooden table spread with mutton stew, pickled pork and Irish soda bread, along with a full silver service and goblets for wine and rum. She finds solace in the glow of the log fire and the candlelight from a candelabra on the table and a chandelier hanging from the high ceiling. Taking a drag of her cigarette, Edith notices her housemate check her black linen and lace gown as it catches on the timber floor. Jaclyn turns and glares at her with eyes so cold they could freeze the warmest heart. Edith shudders.

'Why do you dress like such a cliché, old lady? You might look younger if you tried the colonial look.'

What is wrong with my blouse and pleated skirt? It is good enough for church.

Edith wants to tell Jaclyn her vampirish make-up and all-black look is anything but appealing, especially on someone so young who should be vibrant and full of life. But that would make her as mean as her housemate, and even though she doesn't know these people, she doesn't want them to think she could stoop that low.

'I would ask that you show me some respect in front of guests.'

'Edith, I'm sorry.' Edith notices a warmth return to Jaclyn's eyes. 'You look just fine. Come and sit down. Our guests are waiting.'

I can't bear that food. It's my house. I should be able to eat what I want.

'I'm not really hungry.'

'Please excuse Edith. She's having a bad day,' Jaclyn announces, but the guests appear not to hear her.

'Who is that woman and what are those strange clothes she's wearing?' says a man dressed like a colonial gentleman in a stiff white shirt and cravat, sitting at the head of the table. He seems to be pointing at Edith.

'What's he talking about?' Edith barks at Jaclyn, avoiding the man's gaze. She takes another deliberate drag on her cigarette and faces the fire in protest.

I should be asking who they are.

'Please, don't mind her. She's gone a little loopy,' Jaclyn says.

That's the pot calling the kettle black.

Edith faces Jaclyn again. 'You shouldn't talk about me like that in my house.'

'What does she mean *her* house?' the gentleman asks a woman sitting to his left. She's in her thirties, wearing a white linen and lace night gown.

'Don't worry about Edith,' Jaclyn says, walking around the table offering bread for the stew. 'She hasn't been the same since the fire.'

A flame in the fireplace flares and sizzles like it is talking to Edith. *What fire?*

'Jaclyn, I was never in any fire.'

I wish everyone would just get out and leave me alone.

5

'Edith, if you don't want to join the dinner, I suggest you go up to your room.'

How dare she? Now Edith's blood is boiling. Suddenly she doesn't care about what the strangers think of her. She walks over to the table and stubs her cigarette into the end of a small bread loaf. It is an act of defiance, and it feels good.

'Silly old woman,' Jaclyn says.

'You're one to call me silly. Look at the way you're leering at your friends.'

Jaclyn stands away from the others. Edith has never seen her eat, even when they're alone in the house. At the dinners, Jaclyn seems to derive a sexual pleasure from observing her guests gorge themselves as though they have starved for a hundred winters. It disgusts Edith.

A man busting out of his breeches, true to a character Edith saw in a history book once, slops stew into his mouth with one hand and takes a bite of bread from the other. The gravy drips down his beard and onto his grubby white ruffled shirt as he concentrates on the meal.

A couple dressed as convicts giggle and blush on the other side of the table. The woman, about 25, has a white frilly bonnet and is very pale with sunken eyes and a dark bruise encircling her neck. The man, whose striped shirt is torn and dirty, whispers something in her ear that makes her laugh. They only have eyes for each other. Suddenly

Edith feels like an intruder in her own home. She has no right to be witnessing this intimate moment. Such a moral notion does not seem to occur to Jaclyn, who is looking at the couple with a look of . . . lust?

'I have something very special for dessert,' Jaclyn announces as she disappears into the kitchen.

Still the guests ignore Jaclyn. Edith wonders if dessert might be something she could eat. *Pavlova*. The white meringue dessert piled high with dense whipped cream and ripe strawberries and raspberries sits on a nobbled timber bench in the stone-walled kitchen. Jaclyn takes the large knife Edith saw her sharpening that morning and slowly slices through the berries, cream and crunchy meringue. Jaclyn flinches. 'It's nothing,' she mumbles to herself. Edith wonders what is wrong with her. Jaclyn seems to be unaware of her presence, meticulously cutting five equal slices and placing each on glass cake plates. She brushes right past Edith as she takes the plates out, holding the door with her hip. But alas, all the guests have gone. The room is cold.

Jaclyn drops the plates, sending cream and meringue flying. Berries splatter her dress.

'Edith, I know you did this,' she yells. 'Somehow you always scare the guests away.'

Edith doesn't feel any need to answer. A window clatters against the frame.

'You are so annoying, old lady.'

Edith shrugs.

'I was sure I closed this.' Jaclyn opens the faded curtains.

Sleet carried by the autumn wind flies into her face. She pulls the window shut and restores the latch. She tugs on each of the curtains to close them with a sense of desperation.

'Edith, come here and tell me what you've done. What did you say to make them leave? Why did you open the window?'

Edith is silent. Jaclyn is screaming.

'Edith, you will pay for this.'

Edith looks down at the cigarette in her hand. She cannot remember lighting it. 'What will you do to me?'

Jaclyn sits on one of the old dining chairs and stares at the table. 'I will think of something.'

Edith has had enough and finds herself in the sitting room on the first floor, her favourite room in the house.

She hears a shrill 'Ediiiiith' from the ground floor.

⚭

Edith's footfall does not disturb Jaclyn as she sleeps in the four-poster bed. She watches her, moves within a breath away and Jaclyn trembles. Jaclyn's breathing is uneven, her face distorted in a scowl. Edith is secretly happy that peace does not come to Jaclyn in her slumber. There is satisfaction in believing she might be in a living hell. Edith moves from room to room of her mansion, surveying the fireplaces, the antique furniture, the portraits of her ancestors. She must get that horrid woman out of her beloved Seaview Manor.

Chapter 2

There is a low hum from students milling around the cloisters of the University of Sydney's quadrangle as Mary White walks along the wide stone path that divides the perfectly manicured lawns bathed in sunshine. The smell of newly cut grass exhilarates her being. Suddenly she wants to feel the soft and springy turf under her feet and take in the magnificence of the neo-Gothic structure.

Each of the four lawns is cordoned off with rope to keep people out, but Mary notices students sitting near the famous jacaranda tree in the corner. She gives herself permission to ignore the temporary boundary even though her late mother is in her head, telling her breaking rules has consequences. She slips off her flat shoes and places them on top of a bag of library books. As she lifts the white rope to walk under it, a loud 'caw caw' reproaches her. Mary sees a black crow perched on a gargoyle popping out of the masonry directly in front of her. The stone figure is scowling at her. Suddenly the hairs stand on the back of her neck. Sensing eyes on her, she spins around to see who's watching her. An official-looking woman is striding through the middle of the quad with purpose in her step. She doesn't look at Mary.

Oh, I am just a bit jumpy! Must have been that call from the strange man at the weekend. Could he be following me?

Tuesday is normally a bright spot in Mary's week. She times her visit to the university's main library for lunchtime to drop off interlibrary loans and pick up returns. This gives her time to walk around the quad and have the curried egg sandwich she brought from home. Today she is rattled. Even the egg filling in her sandwich tastes off. Feeling a sense of dread, she throws the second half of her lunch in the bin and heads back to Macquarie Street and the safety of her desk at the city's main library.

☙

Mary works diligently, answering phone calls and emails, cataloguing books, filing. Her job as library assistant is not taxing, and the mundane tasks become like meditation. Her mind goes back to the eerie feeling at the university and the strange caller from the weekend. She sees herself in the recliner in her cosy lounge room, a heavy antique handset to her ear. Silence, then someone clears their throat.

'Mary White?' A male voice falters on her last name.

'Yes. Who is this?'

'Was your mother's name Isabel White?'

'Who is speaking please?'

'I really need to tell you in person. Do you still like hot chocolate? Could we meet at the chocolate shop or the café opposite?'

'I'm sorry sir, I don't know who you are, and I shall have to end this conversation if you don't identify yourself.'

'Please let me explain.'

'No. If you call again, I will contact the police.' She drops the handset on the brass cradle.

The sound of her name brings her back to reality. Her colleague, Andrew, is trying to get her attention. He tells her about a woman who claims she's being blocked from seeing her elderly aunt by the aunt's housemate.

Andrew turns the monitor towards Mary. 'Look at the house. It's like that Gothic architecture you love so much.'

Mary's eyes are drawn to the photo of the grand sandstone house. It has an eerie beauty. Obviously, time has taken its toll; there are vines growing over the house and broken glass in the pointed arch windows, but she knows how magnificent it once was. She looks at the head-and-shoulders photo of the elderly lady and is moved by the sadness in her eyes.

I guess some people have worse troubles than mine.

'Can we speak about something else?' Mary asks. 'Like when you'll come on the tour of Government House with me, or better still a ghost tour at The Rocks. I would love to inspect the colonial buildings more closely.'

'You want to go on a ghost tour to see the buildings?'

'Yeah, I don't believe in ghosts, although today I felt like someone was watching me at the uni. Maybe it was a ghost.'

'You thought someone was watching you?'

'Urgh. I don't feel well.'

Mary runs to the bathroom. She makes it to a cubicle, lifts the inner seat and waits for the involuntary heaving.

'Blah.' Her breakfast and lunch leave her in waves.

She is transported to her childhood when children were tormenting her about her weight. She was about four.

'You're so fat you need a crane to pick you up.' She remembers hearing the chant, running to the toilet and vomiting.

She has had a recurring image of the vision, and it is strange because it doesn't seem to be at a preschool or day care. It is a dark place with rows of beds.

When she walks back into the corridor, Andrew is waiting.

'Are you all right?'

'I think it was my lunch. It did taste strange at the time. I'll be okay in a few minutes.'

'You look really pale. All the blood has run from your face.'

'I'm okay.'

'I'll call you a cab to take you home.'

'I'm fine. I need to get back to work or Jodi-Ann will be angry.'

When their temporary boss appears less than a minute later, Mary thinks that maybe she has placed a camera over their desks. It wasn't the first time she came cruising by their pod for no apparent reason since being hired on a short-term contract.

'Andrew, are you working or daydreaming?'

'Mary isn't feeling well. I was making sure . . . er, um . . . under my duty of care, that she's all right.'

The short manager walks next to Mary's desk and hovers beside her. She puts her hand under Mary's chin and turns her face towards her.

Mary shudders. She has been transported to when she was six or seven and her mother was holding her face, reprimanding her. She hopes Jodi-Ann hasn't felt her repulsion.

'You do look pale. But my policy is if you come to work, you work. Otherwise, stay home. There's no place for martyrs here.'

'Yes ma'am.'

'Jodi-Ann, I think she should go home,' Andrew says.

'Mary, do you need to leave?'

'I'm fine, really.'

'Then we can all get back to work.'

Once Jodi-Ann is out of sight, Mary feels another wave of nausea and runs for the bathroom. Andrew follows her into the ladies. Mary doesn't make it to the toilet and heaves on the grey tiles. She runs over to the paper towel dispenser and pulls several out. Andrew walks up behind her and gently takes them from her.

'I'll clean this up while you wash your face.'

Mary is surprised by his presence. Her mother's voice is saying he should not be in the ladies' bathroom and that she should clean the mess quickly before anyone else witnesses her shame. But in some strange way Andrew is taking the shame out of this incident as she watches him wipe up her bile. The nausea has evaporated.

Maybe I'm not alone!

Mary closes her eyes to savour the moment. She feels firm hands on her shoulders and opens her eyes. Andrew drops his hands by his side and steps back.

'What are you doing?' Mary says, looking at him behind her in the mirror.

'I thought you were going to collapse. You're still so pale.'

'We better get back to work.'

'You should go to the medical centre.'

'I'm okay now. Truly. Thank you for your help.'

'I did what any decent person would have done.'

Andrew pulls a few more pieces of paper towel from the metal dispenser. 'Here, in case you have another episode. I'll go to the storeroom and get a bucket too. You can never be too careful.'

Mary laughs. Perhaps it's a nervous reaction. Andrew responds with a hearty chortle. Jodi-Ann walks by as they leave the bathroom together.

'What is going on here? Both of you, in my office. Now.'

'Jodi-Ann, please. Mary has been sick again.'

'This looks highly suspicious. I expect a full explanation.'

Jodi-Ann marches off, her nose pointed in the air.

'What is she going to do to us?' Mary says.

'Once we explain the situation, it'll be fine.'

They follow their boss, and she turns around to face them when they are in the middle of the open plan office.

'It won't do any good to talk to you together. Mary, I want to see you first. Andrew, go back to your workstation until I call for you. You are not to leave your desk until then, is that clear?'

'It's clear.'

Jodi-Ann turns around and Mary looks apologetically at Andrew.

He mouths, 'It will be okay.'

Jodi-Ann sits behind her desk. 'Shut the door behind you, Mary.'

Mary's hand shakes as she closes the door. She fights another bout of nausea and wills it to leave her.

'Sit down, Mary,' Jodi-Ann snaps, 'and tell me what was happening in the ladies' toilets just now.'

Mary grabs hold of the arm of the cloth office chair to steady herself and remains standing. She wonders why she is so nervous when she has done nothing wrong.

'Well?' Jodi-Ann's accusing tone pervades every word.

'I was sick again, and Andrew was helping me.'

'Mary, why do you bother to cover for that man? He is trouble. Hopeless at his job and a distraction to others.'

'Andrew is . . .'

Mary wants to say many things in Andrew's defence, but Jodi-Ann is staring her down. Fighting the fear and struggling to find her voice, Mary stands up straight with her shoulders back and holds herself firm as she enunciates her words slowly and deliberately in a low, commanding voice.

'I knew I was going to throw up, so I ran to the bathroom. I was too late and was sick all over the floor. Andrew cleaned it up. Those are the facts.'

Mary is surprised by the power in her own voice. She doesn't know where the deep, dark voice came from. Judging by the shocked look on Jodi-Ann's face, her boss wasn't expecting it either.

Jodi-Ann says nothing, and Mary feels strengthened by her silence.

'If that is all, I shall get my things together and go home,' Mary says in her normal voice. 'I wouldn't want to throw up over books the taxpayers have paid for.'

'Yes, of course. Close the door after you. Tell Andrew I am satisfied with your explanation.'

Mary nods and walks out the door. She is a few steps away from Jodi-Ann's office when she bursts into tears, losing her connection to whatever power she was tapping into. As she walks to her desk, she receives a lot of pats with 'Are you all right?' and 'She's such a bitch, isn't she?'

Mary wants to pick up her bag and get on a train for home. Get as far from this place as possible.

Andrew has a worried look on his face. 'Have you been crying?'

'I'm fine. Jodi-Ann said you don't have to see her. She's happy with my explanation.'

'Okay. But you don't look well.'

Mary packs up her bag.

'I'll come with you.' Andrew starts packing things into his satchel.

'I said I'll be fine.'

'Here is my mobile number if you ever need it.'

Andrew hands Mary a piece of paper. She pushes her hand into her coat pocket and drops the note inside.

'I'm feeling much better. You should have seen me in there with Jodi-Ann. For a few seconds I found a strength in me I didn't know I had.'

'You better go. Call me if you need anything. Anything.'

Mary smiles. She sees a warmth in Andrew's face that reminds her of her cat, Hercules, lying on his back on her bed in a spot where the sun is streaming in. She pulls her awareness back to the present moment and hurries out.

Chapter 3

Edith watches Jaclyn surveying herself in the gild edge mirror and brushing her long hair, which shines blue-black like a crow's feathers. Jaclyn bends down to open the antique cabinet and runs her hands along dozens of lipsticks. She studies them, picks one.

'Yes, I think this is it. No. 155 Seductress,' Jaclyn says and snaps off the lid to compare the shade with her turtle-neck cashmere top and red patent stilettos.

'I've always wondered why you dress like a business executive to go to university,' Edith says.

Jaclyn looks behind her. Edith takes a drag on her cigarette.

'At least I change my clothes.' Jaclyn turns back to the mirror and applies the lipstick.

'That's the wrong shade,' Edith says, smiling to herself.

Jaclyn looks in the mirror and pulls her top to her face. She applies more colour, then reaches for another lipstick, then another.

Oh, this is ridiculous, Edith thinks.

A sudden gust of air causes the lipsticks to fall to the floor like cylindrical dominoes.

Surely, I couldn't have done that with my mind?

Frantically, Jaclyn checks the bottoms of each one. She pulls one lid off, unscrews the round solid cosmetic, throws the lid and container on the floor and picks up another one, does the same and then throws it down. She is frenzied in her search for the lipstick, but none is right. Finally, she sits in the middle of the pile, puts her head down and cries.

For heaven's sake.

Edith wills the No. 155 Seductress lipstick to roll from outside the circle towards Jaclyn and stop. This time Edith doesn't question her sudden mind-over-matter power. She is glad it worked.

'There it is.' Jaclyn smiles, then stands, wipes her lipstick off with a tissue and applies the one in her hand.

Jaclyn dusts pale powder over her face to make her skin look bleached. She takes one of a dozen eyeshadows in a dark grey and then applies black mascara over and over to create long curved lashes adorning her big dark eyes.

As Jaclyn surveys her slim figure from head to toe in the long cheval mirror in the corner, Edith hears a creak in the glass that becomes a crack. Then another, and another. Lines spread through the oval glass like spidery veins, making a crackling sound. Entranced, Edith watches Jaclyn's image split hundreds of ways. Blood starts to flow from the cracks and stream down the mirror. Jaclyn does not move.

Edith wonders what is happening.

There is a crashing sound, like something collapsing upstairs, and Edith follows Jaclyn into the hall and up the stairs to the small landing on the first floor.

Crash!

The sound has come from Edith's bedroom. They both walk a few steps up the red-carpet runner. Another crash. Something heavy hits the ground. Edith stands beside Jaclyn in the doorway of her room. The 19th-century dresser has been overturned. The century-old floral jug and bowl are smashed into hundreds of pieces. The four-poster bed looks as though a cement block dropped from a great height and fell through the base, causing all four pillars to collapse into the middle. Only a heavy cedar armoire remains intact.

Jaclyn steps over glass and ceramic fragments, broken frames, overturned furniture and colonial landscape paintings. She checks herself in the mirror inside the armoire and brushes fine grey powder from her shoulders. She smiles at her full-length image.

'Perfect. As usual.'

'What do you mean? You're in a boring grey suit. And look at this mess in my room. What happened here? And where am I going to sleep now?'

Suddenly, Edith wonders where she slept last night and the night before that.

'This house has plenty of rooms. I think you'll find somewhere, unless you'd like an easier life in a nursing home?'

'Over my dead body.'

'Just kidding.' Jaclyn smiles as if she is having a joke with her grandmother, and Edith lets herself bathe in the glow of it.

Maybe she's not so bad.

Chapter 4

The kookaburra's warble begins softly before bursting into a full laugh. Not to be outdone, a couple of magpies begin their call. Mary thinks there is no sweeter song. She guesses it is about 6.30 am by the way the sun's rays filter through the pine branches. She looks down on the rooftops descending into the ravine. Through the window on her left she sees the English oak, its leaves all the shades of a sunset.

On a weekday, she would normally be out of the house by now and on the express train to the city, but she has decided to call in sick, a rarity for her. Her mother certainly would not have approved, especially since she has had no hint of nausea since returning home the night before. Mary lies in a little longer, comforted by the voluminous down quilt and the pressure of Hercules rolled in a ball against her leg, but the events of the past few days gnaw at her.

She gets up, disturbing her Burmilla cat, who rolls over in the sea of pink and crimson flowers. It is cool even for May and Mary takes her pink fleece gown and fluffy slippers from the armoire and envelops herself in their softness. Hercules jumps off the bed and runs ahead of her along the hallway to the kitchen. Hercules, his short, brown-tinged cream fur all fluffed up, cries next to a shiny steel bowl and looks her straight in the eye.

'I know, boy.'

The cat drags his tail around her leg as she takes the lid off a plastic canister with a cursive 'C' on the front. Mary doesn't drink coffee, so the container holds the cat's dried food. Hercules's head dives into the bowl before she's finished pouring the biscuits.

Feeling the cold air biting her ears, she pulls a cord on a radiator above the back door, then heats milk on the gas stove. When it is steaming, not boiling, she pours some of the liquid over chocolate flakes to melt them before pouring the rest into the rose-patterned mug.

Standing on the tiny deck at her back door, her hands cupped around the mug for warmth, she watches the first patches of sunlight waking the daisies and nasturtiums and warming the carnations and roses. She loves this time.

Mary descends the steps from the deck and walks onto the dewy grass towards the lily pond in the middle. The fountain is turned off, but in the warmer months the statue of the white cement goddess pours water from an urn into the pond, which is encircled by a pathway of stones of all sizes arranged like a mosaic.

A magpie flies onto the fence and watches Mary.

'There are lots of worms in the garden. You should tell your friends.'

The bird, still quite young judging by the presence of brown and grey feathers, flies off.

Mary hears scratching on glass and sees Hercules dragging his front paws one after the other on the kitchen window. She cannot let him roam because his breed is intended to live indoors. 'Burmillas are no good on the road,' the breeder told her. 'You let him out and it's likely to end tragically.' Mary is sure Hercules will be content once she returns to the house. Then they can snuggle on the lounge together in front of the gas heater while she does a crossword puzzle or reads a novel.

She takes a seat at the little white round lattice table near the pond. From there she can take in the entire garden. She sips the nourishing hot chocolate. At this moment, she is thinking only of the crisp air on her face and the exquisite beauty of her garden on this sunny morning in her beloved Leura. She would never leave this place if she did not have to earn a living.

From the stillness she hears loud banging. Could it be her front door? Her mother didn't believe in door chimes.

She thought they served as an invitation to people, and most people could not be trusted. Few people ever visited the house while her mother was alive, and no-one visits now she is dead.

Mary creeps up the back steps, hoping whoever they are won't hear her and will be on their way. It is so early, even for Mormons and people collecting for charity. She winces at the sound of the back screen door banging against the door jamb and tiptoes through the kitchen into the adjoining lounge room.

She pretends not to be home. More loud banging sends a chill up her spine. She picks up the receiver of her antique phone to dial 000 and puts it down, realising the police will think her foolish.

'Mary, please open the door. I need to speak to you.' Mary trembles at the sound of a strange male voice.

In her peripheral vision, she sees a person peering through the front window. Her heart thumps in her chest and she slides down behind the lounge.

'Mary, I know you're there. I need to speak to you. I mean you no harm, I promise you. I tried to explain that the other day on the phone, but you wouldn't give me a chance. I had to come.'

'Go away, or I will call the police.' Mary tries to find the power in her voice she had the previous day with Jodi-Ann.

'You have every right to be wary, but I can explain everything. Call the police if you like, but I'm not leaving until I have had a chance to tell you what I need to say.'

'I said, go away. Leave me in peace. I keep to myself. I don't know of anyone who has any business with me.'

'That is where you are wrong.'

The man's tone has softened considerably. The vulnerability in his voice causes Mary to pay attention.

'When people are tied by flesh and blood, they will always have business with one another, no matter the circumstances,' he says.

Flesh and blood? What is he talking about?

For a minute there is silence. Mary thinks the man must have left. She walks over to the window and pulls the white lace curtain back to see a man sitting on the front step with his head in his hands. She is struck with pity for him.

What could he want with me? I don't have any living relations.

She tiptoes to the front door, which has a frosted glass centrepiece, carefully turns the key in the deadlock and opens the door. The man jumps to his feet and Mary takes a step back ready to close the door. A locked screen door still separates them.

'I meant what I said,' says the man. 'I won't harm you.'

His hair is long, stringy and grey to match his long beard. He looks about 65. His skin and features are boyish for an old man. His dishevelled appearance and shabby clothes suggest he may be homeless.

'I don't know what you want from me. I don't have any money,' Mary says, suddenly aware she is still in her dressing gown. Her mother would not have approved of her answering the door in that state.

As if to distract herself from the embarrassment, Mary looks for Hercules, but he's not there. Whenever she opens the front door, he is immediately at her feet, ready to make his escape into the yard. His absence bothers her, but she must focus on the stranger now.

'I don't want anything from you. I came to give you something.' The man opens his right hand to reveal a cameo brooch. A perfectly formed woman's face is carved in ivory on a coral-coloured background trimmed with gold.

'It was your mother's,' he says.

'I don't remember my mother wearing that,' Mary says defiantly. 'What kind of an imposter are you?'

'I'm your father, Mary.'

'My father is dead. He died when I was four. How dare you come here and say these things to me.'

This time Mary slams the door. The abrupt sound must have been heard down the street, and the motion shakes the house. She is surprised by the force of her anger.

Why would someone want to upset me like this?

Has this stranger been stalking her? How long? He knows where she lives. The safe haven her mother created for her, the same haven she has maintained for herself, has been compromised. She can't feel sorry for herself. She must act.

'Police,' she says in response to the prompt.

Mary tells the operator about the unkempt, and possibly disturbed, intruder and her fears that he will come again. Two female police officers arrive within 15 minutes. One takes a statement while the other looks around.

'He didn't try to force his way into the house?' the petite officer says, looking Mary in the eye.

'No, but he looked like he hadn't washed in days, maybe weeks. And he was ranting about being my father.'

'And he's not your father?'

'No, my father died when I was four.'

'Did he verbally assault you?'

'No.'

'Ms White, this may be a one-off incident, or it could be a stalking case. Have you seen him before?'

'No, but he did call me once, saying he had something important to tell me.'

'Unfortunately, we do have cases where a stranger becomes obsessed with another person for no good reason. Here is my card. Please call me if he bothers you again.

You may have to take out an AVO. Do you have any idea of his name or where he lives?'

'No. My life was so peaceful before this. Why me?'

'This shouldn't happen to anyone, but unfortunately it does.'

Mary silently reprimands herself for being so focused on herself. Of course, it happens to other people. Some aren't as lucky as her. Some are too afraid of the consequences to call the police and pay for it with their lives.

'Can you call someone to stay with you for a little while, so you're not in the house by yourself?'

'No. My mother passed away a few years ago.'

'What about friends then?'

'I pretty much keep to myself.'

The police officer looks up from her notebook. Mary can see pity in her eyes. Or is it sympathy for a young, single woman being harassed in her own home?

Mary thanks the officers and watches through the locked screen door as they drive off. She shuts the main door, deadlocks it and pulls the bolt and chain across. Still, if he really wanted to get in, he would.

Mary tries to remember as much as she can of the encounter with the man for clues to his state of mind.

He held his head down a lot, and lowered his voice when Mary was at the door. He seemed not to want to appear threatening. And yet his words were entirely preposterous.

How could he claim to be her father? And if he were crazy, why did he pick on her with this story?

Mary has stuck to her mother's policy not to use the central heating during the day because of the cost, so it is like an icy breeze blowing from a snow-covered mountain when she steps from the toasty warm lounge room into the chilly hall. She wants to go to bed and sleep off this bad experience with Hercules by her side.

Hercules!

'Herc. Herc.' Her calls get louder. There is no sign of him.

In the kitchen she sees a clue. A small opening between the door frame and the screen door.

'Hercules!' she cries out.

Rushing onto the deck, she sees her plump cat, whom she feeds only the finest fresh kangaroo mince and vet-supplied dried food, feasting on a magpie. Feathers are strewn across the grass and the cat is pulling flesh from the bird's frame.

'Hercules, come here!' Mary shouts.

The cat defiantly picks up his prey and takes it behind a hedge where Mary cannot reach him.

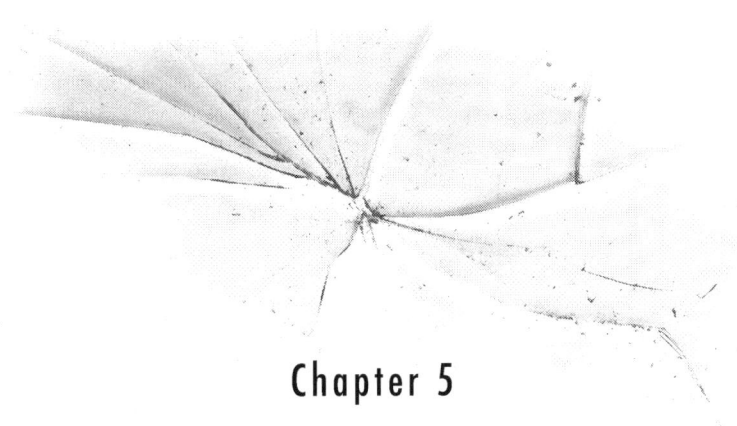

Chapter 5

Edith searches the rooms to find Jaclyn. Her housemate is pulling one grey jacket after another out of her wardrobe. Her bedroom is stark, like Edith would expect a uni student's room to be. The only furniture is the four-poster bed and an old wardrobe that were already there when Jaclyn arrived. Books are strewn across the floor. The wardrobe is crammed with jackets in slightly different shades of grey. Jaclyn is exhibiting the kind of frenzy she did that day with the lipsticks.

'How hard can it be to choose between grey and grey?' Edith can't help herself.

Jaclyn spins around. Her eyes are wide.

'Leave me alone, old woman. What I wear is my business.'

But where are your colonial clothes for dinner with your friends? Edith wants to say.

Instead of replying to Jaclyn, she lifts a jacket from the pile and drops it over Jaclyn's arm. She is expecting a reaction to this action, but Jaclyn pops the garment over her red turtleneck and happily looks for shoes as though nothing has happened.

There is something very odd about this woman.

'Look, Jaclyn, we need to talk about this dinner. After this one, I don't want these people in my house. Can't you have it at a restaurant?'

'What are you talking about old woman? They were here the first Sunday after I arrived. You really are losing it.'

'That's ridiculous. You're the mad one. If only I had realised that when you answered the ad.'

❦

Edith thinks perhaps she should apply the philosophy 'if you can't beat 'em, join 'em' to Jaclyn's Sunday dinner. She can choose to be angry and annoyed, or the guests can entertain her and even tell her what they know about the fire Jaclyn keeps mentioning. All the guests are in the same costumes they wore last time. They are sitting in the same places, making similar gestures and eating the same food.

'Thomas, would you mind passing the salt?' the young woman in convict clothes says.

The rotund man with a ruddy complexion passes her a bowl with salt across the table. She grabs a generous pinch to sprinkle over a large helping of stew and hands it to her companion, who is whispering in her ear.

Edith sits down next to the young woman in the nightgown.

'So glad you could join us,' the woman says, looking right at Edith. 'You weren't happy last time.'

'You haven't been yourself since the fire,' Jaclyn says.

'What fire?' Edith says.

'The one in your bedroom,' Jaclyn replies.

'I don't recall any fire.'

'You were injured. Had to get the doctor in.'

'Oh, yes. The fire.'

Edith decides to play along because she suspects this fire will provide a clue to her housemate's behaviour. She is pretty sure there has not been a fire in the mansion. She will check the entire house after dinner. If there has been a fire, there is bound to be evidence. If there hasn't, then Jaclyn is referring to a fire elsewhere, or in her imagination. Perhaps she knows in her subconscious that she is going to hell.

Edith turns to the woman in the nightgown.

'What is your name, dear?'

'Amelia.'

'Amelia, do you think there's something wrong with me? Jaclyn thinks I'm crazy.'

'Not crazy. You were very crotchety at last week's dinner. You seem brighter today.'

'I'm glad you think so. Are you enjoying the food?'

'Yes, Peter puts on a wonderful feast.'

Edith moves to the chair at the end of the table so she can be closer to the gentleman she assumes is Peter.

'So, you are talking to us now?' the man says.

'I am sorry if I was rude last time. I am Edith Green. And you are?'

'Peter McNamara, architect, landowner, grazier and master of Seaview Manor at your service.'

'The original owner of Seaview Manor.'

Edith reminds herself that this man is playing a character, but he seems remarkably authentic.

'I don't know what you mean by "original". I'm the only owner. Built her myself I did.'

'I know. You had the sandstock brought in from up north and designed the house in the neo-Gothic tradition.'

'How do you know all this?'

'I've done my research.' Edith winks but fails to get a rise from Peter, not even a smile. 'What is this dinner for?'

'I became lonely after my wife, Elizabeth, died and decided to invite some staff and our publican for dinner every Sunday to celebrate all our hard work over the week, just like the ones my wife and I always enjoyed together. It's become a tradition.'

'What's it like living here?'

'Serene. And I'm in love again. We're not open about it with the others, but Amelia shares my bed. Pray don't tell anyone.'

'Oh, I wouldn't.'

Edith looks at Amelia, who is laughing.

'So, you're the host?'

'Of course, as master of the house, I'm the host.'

These actors are so good. They remember the scene so well and can even improvise in character.

Thinking she probably won't get any more intelligent answers from the dinner guests, Edith approaches Jaclyn, who is watching the young convict couple.

'Jaclyn, tell me about the fire!'

At the back of the room, the fire's orange and blue fingers flicker and the hollow logs crackle, almost in anticipation of an answer, or is it a longing to reveal the truth?

'I told you, you're crazy. What fire?'

'The fire you keep referring to.'

'Oh, that? You left your cigarette burning when you fell asleep one night. Don't you remember? If it hadn't been for me walking past at the moment the cigarette dropped onto the bedspread, you might have died. The house would have burnt to the ground, and we both could have died.'

'You didn't drag me out of any room.'

'I can't believe you don't remember any of this. I knew you had dementia. I told your niece today that you were very forgetful.'

'What else did you tell my niece?'

Edith feels her anger return.

'That you like to wander.'

'Lies. All lies.'

Chapter 6

M ary turns in a full circle as she takes in the university's quadrangle, admiring the prominent arches and ornate windows, the copper steeples, the slanted roofs and the main entrance framing the park below. Suddenly a dark cloud moves overhead, casting a shadow over the building and giving her beloved gargoyles a slightly angry look. But it's moving quickly, and soon the quad is awash with sunlight once again. The gargoyles' expressions have returned to mischievous. She breathes easy.

Maybe I can put all the drama behind me, and things can go back to normal.

Mary sticks to her routine of sitting on the bench seat at the edge of the university grounds to have her lunch. As she unwraps the foil around her white bread sandwich, the crackle coincides with a shadow in her peripheral vision.

'Hello,' says a deep voice.

Mary's heart jumps in her chest as she looks up and sees a woman dressed in a suit.

'Oh, I'm sorry if I frightened you.' The woman moves to put her hand on Mary's shoulder and Mary slides along the seat, out of reach. 'May I sit down?' The woman points to the empty space Mary has left.

Mary nods and looks ahead. The woman sits down as Mary bites into half of her sandwich. She is relieved that the ham, tomato and lettuce filling she decided to try instead of her regular curried egg tastes fresh and wholesome.

The woman doesn't say anything, and Mary feels obliged to fill in the silence.

'Did I do something wrong?' she says.

'Not at all. I wanted to say I love the way you appreciate the university's architecture. It's one of the reasons I chose to study here.'

The woman's voice unnerves Mary. 'What, you saw me in the quad?' She immediately places her hand over her mouth in horror. 'Oh, I didn't mean it to come out like that.'

'I can tell you're very polite. But why was a nice girl like you trespassing on uni grounds? I'm sure your mother would not approve.'

'If she were alive, she would not.'

'I'm so sorry.'

'Last month was the third anniversary of her death.'

'And she left you all alone in the world. A sweet girl like you.'

The woman takes a tissue from her shiny black handbag, leans across and wipes a spot on Mary's face. She shivers. It reminds her of something her mother used to do when she was well into her teens.

'You had a bit of tomato on your face,' the woman says.

Tears well up, and Mary gestures for a tissue to halt the stream. Taking one, she is surprised by how young the woman is, late 20s like herself, and yet she acts like a more mature woman.

'I'm sorry I got all emotional. No-one has mentioned my mother in years, apart from a strange man last week.' Mary wipes her eyes.

'Is he a relative?'

'No, I don't know him. I was doing fine and now people want to bring back the pain of the past.'

'I don't want to cause you pain. I want to be your friend. When I saw you admiring the university building, I knew we had a love of architecture in common.'

'You're right. I love the main quad. The little attic windows. The spires. The gargoyles.'

'Oh, I find the gargoyles creepy.'

'Do you work for the university?'

'Hell no. I'm a psychology student. Cut a lecture early because, frankly, psych history bores me. You haven't spoken about your father. What happened to him?'

'He died when I was a little girl.'

'So, you never knew your father?'

'No.'

'That strange man you mentioned might be a secret admirer, or a stalker. Maybe he lied about knowing your mother. Have you called the police? You have to be careful.'

'I really shouldn't be troubling you about this.'

Mary wishes she could talk to someone about what happened with this man, and the past three years since her mother died, but it would be unkind to dump this on a stranger, even a psychology student. Mary checks her mother's old gold watch. 'Oh, goodness. Is that the time? I have to get back to work.'

'Can I give you a lift? I have a gorgeous Buick convertible.'

'No, I always get the bus. Thanks.'

'Before you head off, I didn't catch your name. Let me introduce myself. I'm Jaclyn. Jaclyn Chauve-Souris.'

'I'm Mary White.'

'Of course, you are.'

'Pardon?'

'Oh, nothing.'

Jaclyn takes a small box from her bag. She opens it to reveal four foil-covered chocolates and offers them to Mary. 'Never take lollies from strangers,' she can hear her mother telling her eight-year-old self. Mary shakes her head to refuse the sweets. Jaclyn takes one from the corner and offers the box to Mary for a second time. Mary declines, wondering if her new acquaintance will think her rude, but she really doesn't want it. She notices Jaclyn doesn't eat the one in her hand either.

'Where are you off to, Mary White?'

Grateful she hasn't caused offence by her refusal of the chocolate, Mary smiles. 'Macquarie Street. I work at the library.'

'And you come here every Tuesday?'

'How did you know that?'

'I'm pretty sure I've seen you here before on a Tuesday.'

'I deliver books for interlibrary loan every Tuesday and pick up any returns. I have to deliver these now as a matter of fact,' Mary says, standing and pointing to a bag full of books.

'It was nice to meet you, Mary White. Maybe I'll see you here next Tuesday.' Jaclyn smiles, and Mary pushes the thought of any niggly comments her mother might have made from her mind.

'Maybe,' Mary says, picking up the heavy bag and setting off without looking back.

☙❦☙

Mary has a spring in her step as she enters the university library. Jaclyn seemed nice and genuinely interested in her.

No-one ever asks me questions about myself, except Andrew, but what else are workmates going to talk about?

'Delivering books on interlibrary loan.' Mary flashes her ID and an involuntary smile at the male library assistant and hands over the reusable supermarket bag.

'I hope your car is handy because we have a lot of returns for you today.'

'I should be all right.' Mary reaches for a folded bag from her tote.

The assistant brings a trolley load of books and returns her original bag.

'Luckily, I brought another one of these.' Mary holds up the second bag.

'Did you bring two more?'

'I did, but will I need them?'

'Sure will.'

'Might have to make another trip then.'

Mary wonders what Jodi-Ann will say if she has to come back. Probably something like: 'That's what the fleet car is for.' Mary always takes the bus because the only car she's comfortable driving is her mother's old-model Volkswagen

Beetle. And, until now, she's always been able to transport the books in one or two bags.

'I am only going to be able to take two bags at a time. Would you be able to keep the others until later today when I can come back for them?'

'No problem.'

'That won't be necessary,' says a distinctive female voice.

Jaclyn?

Mary turns around to see the woman she met only moments ago smiling at her as though she has known her since childhood.

'My car is outside,' Jaclyn says. 'I will take you. I'm sure that would look better with the boss, wouldn't it? They usually don't like you to be away for too long, am I right? I'll bring the Buick up closer, so we don't have far to walk.'

'That is really nice of you,' Mary says.

'Just a random act of kindness. I do them all the time.'

This young woman wants to help her. Even her mother would have been hard-pressed to give her a reason why she shouldn't accept the ride.

When Jaclyn returns, she tests the weight of each of the bags and then takes two with ease. Mary struggles under the weight of the remaining two.

Outside the university library, Mary looks for an impressive vintage car. She imagines it to be bronze, burgundy or olive green and gleaming, like Jaclyn's shiny lipstick. But she can't see such a car anywhere.

'It's that one over there.' Jaclyn points to an old rust bucket. It looks like the doors are about to fall off and hasn't been painted in 40 years. 'Isn't she a beauty?' Jaclyn says.

Mary wonders why she had imagined a magnificent car. Was it because of the way Jaclyn originally described it as 'a gorgeous Buick convertible'? Why should those words alone conjure up something wonderful, beautiful and chic from another era?

'It has a certain charm,' Mary says, relying on one of her mother's polite expressions.

Jaclyn pulls the cream-coloured top down to reveal more rust and torn leather. Mary looks for a place to put the bags of books in the back and notices a porcelain doll on the seat. It seems familiar. Its long brown curly hair is like her own. Did she have a doll like it? The doll's long tartan dress and vintage look fit the image of the Buick, but nothing else about it being there seems right. Mary resists the urge to pick it up to inspect it more closely. She walks around the car to place the bags on the other side. She doesn't want to damage the doll. Jaclyn has left the other two bags by the car. Mary can see no other way but to pick up the doll to make way for them. Jaclyn snatches the doll from her hands. The violence of the motion shocks Mary.

'That's mine,' Jaclyn says in a child-like voice.

'Oh, I was just moving the doll to make room for the extra bags.'

Mary feels a strong sense of this happening before. But how could it have? She didn't even own any dolls when she was young. Jaclyn throws the doll onto the floor in the back. Mary wants to retrieve it. She wants to cry but holds back the tears, reprimanding herself for being so silly. It's only a doll.

Suddenly the Ring-a-Ring o' Rosie nursery rhyme starts playing in her head. The memory is comforting and yet eerie. She puts it out of her mind.

Mary looks at the sky and wonders if the dark clouds looming overhead will burst open while they are on the road.

'Could we put the top up in case it rains?' Mary says. 'I'm not worried about getting wet myself, but I wouldn't want the books to be damaged.'

Or your lovely doll, she wants to add.

'You worry too much, Mary White. You'll love having the wind in your hair.'

'That does sound fun.'

Mary opens the passenger door. It creaks and grinds. There are cobwebs and grime in the door frame. A rusty spring is popping through the seat, and Mary sits to the left of it to avoid tearing her skirt. She tries to ignore the pile of rubbish on the floor and focuses on the kindness of the driver, who may be saving her from certain humiliation at the hands of her boss. Mary reaches for empty air where the seatbelt should be. She checks for a seatbelt socket. Nothing.

The car lurches as Jaclyn takes off. Once they are on Parramatta Road, she swerves in and out of lanes, with Mary clinging tightly to the top of the door to stop herself from being thrust into the driver. She wants to ask Jaclyn to slow down but can't. Her mother is in her head: 'You got into the car. You must take responsibility for what happens.' As they are about to hit a bus pulling out of the curb into their lane, Mary closes her eyes and waits for the crash. Instead, she feels a swerve and then a pulling forward, a screech of brakes. She is pushed back in her seat as the car comes to a sudden halt. She opens her eyes to see a red light.

Mary wonders how old the brakes are.

'I love driving,' Jaclyn says. 'Wanted to be a racing car driver once. Did you like that stop? Great brakes, huh?'

Jaclyn makes a U-turn at the lights near the Botanic Garden and parks in a bus zone outside the library.

'I won't go in. I'll stay by the car while you unload,' Jaclyn says.

'Of course.'

Mary takes the two heaviest bags in the lift to her office. She is breathing heavily but straightens her posture, so she doesn't appear overwhelmed by the weight of the books. Andrew is at the lift when the doors open and immediately takes one of the bags.

'Whoa!' he exclaims, letting the bag drop to the floor. 'Mary, why didn't you call me to bring the trolley down?'

'I'll be right,' she says, picking up the second bag. 'But it would be good if you could get the trolley. There are two more bags downstairs.'

'There's more? How did you even get them here?'

'A student from the university gave me a lift.'

'Did he now?'

'*She* was being kind.' Mary blushes but doesn't understand why she feels defensive.

'Sure,' Andrew says.

Mary walks quickly to her workstation and places the bags on the floor. Like an irritating child, Andrew pushes the trolley towards her. Mary uses her leg to stop it from hitting the desk and it catches her shin.

'Ow!' she moans.

'Oh, Mary. I'm so sorry. I was just mucking around.'

'I better get this trolley downstairs. Jaclyn is parked in the bus zone.'

'I'll come and help you.'

'There's really no need.'

'I insist. I'll take the trolley.' Andrew pulls the trolley back and directs it to the lifts.

Neither of them speaks as they travel down to the main entrance. Mary walks briskly to the car, with Andrew pushing the trolley far enough behind not to hit her again.

'Interesting car,' Andrew says. 'A vintage Buick convertible coupe from the 1930s. Could use some TLC!'

'Sorry I took so long,' Mary says.

'Your friend here kept you chatting, no doubt.'

Mary notices Jaclyn size Andrew up in a dismissive fashion, but he responds with a smile and puts his hand out. 'Andrew Garcia.'

'Yeah.' Jaclyn ignores the gesture and doesn't glance at Andrew again.

Mary silently pulls the bags onto the trolley. As the second one hits the metal, Andrew wheels them off.

'Thanks so much, Jaclyn.' Mary smiles.

'He's not really your friend, is he?' Jaclyn frowns.

'Ah, I work with him. That's all.'

'Good. I don't get a good vibe from him.'

Mary doesn't know how to respond. She knows Jaclyn shouldn't say such things, but she doesn't know why she is bothered by it. She dismisses the thought.

'Well, I'll head back to uni. I've missed a lecture.'

'Oh, I'm sorry.'

'You owe me.' Jaclyn laughs.

Mary can't tell if she is joking and feels uncomfortable by the words. One of her mother's continual instructions playing in her head is never to be in debt to anyone.

Jaclyn pulls out from the curb and toots the vehicle's old-fashioned horn.

As Mary returns to her workstation, the events of her lunch break flash in her mind.

What happened? I broke Mum's rule never to trespass, and I made a friend. That can't be bad.

Andrew is back at his desk, the trolley between them.

'Who was the she-devil?' he asks, getting up to put a pile of economic journals on the top tray of the trolley.

'She's my friend.' Mary neatly places science journals next to the existing stack.

Andrew looks at her curiously. 'Since when?'

'Since this morning.'

'She's bad news.'

'Why would you say that?'

'Did you see the way she looked at me as though I was dirt on her shoe?'

'I don't think she likes you.'

'She hardly even spoke to me to make that call, but I'm relieved to hear it. How could you be interested in her friendship?'

'She's caring.' Mary turns her back on Andrew to pick up more journals.

'She'd eat her own young.'

'Please don't talk to me if you're going to keep speaking about my new friend like that. She did me a favour.'

'I'm sorry, but I think you can do better.'

'I think we should agree to disagree.'

Mary goes back to stamping journals with the library details and wonders what Andrew means that she can do better. She has no real friends now, so one is better than none. And how is Andrew able to sum up a person with such little information? Her mother used to tell her that people could seem disagreeable one minute and completely charming the next, so it was virtually impossible to tell what they were really like. Mary doesn't think she is either disagreeable or charming, just somewhere in the middle. Constant, like her mother encouraged her to be. Not too hot or too cold, just right, like in the Goldilocks and the Three Bears fairytale, a story her mother read to her often as a child as a reminder of the perils of trespassing. What does Jaclyn see in her? How did she make up her mind so quickly that she would make a suitable friend? She likes excitement all the time, so what could Mary offer?

Jaclyn is a woman of the world who knows her own mind. Who am I to question who she wants to be friends with? I should be grateful she chose me.

❦

A lone flying fox flies over Macquarie Street. Mary continues to watch it while she walks in the direction of the train station. In human terms they are ugly creatures with their bald heads, beady eyes and webbed wings, but at the same time Mary thinks there is something hauntingly beautiful about them when they are in full flight against the twilight sky.

Chapter 7

Edith wonders what has Jaclyn so agitated as she paces up and down in the sitting room, rubbing her shoulders in the icy air. None of the usual autumn sunlight warms the room. In fact, the natural light is dull on account of heavy, dark clouds. Jaclyn pushes the bottom corner of the landscape painting near the grand piano to correct its slant.

'I checked them only last week and they were fine,' she says aloud. 'Maybe there was a tremor while I was at uni.'

'I did it,' Edith says. 'I put all the pictures on a slant.'

'Edith, where are you hiding? Don't play with me. You're being ridiculous.'

'You should stay out of my favourite room. I told you some areas of the house were out of bounds.'

Jaclyn moves to the centre of the room and surveys the entire space. Edith knows she won't find her behind the gold velvet curtains.

'I'll find you, and when I do . . .' Jaclyn says. 'Maybe the old spinster is behind the lounge.'

Who is she calling an old spinster, the little cow?

Edith keeps herself still as Jaclyn bobs down and looks through the curved giltwood legs of the Louis XVI lounge. Then behind the piano. A tassel slips to the floor. Jaclyn covers her mouth as though she is surprised.

'You missed me.'

Jaclyn spins around as Edith settles into a tapestry chair. Jaclyn jumps slightly, then straightens. Edith is enjoying this game immensely.

How did you do that?' Jaclyn demands.

Edith leans back and crosses her legs. She holds Jaclyn's gaze. Her grin broadens.

'I have many hidden talents it seems.'

'Are you a witch?'

'How dare you? I am a good Christian woman.'

Edith can feel her face red with anger. How does this woman know how to press her buttons that she can go from frivolity to anger so quickly?

Jaclyn crosses her arms over her chest and taps her foot. 'I came up here to think. Could you leave me alone? Now!'

'Jaclyn, this is my spot in the house. You have more than 10 rooms to choose from, why take mine?'

'You always say you do your best thinking here, and I need to work some things out.'

'Like what? Maybe I can help you.'

'You can't help me, old woman.'

'Try me!'

Jaclyn sweeps past Edith and stretches out lengthwise on the ornate lounge, placing two cushions behind her back against the curved, padded arm rest.

'If you must know, there is this friend from uni. Her name is Mary White. She's been through some difficult stuff. Her mum's dead and she's been harassed by a strange man. She lives all alone. Bit of a mousy type, but I know there's a beautiful woman under there somewhere and I can help her.'

'You should invite her to Seaview Manor,' Edith says.

Jaclyn shoots a look of disbelief at Edith.

'Really?'

'It is nice that you want to help her. I am sure she would love it here.'

'She does love Gothic architecture. She would love this house. I will invite her to Sunday dinner.'

'That sounds lovely.'

'See, Edith, you can be nice when you want to be.' Jaclyn gets up and straightens each painting in turn. 'Mary will love this room.'

'I am really looking forward to meeting her,' Edith says.

Jaclyn goes back to the antique lounge and this time puts her head on the cushions and falls asleep.

Was it something I said? It is as though she takes energy from anger and fear and is depleted by kindness. Maybe if I wake her up, I might get some answers.

'Jaclyn. Jaclyn.'

'What? How long was I asleep?'

'An hour or so.'

'I still feel really sleepy.'

'That's okay. Close your eyes. I wanted to ask you a couple of things.'

'All right.'

'Why did you say you saved me from a fire?'

'I don't know what you're talking about. The fire was a long time ago before I met you.'

'Tell me about it.'

'It's a bit hazy.'

'Imagine you are back in the house. It was a house, wasn't it?'

'A fisherman's cottage.'

'Where was the fire?'

'In the bedroom in the attic.'

'And you were downstairs?'

'No, I was outside. The smoke was too thick. I couldn't get back into the house.'

'But you knew someone was inside.'

'My housemate.'

'Male or female?'

'Female.'

'Age?'

'About 25.'

'How did the fire start?'

'I think it was a cigarette or a candle.'

'You don't know which?'

'She smoked in bed, but she also had lots of candles.'

Speaking to Jaclyn this way, Edith has her under her control as though she has hypnotised her. She doesn't know how long she has before Jaclyn goes to sleep or wakes up and realises what is happening.

'Tell me about the last time you were in that bedroom in the attic. What were you feeling?'

'I was angry. Really angry.'

'Was your housemate in the room at the time?'

'No, she was out with friends. She didn't invite me.'

'Is that why you were angry?'

'No, she kicked me out of the house. She said I had to be out before she got back.'

'And you wanted revenge?'

'I had done so much for her. I'd made her into a new woman. She was a frump before she met me with no friends and no boyfriend. Then as soon as she turns her life around, she kicks me out.'

'Did you go up to her room a lot when she wasn't home?'

'I had to make sure she wasn't smuggling in any more of those daggy op shop dresses. She picked this certain tunic style that made her look so overweight.'

'And what other things did you look at while you were in her room?'

'I borrowed some lipstick.'

'Red, no doubt?'

'Yes, after I helped her with the makeover, her mother bought her some expensive brands.'

'Did you steal any?'

'Between friends it's a long-term loan.'

'What else did you look at? Did she have photos of her new friends and her boyfriend?'

'Everywhere.'

'Did seeing these photos make you mad?'

'Yes. I knew they were all off having fun, talking about me behind my back. Saying nasty things.'

'Why did you go up to the attic bedroom that last time?'

'I knew she had two grey suits that were my size because I was with her when she bought them, and I decided I deserved to have them as payment for my services. I also took some red underwear and stilettos.'

'And you were going to pack your things and go before something caught your eye?'

'On the dresser was a pack of cigarettes. I loathe smoking and I scrunched the packet up and put it in the little plastic bin with the swing lid. There was also a lighter and three candles. I lit each candle and said a curse for my housemate, her pretty boyfriend and her smarmy friends.'

'What else did you do before you left the room?'

'I found some scissors, pulled the bedding back and cut a hole deep into the mattress at the bottom end. It was easy. I took a piece of the stuffing and lit it with the lighter. It didn't go up in flames, just smouldered a bit. I dropped that in the hole, covered the rest up with the stuffing and put the sheets back in place. Then I left the room.'

'What happened after that?'

'I remember being outside the house. An ambulance came and took me to hospital. I was treated for smoke inhalation.'

Suddenly Jaclyn opens her eyes. The story isn't complete. Edith wants to know if the firefighters got to the woman in time.

'Did I doze off?' Jaclyn asks.

'You did.'

And now I may never know how the story ended.

Chapter 8

Mary is walking through a wooded forest, light streaming gently through the autumn leaves. She hears robins singing. Her heart feels light. She skips, stopping to pick wildflowers along the stone path. Suddenly everything goes dark. Bats are flying around her as her eyes adjust to the minimal light. It is cold and damp. A cave. Mary is not scared. Something is compelling her to walk further into the darkness. She hears water dripping and wings flapping. She is surprisingly calm for someone who is in the dark and doesn't know where she is or how she got here. She is stepping on small rocks now. They are jabbing her soft, bare feet, and she treads more carefully to avoid the prodding. A draft blows on her face. She takes another step, and another. Suddenly stepping into nothingness, she free-falls in an abyss. Falling. Falling. She tells herself she is not likely to survive this. It is all right. There are worse things than death, like what comes just before it. And she will lose consciousness first.

◦❦◦

Mary wakes with a jolt, eyes wide open. She is exhausted though relieved that she is safe. Was she dreaming all night? How did her mind rationalise the irrational? What does it mean? Is it related to the crazy man claiming to be her father? Every scene is vivid in her mind. She does not dream often and when she does the images can normally be explained as wishful thinking. Happy dreams where she finds treasure under her bed or takes possession of a litter of kittens. Mary shakes her head to throw off the terrifying scenes.

Clouds muffle the sunlight. The light is straining and casts her room in a sombre hue. The chill in the air bites her ears, and she pulls the doona over her head. Hercules scratches at the door and meows.

Mary wonders why the door is closed and remembers that Hercules disturbed her during the night, and she put him in his basket in the other room. She lies there cocooned in warmth. Hercules's pleas become more insistent. More scratching. She knows he is dragging his front paws down the paintwork. She thinks Hercules will relent if she ignores him. But the scratching becomes more frenetic, and the cries grow louder.

'Herc, I'm coming.' Mary throws back the covers. As if he is making sure she won't renege, his meows have escalated to the likes of loud human baby cries.

Mary opens the door. Hercules walks past her and jumps on the bed. Mary gets back into bed and pulls up the doona. Hercules lets out one short 'yow' and curls up next to her, closing his eyes in contentment. She strokes him around the cheek. He opens his eyes briefly and the purring deepens. Mary lies back on the pillow and closes her eyes, but cool air touches her cheeks and takes her back to the dark, damp cave of her nightmare. She opens her eyes and sits up, preferring the reality of her room, even if it is darker than normal. Hercules lifts his head and looks up at her. He puts his head back over his front paw. He has misread the situation. Mary is unsettled by the images from the nightmare that fill her mind when she closes her eyes. She wants to get up and do something.

She looks around the room. Everything is exactly the way her late mother positioned it, right down to the antique water pitcher and bowl on the dark dresser set against pale green walls adorned with McCubbin and Roberts prints. It all fits together nicely and suits the house, but is this her style? Would she even know where to start to redesign it? She takes the cream pitcher from inside the deep bowl and puts it in front of it, slightly to the left. Even that is an act of defiance.

As she showers and dresses in pre-loved trousers, a long sleeve shirt and a jumper, Mary wishes her mother hadn't forbidden her from owning a pair of jeans, second-hand or otherwise. Her mother never gave a reason, and Mary didn't ask for one. She vacuums, sweeps and dusts before cleaning the bathroom. She has been completing these tasks since she was 12. Only today she has finished them by 8.30 am.

As Mary strolls around the house to see if she has missed anything, she becomes aware of Hercules's cries behind her. She still hasn't fed him.

She watches Hercules gulp his kangaroo mince and swallow his biscuits. Mary tries to restrict him to smaller portions to counter his increasing weight, but at times she can't resist his pleas for extra biscuits. Her heart feels warm as she sees him enjoy his food. When he is finished, Hercules follows Mary into the lounge room where she lights the gas faux log fire in the house's original fireplace. The cat immediately curls up on the '60s floral rug her mother bought at an op shop.

Mary picks up her novel from the antique coffee table, sits on the floral lounge and swings her legs up on the seat, her back resting against the arm, her legs bent and her slippers resting on the fabric. She ignores her mother's voice chiding her for spoiling a perfectly good lounge for her own selfish reasons.

The yellowing plastic on the old hard-cover book of *Rebecca* by Daphne du Maurier is cold to touch. Her mother had covered all their books in plastic to help protect them. She had a cover or device to protect just about everything. Even the couches had all been covered in plastic until Mary tore it off a few months back. Her mother would have hermetically sealed Mary if she could have. Perhaps in a way she did, and whether it is because of her mother's protection or simple good luck, Mary has kept out of harm's way. Until now, even her subconscious has protected her by not presenting horrifying dreams as she slept.

Feeling restless to the point where she can't even focus on the words in her favourite book, Mary decides a wander around the village might calm her. She puts on her mother's trench coat, which is hanging on a hat stand near the front door, and wraps a woollen scarf around her neck to face the cold, then drives up to Leura. The car park is nearly full. The cooler months are the most popular with tourists, who come for a proper winter experience including log fires and comfort food like the famous flowerpot scones.

Today, despite the rain, the mall is alive with people. She is pleased to be out among them. If something happens to her, there will be many witnesses. Immediately, she admonishes herself for being a drama queen. What can possibly happen here?

Her first stop is a gift shop filled with an array of pretty items displayed in perfect combination – floral stationery, crystal jewellery and silk skirts. The soft scents from candles and diffusers in vanilla, patchouli and sandalwood lift her senses as soon as she enters. She buys a bottle of her favourite vanilla-scented bubble bath.

Her next stop is the nursery, the Japanese maple trees creating a pretty setting for the potted colour.

'Hi, Mary, we haven't seen you for a while,' the female owner says.

'Aren't the miniature carnations lovely?'

'Yes, they are good this year. Are you only after flowers, or are you interested in herbs too? They are particularly good at the moment.'

Mary smiles. 'I could use more basil and parsley.'

Nothing pleases her more than being the new owner of plants. Big or small, it doesn't matter, because as soon as there's a break in the rain, she will have her hands in the earth and be planting and nurturing life.

After depositing bags under the bonnet of the mustard-coloured Beetle, she walks through the mall via the lolly shop where she picks up a rainbow spiral lollipop and a bag of musk sticks.

Mary walks into her favourite café on the corner of the mall. She has known the waitress who greets her since she was a young girl, which is also how long she has been having the flowerpot scones.

No place feels as warm and safe as home. Right now, it feels safer than home.

This is normal. Nothing is going to happen to her. The strange man would have seen the police drive into her street. He will know to stay away from her.

The waitress leads Mary to a little table in the front window. The pink gingham tablecloth appears to have been freshly laid for her.

'We saved your favourite spot,' she says. 'Would you like a menu, or will you have your usual?'

Mary asks to see the menu. She studies the warm drinks and variety of food, but she's too distracted to choose and settles on her regular hot chocolate with marshmallows and a flowerpot scone. She picks up a newspaper from the counter and takes it to her table. Instead of reading the news, she goes straight to the lifestyle pages.

Mary's concentration is disturbed by a knock on the window. She ignores it at first, thinking it must be for someone else and keeps her head buried in the latest cosy looks for the home, but the knocking is insistent. Her curiosity forces her to look up. Before her, with his face pressed against the glass, is the old man with the stringy hair and beard who had been ranting at her front door. Her jaw drops in surprise. Now he is smiling and waving at her. His eyes are hollow and sad, his smile child-like. He looks more mentally deficient than a crazed killer. She wants to put the newspaper between her and the intruder again, but it's too late.

Her mother is in her head cautioning her to get up and escape through the back, but another voice is coming through. It is telling her this is a lonely man whose tragic story is written in the deep tracks across his face. And she is in a public place with people all around. Maybe he just needs nourishment.

The man points to the door and asks with his eyes if it is all right with her if he enters. Mary gives a polite nod in agreement. The man mouths 'thank you' and then slowly and quietly enters the café with his head slightly bowed.

This time the man seems shorter, less imposing.

'May I?' he says, putting his hand on the top of the wooden chair ready to pull it out.

'Sure.'

If this man is not right in the head, then she must be careful. She puts her hand up to get the attention of the waitress.

'So, Mr White, will it be hot chocolate with marsh-mallows for you today?' she says directly to the man.

White! Mary's own surname screams in her ears.

'You two know each other?' Mary asks the waitress.

'Yes. Mr White is a regular.'

'We share a love of hot chocolate, my dear.' The man's voice is smooth, and his face has softened to the point where he is almost handsome despite his unkempt look and missing front tooth. 'May I also have a flowerpot scone? Mary, have you ordered? This is on me.'

'Mary has ordered exactly the same as you,' the waitress chimes in before heading to the counter.

The man nods his head several times as if he already knew. Mary wonders if he has been stalking her at the café. Will all her favourite places be off limits now?

'You don't have to pay for me,' she says. 'I can take care of it.'

'I insist. It's the least I can do for allowing me to sit with you after I caused you that trouble the other day.'

'Did you follow me here?' A frown creases Mary's brow.

'No, I swear. I come here every Sunday at this time. Ask the waitress. She'll tell you.'

'I guess I have to believe you. Was it you who rang me two weeks ago?'

'Yes.'

'Why?'

Because Mary is being reasonable and her café companion seems to have gained some sense of decorum, she expects she will get the truth now, not some farfetched story.

'The day I called you . . . actually that doesn't matter. I should first tell you about your mother.'

The man smiles at the waitress in a fatherly way as she places mugs of hot chocolate in front of them.

'I don't see where I fit into all this. I don't even know you.' Mary stirs a marshmallow into her drink and licks the teaspoon.

'Mary, I don't expect you to forgive me for what I've done, but I know it's important for you to know so you can get out there and live your life.'

'I don't know how anything you've done could possibly have anything to do with me.'

'I should start at the beginning.'

'Okay.'

This single word of consent belies the ideas racing in Mary's mind. He is an eccentric man who knew her mother and doesn't have anyone to leave his home to. He wants to marry her so he can say he was married before he died. He has a mental illness and has taken a shine to her.

The last one seems to be the best explanation.

But why did the waitress call him Mr White? It is a common name. Maybe that's where all this nonsense started, in the coincidence around their names.

The man has paused and seems to be waiting for a signal to continue.

'Go on,' Mary says.

'I met Mary White at a dance at Blaxland in the winter of 1984—'

'Wait, Mary White, the same name as mine? My mother's name was Isabel White.'

'Yes, dear, I know. I will explain. My romance with Mary was the kind you know will last forever.' The man looks into his mug, takes a sip and continues.

Mary is eager for him to get to the point.

'We spent every waking minute together. It was a blessing because neither of us had thought we'd ever find the one. I loved that woman from her smile to the way she said my name. I loved everything about her. She had a glow, a radiance that seemed to touch everyone and everything around her. Animals adored her. She was not attached to material things apart from sentimental items that had been handed down through the generations like a piece of jewellery. She loved helping people. She was always on the stall at the church fair, and the night before she'd be up all night knitting covers for coat hangers or making cakes to sell. And what a cook she was. She made the best roast in the world. The most succulent meat, the crispiest skin on baked potatoes. The Sunday roast was an event I looked forward to the whole week.'

'She sounds like a wonderful woman, and you must have had a great life, but what does this have to do with me?' Mary shifts in her seat.

'I will get to that. I forgot to mention our wedding. The day she walked up the aisle and said she'd be mine forever was the happiest day of my life. Boy did she look beautiful. We didn't have the usual teething problems. We were two peas in a pod. I liked what she liked and vice versa. We both chipped in with the work around the house. We were the ultimate home bodies, and we loved being together. We had found our other half. So, when Mary told me she was pregnant, it was like the ultimate gift. A child was to be born out of our happy union. Another person to love as much as we loved each other.'

This story is more like an audio book of a novel than real life.

The waitress interrupts the man's story, placing two small terracotta pots with a bulbous scone popping out the top on the table, alongside bowls of berry jam and cream. Mary has mastered the art of eating these novelty scones and slices the top off before layering the spreads, jam first. The man follows suit.

'Sorry,' Mary says. 'Continue with the story.'

'Where was I? That's right, Mary's pregnancy. She had a difficult time and became moody, which was unusual for her. I put it down to the hormones. While her tests were all normal, she kept telling me she was worried that something wasn't right. She could feel it in her waters. I tried to reassure her that the doctor would tell her if anything was wrong.

'I failed her, Mary. I should have listened to her and taken her to a second doctor, but I didn't. Three weeks before the due date, she had to be rushed to hospital for an emergency caesarean section. She lost a lot of blood and her blood pressure plummeted.'

The man lowers his head for a minute. Tears stream down his cheeks.

'I lost the love of my life that night,' he says.

'And the baby?'

'The baby survived. But I was so devastated I refused to even look at it for the first few days. They told me I had a beautiful baby girl, but I didn't care. That demon child had taken my beautiful Mary away from me. The nursing staff contacted Community Services and were about to hand the baby over to them when I came to my senses and brought you home.'

It takes Mary a couple of seconds to register what he is saying. 'What? You mean . . . ?'

'Yes, I named you Mary after your mother. I promised her spirit, and you, that I would protect you and care for you for the rest of your life. Something else I failed at.'

'This is too much.' Mary signals to the waitress and orders another hot chocolate.

'I have a lot to tell you, Mary, and a lot to make up to you in a short time.'

'So, you're saying that your wife was my real mother. Then who is the woman I have known all my life as "Mother"? Who is Isabel White?'

'I met Isabel at church. She was always looking for someone she could help, someone who was weaker than she was. She used to bring me cookies and home-baked bread to the Sunday service. Eventually, she started coming round and making me meals at home.'

'Making you meals? Who was looking after me?'

'I was getting to that. When you were about six months old, I gave up. I couldn't bear my grief and the responsibility of looking after you, so I gave you to Community Services. We had an agreement they wouldn't adopt you out to give me a chance to see if I could get my life back together.'

'How long was I in care?'

'Until you were almost four. After Isabel moved in with me, she told me she couldn't have children and I told her about you. She convinced me we could all be a family and give you the love and protection you needed. At the time, you were in a home with 20 or so children.'

'An orphanage?'

'They called it a residential home.'

'How do I know that any of this is true? You have to understand how ridiculous this all sounds. You could be some psycho with a warped story.'

'I have evidence of our life together – photos, household bills, a bank book. I can bring it here if we could meet again.' The man reaches into his back pocket and pulls out a worn leather wallet. He lifts out a picture.

'This is you on your fourth birthday. I picked out that pink fairy outfit. You were serving pretend hot chocolates in your new plastic tea set.'

Mary stares at the picture. Along with the bullying, it is one of her earliest memories. She remembers how proud she was placing actual pink and white marshmallows on the plastic saucers of the teacups for the imaginary drinks. A man stands with the woman she believed was her mother. He has a big smile. Mary's heart breaks, as much for the man who has been denied a daughter as for the girl who was denied a father.

Chapter 9

Mary is aware of Jodi-Ann's staunch policy about conducting personal research in work time, but now she has a burning desire to find out about four lost years when she was essentially an orphan. She can deal with her boss's objections later. She hates to ask Andrew to take on her work entering stacks of academic papers in the database, but he doesn't seem to mind, judging by the number of questions he's asking about her father, her step-mother and her birth mother. He seems at least mildly curious to find out about her time in the orphanage too.

'I'm sorry that all these revelations have been so shocking for you, but who would have thought that your background would be so intriguing.'

'I wish I didn't know any of this. At least when I believed Isabel was my mother, I had a sense of where I came from. Now I have no idea who I am.'

Saying her name in the third person makes the only mother Mary knew for more than two decades sound like a family acquaintance, but it is only right that she put some distance between them now. Mary was her real mother. She sacrificed her life to bring her daughter into the world.

'I wonder what traits of my birth mother I inherited?'

'You can ask your father,' Andrew says.

Mary trawls the internet for any mention of children's homes that may have been open in the early 1990s. She finds several in Sydney. One in the inner west, Fairy Glen Home for Children, has a decidedly Gothic look and seems oddly familiar.

'This one had children of both sexes and all ages,' Mary says.

'Oh, that looks creepy. No wonder orphanages had a bad rap. They were dark and dreary places.'

'I love the building. It would have been beautiful when it was first constructed.'

'Maybe that's where you got your passion for this kind of architecture, especially if it was your first home. It was probably haunted, which might explain your fascination with ghost tours too.'

'Ha ha.'

Mary and Andrew laugh. Andrew holds his hand over his mouth.

'Wouldn't want to wake the fire-breathing dragon,' he whispers.

'No, we can't. I have so much more to find out, but I think this home may be a lead. Could I borrow your phone to go out and make some calls?'

'Mary, you need to get yourself a mobile.'

'I know. I never really needed one before.' The voice of Isabel saying mobile phones – anything electronic, for that matter – are the work of the devil still plays in her head.

Mary writes down the number for a support organisation for former state wards and foster children, and Andrew hands her his phone.

'Thank you. I promise I will take on more of the workload when I get back from lunch.'

'You'd better.' Andrew gives her a cheeky look that takes her aback, even makes her feel a little self-conscious. She knows he would take on more of her work if she asked him.

But why would he do that? Oh! No, he's just a friend.

꧁꧂

Walking towards the glass doors of the library's main entrance, Mary is stopped by a husky female voice calling her name. *Jaclyn!*

'Hey, Mary. Great. You're here today. I thought we might be able to grab a bite.'

'This is a surprise,' Mary says. 'I have about 30 minutes, if that's okay with you.'

Mary is taking a one-hour lunch break today. Despite all the lectures Isabel gave her about never telling a lie for fear of being struck down, Mary thinks it is not so bad to tell a small one. She doesn't want Jaclyn to think she treats research into her past as more important than creating a bond with a new friend.

'That suits me perfectly,' Jaclyn says.

Mary feels her mind is playing tricks on her. The way Jaclyn is looking at her – the eyes narrowing and the nose pointing in the air, her face decidedly triangular – reminds Mary of a bat.

'Shall we go to the café across the road then?' Mary has never been there, since she always brings lunch from home, but Andrew has said they make a 'pretty mean burger'. She hopes it will meet with Jaclyn's approval since she seems very definite in her opinions and wouldn't shy away from saying if she didn't like it.

'Anywhere is fine as long as they have good coffee.'

Jaclyn links arms with Mary. Instead of being the one to lead her new friend across the road in the direction of the café, Mary feels as though Jaclyn is pulling her along. Something about this makes her uncomfortable, but she pushes the thought to the back of her mind, telling herself she is overthinking things. After all, the café is clearly visible from where they are standing so it makes sense that Jaclyn knows where they are going. And what is wrong with friends linking arms? Jaclyn just wants to make her intention of friendship known.

Jaclyn chooses a table on the street. Mary orders a beef burger and hot chocolate and is surprised when Jaclyn shuns the menu and asks for only a 'skinny latte'.

'Oh, I thought you wanted to have lunch . . .'

'It's carbs and sugar that put on the kilos you know.'

Convincing herself this wasn't intended as a dig at her, Mary tells Jaclyn she would have suggested takeaway drinks to have in the Botanic Garden instead.

'We'll have to do that next time. Maybe we could get in a run.' Jaclyn's smile radiates, and Mary feels privileged to have her attention. She isn't keen on the idea of a run though. She walks at a good pace normally, but getting into active wear and running around the gardens at lunchtime or any time for that matter is not something she ever sees herself doing.

Maybe Jaclyn would be happy to do that on her own.

'You know the principles of calories in and calories out?' Jaclyn continues. 'When I'm not studying, I'm exercising. You could call me an exercise freak. I can share some things with you. Be your personal trainer even. I wouldn't charge you. Just a coffee now and then.' Jaclyn laughs.

'That's nice of you, and I appreciate why people would be excited by all that activity, but it's not for me.'

'That's okay. We can start small and work up, or not. Up to you. I know. What about a girls' spa and shopping day?'

'Yes, that sounds nice, although I've never had a massage before. I think I would feel a bit awkward being naked.'

Mary wonders if she sees Jaclyn roll her eyes at this confession but tells herself it is in her head. Her friend is only wanting to help her experience more from life, and it is probably time she extended her world beyond her home, work and the Royal Botanic Garden.

When the burger is placed in front of Mary, Jaclyn is looking at the bun and its meat and salad contents intently. It is hard to tell if she is judging her choice or envies it. Mary wants to hold the whole burger in both hands and take a big bite, but she is feeling self-conscious opposite Jaclyn who takes small sips of her latte. Instead, Mary cuts the bun in quarters and handles a small portion between her fingers, as she wraps her mouth around it and tastes the warm, salty patty that is perfectly accompanied by the crisp lettuce, sweet beetroot and juicy tomato. How long is it since she has had a burger? Maybe once when she was a child. She gets lost in the deliciousness.

'You seem to be really enjoying that burger,' Jaclyn says, bringing Mary back to the present moment.

'It is so good.'

'I can see you like to soothe with food. What's been happening?'

Mary takes a few seconds to answer. Should she tell her new friend about the sudden appearance of her father and her stepmother's lies?

'It's okay, Mary, I am not only your friend, I am a psychology student. I'm learning to help people just like you.'

'Like me?' Mary takes a sip of her hot chocolate that is now lukewarm.

'People who have lost someone dear to them.'

Mary has suddenly lost her appetite. She doesn't want to talk about how hard it was to lose the only mother she has known and then find out she wasn't her mother at all. How can one put such betrayal and heartache into words? Jaclyn is asking too much of her.

'Look, I really must go. We should talk about this over a cup of tea at home, not on a public street.'

'You could come to my house. You would love it. It's this amazing mansion in the neo-Gothic style. It's called Seaview Manor.'

The words seem implausible at best. How could a woman of 20-something years live in a mansion and in the exact style of architecture Mary likes?

'Your house is a neo-Gothic mansion?'

'Yes.'

'Obviously it's on the sea if it's called Seaview Manor.'

'That's right.'

'It sounds lovely, but I was thinking I'd be more comfortable talking about personal things at my place.'

'Where are you?'

'In the Blue Mountains.'

'That is quite a distance from the eastern suburbs. Give me your address, and we'll work something out. Then maybe once I've seen your place, you can come to mine.'

'Yeah.'

Mary pulls out her native flowers diary from her tote and rips out a page at the back to write her address. She can't seem to find her pen, which coincides with a nagging feeling that Jaclyn is still a stranger and their relationship isn't at the stage of extending an invitation to come home to tea. Still, she digs deep in the bag and finds a capless biro.

She reassures herself it's okay. Jaclyn is studying psychology to help people like her. With everything going on, it wouldn't hurt to run it by someone to help her process it.

'Wonderful. Pop down your work and home phone numbers too so we can arrange a time.'

Feeling happy to be cementing a new friendship, Mary writes the numbers.

'And your mobile?'

'I don't have one.'

'What do you mean? It's in your bag.'

'Oh, I borrowed this one from Andrew.'

'Andrew?'

'You met him the other day.'

'You should be careful who you allow to do favours for you, especially men, because it gives them a hold over you. You need your own phone.'

'Andrew is sweet. He wouldn't ever be like that. And, yes, I know I need a phone.'

'I wonder how you've been able to live without one. I will help you choose one.'

Mary hands the notepaper to Jaclyn, who reads out the address and numbers back to her. She has a child-like glee in her eyes.

'When I come, I will bring all my make-up for you to try. I can't wait to see what you would look like with some eyeshadow and lippy.'

'If you'd like.'

'I have to be off to meet an associate professor. Are you right to fix this up?'

'Sure.'

Mary pays at the counter and wonders what it was about Jaclyn's demeanour and actions in the past few minutes that seemed odd. Wanting to do her make-up when clearly

Mary doesn't wear any? Assuming Mary would pay? Meeting up with an associate professor? The way she said it made it sound like a romantic encounter.

I am overthinking things. She is lovely, and she is my friend.

Thinking the words 'my friend' gives Mary comfort. She has someone in the world other than herself that she can lean on at this difficult time.

❧

After eating only half of the burger and hardly touching her hot chocolate, Mary feels energised rather than her usual afternoon food coma. Maybe it was also the fact that she was out socialising. Andrew drops keys on the desk with a clang, disturbing Mary's happy mood.

'Is everything all right?' she says.

'I could ask you the same thing.'

'I'm really good.'

'Yes, I saw you with your new friend.' Andrew makes the sign of air quotes to emphasise 'friend'. 'If you are going to lie about why you need to borrow my phone, at least make your rendezvous in a more discreet location.'

Mary is lost for words. Andrew has never used such a tone with her, let alone been angry with something she has done. And why is he upset she has met with Jaclyn? Why should he care?

'I don't understand why you're angry. I had every intention of ringing the support group, but Jaclyn surprised me and we had lunch. I even told her I could only do 30 minutes, but the service was a bit slow and we got talking.'

'That woman is trouble.'

'How can you say that?'

Andrew pauses for a moment. 'Look, Mary I'm concerned for your welfare. I think she is bad news for you. I feel it in my bones. I can't explain it.'

'You haven't talked to her the way I have. This is my life, and it is time I made decisions for myself. Not my stepmother, not Jodi-Ann, and not you.'

Suddenly Andrew looks forlorn, and Mary thinks she has pressed the point too hard. He doesn't say any more, just sits down and starts reading something. Mary opens her mouth to apologise for how forcefully her words came out, if not the words themselves, but decides against it for fear it would only make things worse. Maybe they need time for things to blow over. Mary takes a pile of science and mathematical journals from Andrew's trolley. At least she can lighten his load as she promised.

The phone rings on her desk. She wonders if Jaclyn has decided on possible weekends to come to her house.

'You've called the library. Mary White speaking. How can I help you?'

'Mary?'

'Yes. Mary White speaking.'

'It's Tony White, your father.'

'Oh, Tony, hello.'

Andrew looks up from what he's doing.

'It's my . . . father,' Mary mouths to him.

'Sorry to disturb you.'

'Yeah, I can't talk. I'm at work.'

'I know, but this is important. I need to see you.'

'Could we meet after work?'

'I thought we could have a meal at the soup kitchen near Central.'

'Have you been following me?'

'No.'

'Have you been drinking?'

'Maybe a little bit.'

'I have a lot of work to do, but I will try to meet you at Central at the Eddy Avenue entrance at 6 pm.'

'Oh, thank you, Mary.'

She hangs up the phone.

'Everything okay?' Andrew comes around to her desk.

'Is anything in my life normal?'

'It seems not to be at the moment.'

'Tony wants me to have dinner with him at a soup kitchen.'

'At least now you can ask him more about your mother. Do you want me to come along for moral support?'

'No, I have to do this on my own.'

'Hey, I'm sorry about before. I should have known that Jaclyn surprised you and you weren't deliberately deceiving me. It's not in your nature.'

'Thanks, Andrew. I would never lie to you.'

'We have each other's backs.'

'We do.'

She wants to hug him, but in the three and a half years they have worked together, they have not shown that kind of affection. Besides, Jodi-Ann would never stand for it.

෨෯

Sitting across from her father in an austere soup kitchen, a piece of food caught in his beard, Mary's heart swells with a pity she has never felt for anyone before.

'It is so good to have the chance to see you again,' Tony says, tears welling up in his eyes.

'It's okay.'

Tony wipes his eyes with the back of his hand, leaving dark smears across his face. 'I wonder how things would have been if your mother hadn't died, or if I hadn't given up. We could have lived as a happy family.' He bends over, holding his head in his hands.

Mary leans across and places a hand on his shoulder. He covers her hand with his and straightens up to look her in the eye.

'I know I should be well and truly over this, but now that I've met you again, I can't stop thinking how I've let you down over the years. I've missed out on so much. What a mess I've made of my life.'

'Well, today is a new day.'

Tony's sudden grin with the missing front tooth gives him an endearing quality.

For a while they eat in silence. The thick pea and ham soup is particularly good. It tastes home-made with a richer, stronger ham flavour than the watered-down can variety she remembers from childhood. Why should that be a surprise? The homeless deserve to eat as well as everyone else. She wonders if they will share the recipe.

Tony pushes his bowl aside and looks into Mary's eyes. 'I have so much to tell you about your early years. Is there anything you'd like to know?'

The questions come flooding into her mind, and she doesn't know where to start.

Being in care!

She asks Tony about the residential home where she lived for those early years of her life. He confirms it is the building she found on the support group's website in inner western Sydney that has since closed. So now she can ask the group directly for help to obtain her files. She asks him to tell her everything he can about the time he and Isabel picked her up from the home. He has answers for every question. She was a quiet child and hugged them tightly when they arrived to take her home, seeming to be so appreciative to have a family. The other girls were standing in a row, apparently under orders from the carer in charge, a stern woman, and there was an obvious tension between the children and Mary. She had to be coerced to farewell each one individually, which didn't seem in keeping with the loving nature she had demonstrated in the greeting she'd given Tony and Isabel. Then, when she came to the end of the row, the last girl started screaming her name and couldn't be consoled.

'You did a remarkable thing, almost as though you had done it before. You patted her on the back and said "Your mummy is coming. Your mummy is coming." The girl immediately became silent. I knew at that moment you were a very compassionate person, just like Mary, your mother.'

Mary's eyes fill with tears at the love the young girl, who happened to be herself, showed an orphan who wasn't the one chosen to go home with a family. She knows that as well as finding out as much as she can about those early years in the home, she should see if she can find that little girl and learn what happened to her.

'I know you feel bad about everything, but I want to thank you for getting me out of there and giving me a home that I continued to live in even when you had gone.'

'That is a small mercy, but a mercy all the same.'

'I have flashbacks to being tormented and bullied by young kids and I have often wondered where I was. Now I realise it was the residential home.'

Tony's eyes fill with tears again.

'What happened after you picked me up? I have no memory of you.'

Tony starts to cry. 'I don't know how to tell you this.'

'Take your time.' Mary feels compassion for the man. It reminds her of what he said about her grace towards the little girl who was left behind in the home.

'Not long after you came to live with us, I started drinking heavily. You reminded me so much of your mother. I numbed the pain of her loss and the burden of caring for a vulnerable child with whiskey. I would drink myself unconscious, and Isabel would put me into bed and take care of you. She doted on you as though you were her own.'

'What happened?'

'One night, maybe three months later, I came home rotten drunk from the pub. Some of my belongings were on the front lawn. Isabel kicked me out. She kicked me out of the house I had bought, the house I shared with your mother. Isabel said I was a drunk and if I didn't leave your lives, she would report me to Community Services, and I would be forcibly removed from the home. After Mary died, I became a coward, and it was easier to go than to fight. Besides, I had nothing to recommend me. I was a bum and a drunk. I wasn't fit to be a father.'

'So, you left me in the care of a woman who was no blood relation?'

'I regret that every day, though I am glad to see you turned out all right.'

'But my whole life was based on a lie.' Mary swallows a mouthful of soup.

'I thought it was better that you were with someone who truly cared for you than an irresponsible drunk like me. It took me about 10 years to kick the drink, get a decent job and put my life back together, but Isabel refused to let me see you. She said the shock would be too great. I didn't know she'd told you I'd died.'

☙❦☙

Mary leaves Tony at Central, where he has a bed in a shelter for the night. Once she is home, she removes her sneakers and coat, puts Hercules on her bed and gets under the covers fully dressed. Then she starts to howl, and howl. Hercules nudges her to go under the covers. And she howls some more, comforted by his softness under her arm. She laments how cruel life has been to her, making her live under the control of a domineering stepmother rather than the warm embrace of two loving parents.

Chapter 10

Edith decides the only way she will protect herself and get Jaclyn out of Seaview Manor is to play along with her housemate until she works out a proper plan. Jaclyn appears to be happy today, and Edith knows she is probably more pliable in this state.

'Why so chipper?'

'I have a new friend. Her name's Mary.'

Haven't we already had this conversation?

'That's lovely, dear. Let's go into the sitting room, and you can tell me all about her.'

'I thought I wasn't allowed in your favourite room.'

'I can make exceptions now and then.'

Edith guides Jaclyn to the sitting room. Talk of Mary was only a decoy to get Jaclyn to sit down and be calm. Jaclyn is restless on the antique lounge, fidgeting like an excited child.

'That is good news about your new friend.'

Jaclyn giggles. 'You should see this girl. a real frump. She's overweight. Completely no dress sense. A doll for me to dress and play with.'

'I see.'

'I've got such great plans for her. Extreme diet. Great clothes. You should see what she wears.'

Jaclyn's eyes are cold and glazed despite her animated language.

She sniggers. 'Dresses like she's an old woman. Skivvies and pants. It is so sad.'

'She can really use your help then.'

'Great hair though. Long and luscious and those curls.'

Edith wonders about this poor girl, who thinks Jaclyn is a messiah who has the answer to her mundane life. At least she's young and not an old fool duped by Jaclyn's youthful exuberance.

Or was she betrayed by her own need for some help and company and perhaps to recapture some of her lost youth?

Edith brings her thoughts back into the present and realises this innocent girl, Mary, may help her get Jaclyn out of the house.

I wonder what this girl sees in Jaclyn?

'Someone's at the front door,' Jaclyn says, jumping up. 'It must be a parcel I ordered online. Stay here, Edith. No need for us both to go.'

Edith hears a key turning in the door. Jaclyn has locked her in.

⟨❦⟩

Edith is moving through a long passageway to the back door. It's as though the corridor will never end, but eventually she finds herself in the back garden. She can't remember when she was last here, or when the garden became so overgrown, but out here, away from the intense heaviness of the house, she feels free. She sees the gum where she used to swing on a thick rope tied to a sturdy branch. Her childhood has been vivid lately.

Suddenly Edith has the sensation of floating. Past the gum tree. Past the angel fountain, which hasn't been running for years. She stops at the fountain a moment and thinks she sees an angel in a brilliant white robe with magnificent wings.

Edith closes her eyes, and the angel is in her mind's eye, beckoning with a beautiful hand and overwhelming love in his eyes. His pull on her is impossible to resist. She follows the winding, overgrown path to the magnificent being with an aura of pink-gold light as he turns to walk further down the pebble stone path. Edith is compelled to follow.

The landscape has a misty quality. While before she felt like she was floating, now she is buoyed by the immense warmth of the angel's love, which envelops everything around him. She is completely at peace. It has been a long time since she has felt like that. She was angry and agitated for so long that she didn't know any other way to be.

The angel leads her to a shady spot where the trees are overrun with pest vines that are choking them. Edith feels heavy. The angel turns to face her and radiates love. She feels better, but why can't she smell the dampness, moss and rotting leaves?

The angel's mouth does not move, but in her mind she hears: *No matter what happens, everything will be all right.*

He leads her deeper into the shadows and stops at a patch of ground where a tarpaulin is covering a mound. He points at it. Still, he doesn't say or do anything. Unaided, a corner of the heavy material begins to lift and roll off the item it is covering.

At first the scene is fuzzy. Edith does not know what she is looking at. Then, as though her focus has suddenly sharpened, she sees a woman's feet. The tarpaulin, pulled by an invisible force, reveals stockinged legs, a navy skirt, a white blouse. This all seems familiar to Edith. She does not want to see what comes next but cannot turn away. The tarpaulin hovers at the neck. Edith looks at the angel for . . . comfort? An explanation?

She feels his love intensify and her fears melt. She knows he is preparing her and that she must be still for a moment.

She is completely calm as the sheet uncovers a face. And the face, though decayed, is unmistakably her own.

I'm dreaming. I will wake up at any moment.

Edith wants to scream, but she has no voice. She wants to punch the air, but she has no strength.

The angel opens his huge wings and beckons her to him.

Edith wants to run to him, but she's glued to the spot. And yet she is now enveloped in a soft warm energy. Her mind can't make out how she got here. She is standing in a pink fluffy cloud alone with the angel, but she can feel the firmness of a loving hug around her. She experiences a warmth throughout her being that relieves her of her trepidation, if only for a moment.

The angel holds his hand up to Edith's forehead and she feels warm energy in the centre. Scenes start to race through her mind. She is watching them from outside the scene. She sees herself open the big front door. A woman with long black hair and bright red lipstick on her pale face appears in response to the advertisement for a boarder. The woman demands to see her room. Edith tries to say she would like to think about whether she really wants a boarder, but the woman says an old lady like her must need a young person to look after the place. In Edith's moment of hesitation, the woman makes her way up the stairs.

Whoosh. Her mind takes her to a few days later when the woman returns with a single suitcase and a beaten-up vintage car. Edith wonders if that is all the woman owns in the world or if she can expect a removalist truck to turn up later. She greets her new tenant warmly, but the woman walks past without acknowledging her.

The film in her mind suddenly shows her in her bedroom. She is lying on her four-poster bed reading *Wuthering Heights*. She has read it before, but she rarely remembers anything after she has finished it. A storm is brewing outside, and the autumn wind is rattling the closed window, but she feels safe inside. Time speeds up, and the door bursts open. The woman is standing in the doorway, her hair dishevelled and her black shirt half hanging out of her skirt. She is barefoot. She has crazy, bloodshot eyes.

Edith puts the book on the bedside table. Her heart is pumping wildly under her white blouse, belying the calm exterior.

The woman lets out a bloodcurdling scream and runs towards Edith. Instinctively, Edith slips off the bed and ducks as the woman lunges for her. The crazed woman pulls over a dresser and all the items come crashing to the ground. The fancy brush, comb and mirror, the antique water jug and bowl, the timber inlay jewellery box. The big mirror over the dresser hits the corner of the bed and cracks. Edith's leg is caught by the corner of the chest of drawers. She's trapped. The woman is emptying out one of two armoires, spilling the clothes on the floor on the other side of the room. Edith desperately pulls at her leg from beneath the heavy chest. The woman pulls at the centrepiece of the empty armoire and jumps clear as the antique furniture piece falls on the bed, making a harrowing sound as the bed frame starts to give way. Edith pulls harder on her leg, breaking free before the bed collapses. Blood streams down the skin where she has torn it.

Like an animal that has picked up the scent of blood, the attacker turns her head sharply in Edith's direction, her eyes mad and red. She kicks the dresser's mirror which separates her from Edith, and it shatters. The woman pulls a large chard of the glass from its frame and holds it up for a moment, studying its raw edges in the light. Too far from the door to escape, Edith has stopped her struggle. Resigned. She wonders why she is not like the animal that will continue to battle to live right to the end. She knows nothing more can be done.

'May God have mercy on your soul, and mine.'

Edith wakes sitting in her favourite Louis XV bergère chair, wondering what kind of a wild dream she's had.

Did she just see a vision of her death at the hands of Jaclyn? She must do everything she can to stop her!

Chapter 11

Mary takes an early train, connecting at Central to Martin Place. She crosses Macquarie Street and walks past Sydney Hospital and Parliament House. A man is standing outside the big black iron gates holding a placard about being thrown out of public housing onto the street. He reminds her of Tony.

She doesn't want to think about all that right now. She looks at the sky above, a fresh blue, cleared of the pollution haze by the rain. Fresh beginnings.

She walks past the library and marvels at the big banners advertising an exhibition of the great maritime explorers coming soon. She is looking forward to that one, particularly the botanical drawings of Joseph Banks.

Mary wants time to wander around the Royal Botanic Garden before Andrew arrives for their breakfast picnic. The picnic before work was her idea, which surprised her even though she knew it sprang from the conversation with Jaclyn. Her life is so regimented, she hasn't needed ideas for novel activities. Andrew is bringing the bacon and egg rolls and hot drinks, and the picnic blanket. He said he wanted to make up for overreacting to her lunch with Jaclyn.

As Mary walks into the gardens at the Macquarie Street entrance, she takes in a huge gulp of air and lets it out with a sigh. She meanders through the rose garden. The blooms are finishing. There are still a few. Soft pink. Lilac. Velvety red. A sweet old-fashioned scent draws her to the red roses, and she holds one in her hand to breathe it in fully. Mary follows the path lined with statues to the fernery. She can sit quietly for a few minutes. The air is cool outside but inside the fernery it is temperate.

She tries to imagine which of the plants she will add to her garden. That is what she must do – plant seeds and watch them grow. She wonders if her birth mother had a green thumb. Tony doesn't look like he would know anything about plants.

Mary walks back in the direction of the pavilion in the herb garden as Andrew arrives.

Does he always look this good?

She pushes the thought to the back of her mind. Still, she notices the freshness of his clothes, his clean-shaven face and slightly spiked haircut. The crispness of his white business shirt that is open at the neck and neatly tucked into well-fitting grey trousers. The shy smile. The cute dimples.

She can't be thinking like this. He's her work colleague. Besides, Andrew would never be interested in her. It's silly.

I have to be happy that he wants to be my friend. We're friends, aren't we?

'Hi, Mary. What a beautiful morning.'

They set up the blanket on the grass near a fragrant rosemary bush. The bacon and egg are still warm in the bun. It has a lashing of barbecue sauce she wasn't expecting, but it adds a fruitiness that makes it even more delicious. The hot chocolate is soothing.

'There's something different about you, Mary. I'm not sure what it is.'

Mary looks into Andrew's brown eyes for what is possibly the first time. The lingering eye contact shocks her. He is looking back at her, waiting for her reply. She doesn't have words. Is she different? Has the news that the woman who reared her was not her mother and that her father was alive this whole time changed her?

'I thought I had so much in common with the woman who pretended to be my mother, our likes, dislikes, the books we read, our love for gardening and being at home.' Mary pauses. 'But it was all a lie. Is any of that me?'

Mary starts to cry. Andrew gives her a clean handkerchief from his pocket.

'I don't think you can feign a passion. Look at how much you love these gardens. That is part of who you are.'

'Is it?'

'Of course, it is. And your devotion to Hercules,' Andrew says. 'How is he?'

The question shocks Mary with its normality. She relaxes.

'Wonderful. Hercules is simply wonderful. It doesn't matter what happens, I can rely on him to be there.'

'I have to meet this character. Why don't we go for a walk. I've heard it helps move the emotions through.'

As they pass the kiosk-style café near the giant water gum, Mary suggests they pick up more hot drinks, her shout this time, to take to the office. She secretly wants to spend more time with Andrew. A pigeon is scouring the floor for scraps around the feet of a young family. As they wait for their long black and hot chocolate, Mary watches the bird's little head bob up and down and wonders what it would be like to live on pure instinct, living in the absolute belief that your needs will be taken care of with no fear of the future.

'He's pretty tame, isn't he?' Andrew says.

Mary smiles at Andrew, nodding in agreement.

'If only life were that simple,' she says.

'If life were that simple, it wouldn't be very exciting.'

On the way back, Mary is captivated by the Oriental Garden and stops to gaze at the various petite plants.

Simplicity versus excitement, she thinks. She feels like light has been shed on a mystery. If we have simplicity, we lack excitement and vice versa. A simple life is a quiet life.

That's what Isabel wanted, but is it what I want?

Andrew is a fair way ahead of her. She starts to run, holding her thumb over the opening in the lid on her takeaway cup. At that moment, Andrew turns around to look for her and stops.

'You were right there, and then you weren't,' he says.

Mary laughs. 'I should have warned you about that. I lose myself in these gardens.'

'Look at this place in the heart of the central business district. Why wouldn't you? We are so close to it, and yet I hardly ever come here.'

Her heart has been transformed. After crying for days, her lungs, chest and eyes were strained until only a few tears could be wrung from her body. Now it's different. Her stomach is nervy, and her head feels light. She is sharing her gardens. Walking around on her own, she can devote her attention to the foliage, the trunks and branches and the flowers. Now the experience is a backdrop for her new focus, the fall of Andrew's shirt over his shoulders and back. How is that so appealing? It's the setting for a state of wellbeing, drifting through time and space, thinking life is wonderful and nothing exists except this moment. What more should there be? She is excited and calm at once.

Mary draws up next to Andrew and walks close enough to notice his aftershave. The long sleeve of her blouse brushes against his shirt sleeve as she lifts her arm to point to some flying foxes. Andrew smiles. Mary hopes it's only slight embarrassment at the accidental touch and not recognition of their first intimate moment. She smiles back. She can't help herself.

We're friends. Just friends.

'What do you think of the flying foxes?' Mary says.

'Only a mother could love them.'

'I'm fascinated by them.' Mary pauses to watch the few bats that are left. 'It's a shame they had to employ the dispersal program,' she continues.

'The people here are conservationists, so if they thought the flying foxes were doing too much damage to the gardens, then they did what they had to do to discourage them.'

'But isn't it amazing that these creatures live wild in a city like Sydney?'

'It is. Not many people would appreciate that.'

Mary doesn't know much about Andrew. He lives alone. He doesn't seem to have a girlfriend. He certainly doesn't talk about a girl or have a photo on his desk. His parents are living, but he isn't close to them. She doesn't know about his hobbies.

'What do you think we have in common apart from work?' She speaks her thoughts aloud and immediately regrets it.

'Not ghost tours, that's for sure.'

'People don't really see ghosts on the tour. It's more about the buildings and the stories of the times.'

'I was only kidding. I would love to share the ghost tour with you.'

'Really?'

Mary is surprised by the exuberance in her voice and her instinct to hug Andrew. She stops herself in time.

'How about we book the 7.45 pm tour next Saturday?'

'So, you've been researching the tour?'

'Well . . .'

'How else would you know the exact time?'

'I thought it might be a way to cheer you up after everything that's been going on. I can put aside my fears about the air temperature dropping and the hairs standing on the back of my neck when a ghost is present.'

'Stop! You're scaring me.'

'You're the one who wants to do it.'

His smile is warm and cheeky, showing both amusement and an interest in her. Why hadn't she noticed this before?

'Okay. Next Saturday it is.'

After talking about it as a possibility so often to Andrew, now she's apprehensive.

It's only two hours. Andrew will be with me.

'Okay it's a date . . . you know what I mean,' Andrew says.

A blush extends across his face. Mary feels her face warm at the sight of his red cheeks and the sound of his embarrassed giggle.

Oh God, my cheeks are burning up. How do I stop it?

'You can stay at mine, so you don't have to drive home.' The redness in Andrew's face deepens.

'There must be a cheap hostel in The Rocks.'

Oh no, will he think I'm inviting him to stay with me at a hotel?

Mary feels the heat in her face intensifying. She looks at her watch.

'It's 10 past nine. Jodi-Ann will be breathing fire. You know what a clock-watcher she is.'

'I'll go in first and take the heat.'

'You don't have to do that.'

'We can't go in together.'

'You're right.'

Andrew starts walking quickly, and Mary stops for a few minutes to give him time to get to his desk.

Chapter 12

It is Friday night, and Mary is already wishing away the weekend. She is smiling, going over every look, word and moment spent in the Botanic Garden with Andrew earlier in the day as she drives home from Leura railway station. It's dark, yet peaceful. She loves this area. She is happy, buzzing. Her rumbling stomach brings her back into the everyday.

Mary gets out of her car and manually opens the large hinged wooden door on the old garage before driving in and parking. A shiver comes over her as she turns off the lights. Something is different. The peace is gone. Replaced by hairs on the back of her neck. In the cooler months, she always drives home from the station in the dark. She has walked through the old garage in blackness too many times to count and never been spooked like this before. Maybe it's all the talk about ghosts with Andrew.

Mary walks out the front and the street is lit only by bright moonlight. A sudden breeze on her cheek sends a chill down her spine as she walks around a baby flowering cherry tree and heads for the front path. Moonlight shows the path to the door, but the rest of the porch is in darkness.

Another shiver. Must be the cold air.

As she puts a foot on the path that runs through her front lawn, she senses a presence. Someone is watching her. She quickens her pace to the front door, straining to hear anything unusual. Silence, but not a peaceful quiet. Something is wrong. She's made it to the porch. Now she must get inside. Involuntarily, she darts a glance to her right. Someone is there. A figure shrouded in darkness. There is a thud in Mary's chest. Her heart rate quickens. She spins around and runs down the path, feeling in her jacket pocket for the car keys.

'Mary,' shouts a desperate woman's voice. 'It's me, Jaclyn.'

Mary stops on the footpath. The woman walking out of the shadows is indeed Jaclyn. The sinister stranger is suddenly familiar in the light.

'Oh, Jaclyn. You scared me half to death.'

'Come here.'

Jaclyn puts her arms around Mary as if to comfort her. Mary shrinks at the touch. She finds no comfort in the embrace. No friendship. No warmth. She wishes Andrew were here. Jaclyn holds Mary a little tighter, and Mary wills with all her might not to pull away.

'Let's get inside before we both freeze to death,' Mary says, while wishing Jaclyn would go home instead.

'I like it in the dark. Can't we sit out here and talk?'

'I really need to feed Hercules . . . my cat.' Saying his name out loud gives her strength. She makes a move towards the door. 'The poor boy will be starving.'

Mary puts the key in the lock of the screen door. The lock sticks.

'Stupid lock.' Mary rattles the key. Finally, it gives. 'I thought we were going to arrange a time for you to come over – for tea on the weekend.'

Mary has the screen door open and the key in the front door. 'You know Jaclyn, I am quite tired. I think I'd like to go straight to bed. Do you think we could meet up for coffee one lunch time next week?'

'You want to get rid of me. Did that nerdy colleague of yours say bad things about me? You should watch him.'

'Nobody has said bad things about you. I've had a rough week, and I need to be alone.'

'What you need is some TLC, and I need a place to stay for the night. I can't drive home now. Have you forgotten how I helped you out the other day?'

Mary is trying to think of an out but can't find one. If she refuses to let Jaclyn into the house, her visitor will get angry and make a scene. After all, Mary did give Jaclyn the address, so it isn't unreasonable for her to think she would be welcome.

She tells herself everything is okay. She is freaking herself out because she thought it was someone else. If it was daytime, she wouldn't feel like this. Jaclyn is her friend.

'You can stay in the front room. I changed the sheets a couple of days ago. Staying busy helps me keep my mind off things.' Mary turns the light on in the front foyer and puts the key in the lock at the back of the door, a habit from when Isabel was alive in case they needed to escape a fire. She can hear Hercules crying from the kitchen.

'Funny hallway,' Jaclyn says as Mary leads her through the house. 'I wonder why they made it crooked like this.'

'I don't know.'

When Mary opens the kitchen door Hercules is waiting and sneaks through as soon as he finds a gap.

He hisses loudly at Jaclyn. His tail flairs up like a bottlebrush, and he bares his teeth.

'Hercules, stop that.'

Jaclyn jumps behind Mary for protection.

'Hercules, in the kitchen now!' Mary yells.

The cat runs in the direction of her bedroom.

'He's probably under the bed by now. I'm so sorry about that. He's not used to having anyone in the house.'

'Oh, it's all right. Cats normally come round in the end. He's very beautiful.' Jaclyn is standing near the laminated dining table for four.

'Please sit down. Would you like some cocoa?'

'Can we go out and get a coffee or something stronger?'

'Everything closes pretty early in Leura. I've probably got Baileys somewhere. I think Isa— Mum kept it in the liquor cabinet. I could put some in instant coffee.'

'It will be well aged then. Didn't you say your mother died three years ago?'

Mary wishes she hadn't mentioned Isabel. She's conflicted about her stepmother, but hearing her passing used as a time stamp for alcohol is upsetting.

Jaclyn drinks the coffee mixture quickly.

'Any more?' she says.

Mary gives Jaclyn the Irish cream bottle and then microwaves herself leftover stew to pour over toast the way Isabel used to. Stew on toast always comforts her. She takes the plastic container from the microwave with two oven mitts to avoid steam burns. When she turns around to put the container on a cork mat in readiness for the toast, she sees Jaclyn head down on the table, apparently out of it.

Mary calls Jaclyn's name three times and on the third Jaclyn opens her eyes but is very drowsy. Mary holds her by the arm and helps her up, grateful for Jaclyn's slight frame. She is so skinny and bony, probably anorexic. Jaclyn rises like a sleeping child and lets Mary guide her to the front bedroom. While holding Jaclyn's arm with her left hand, she pulls back the floral bedspread with the right and guides Jaclyn into bed, on top of the blanket and sheets and pulls the bedspread over her. She opens the armoire, takes a woollen blanket from the top shelf and places it over the bedspread on top of Jaclyn. She seems peaceful.

What was I worried about? Everything is fine.

ಎ⁖ಎ

Mary wakes naturally with the light, though it is an overcast day, all the better to snuggle under the doona with Hercules. She remembers Andrew's last words to her at the end of the workday. 'You are such a talented botanical artist.' Apart from a photo of Hercules, the only decorative item on Mary's desk at work is a small line drawing of a Sturt's desert pea, framed and sitting on a miniature easel. She drew it while Isabel was still alive. Her stepmother said it was her best drawing. That was one of the few compliments Isabel ever gave her, possibly why she cherishes it so much. She's not used to getting praise, so Andrew's words warmed her heart more than he could know. A loud noise of something dropping disturbs her happy thoughts. Someone is in the house. *Jaclyn!*

Mary finds her guest sitting at the kitchen table. She hopes they can have a quick cup of tea and Jaclyn will be on her way. If she can't be with Andrew, she wants to be on her own today.

'Good morning, Jaclyn. Did you sleep okay?'

'Off and on. I was waiting for you to get up. I'm hoping you'll take me to see the sites today.'

'It's probably more a hot chocolate and flowerpot scones day.'

'You know I don't eat carbs.'

'The flowerpot scones are to die for. They bake them in little terracotta flowerpots. Each one has enough for three people.'

'Really, Mary, that is something we shall have to work on with you. If you are going to attract a man, you'll have to lose at least 15 kilograms.'

'I am happy the way I am.'

'How can you be?'

Mary looks at Jaclyn's skeletal frame and imagines that her own size 14 build must seem elephant-like by comparison. She wonders how Jaclyn can be happy with her bird-like features but immediately chides herself for judging another person. That's not who she is.

'I am coming to terms with who I am. I have so many issues needing answers, but my body is not one of them. I'm happy with it.'

'You don't want to be eating too many of those scones, or you'll be the size of a house.'

How can she talk to me like that?

'I guess life is a continual balancing act. I will concede I need to walk more.'

'Perfect. You go and get dressed. Then we'll go for a brisk walk to clear the mind. That will work up an appetite and you can come back and make some breakfast. I don't eat breakfast, of course. Do you have any herbal tea?'

'Ah, no.'

'I'll get some today.'

Mary feels an invisible force pressing on her. She sees a pattern. She felt it when her mother barked orders at her and has the same reaction when Jodi-Ann makes comments about how she should dress for her age. She thought that was how it was for kids and employees. Apart from Hercules's ability to twist her around his paw, she should be able to feel free from pressure from others in her own home.

'I have to find a way to get Jaclyn to go home,' she mutters as Hercules lifts his head when she enters her bedroom.

Mary dresses in black trousers, a white skivvy and red jumper. She has comfortable flat leather shoes. She doesn't put on runners or hiking boots because that would give Jaclyn the impression she wants to go on a proper hike. There's no harm going for a walk around the block.

She picks Hercules up from the bed and takes him into the kitchen. He hisses when he sees Jaclyn at the sink with a glass under the running tap. Jaclyn turns around and glares at Mary. She puts the cat down.

'Naughty boy,' Mary points her finger at the cat. She turns to Jaclyn. 'He hasn't had his breakfast yet.'

'That cat eats too much. Look at him. He needs to go on a diet.' Jaclyn turns off the tap and drinks from the glass.

'He's fine,' Mary mumbles under her breath.

'This look of yours is very Christmas in July, and not in a good way,' Jaclyn snarls.

'Look, Jaclyn, I think I need to be frank with you. I don't want to go for a walk or see the sights today. I've been through a lot. I want to stay at home and rest. I'm not feeling well, and I'm in no mood for company.'

'You can say that again.'

'It's sweet of you to understand.'

'Next time I'll expect to see all the sights. But you can make it up to me now. Come to Sunday dinner.'

'Okay,' Mary says, managing a smile.

'No, I've changed my mind. I really want to go to a lookout.'

'But . . .'

'No buts. Have some breakfast.'

'What will you eat?'

'I told you I don't do breakfast.'

'Jaclyn. I really don't want to go out in this cold. You have your car. You can drive yourself down. It's easy to find Echo Point. All the signs lead you there.'

'I would think that after I helped you the other day this would be a friendly thing for you to do in return.'

'Okay.'

Mary can see no way out but to agree. The word 'okay' sticks in her throat like the dry Weetbix her stepmother once made her eat when they ran out of milk. Mary feels weak. There must be something she can do or say to make this woman leave. What if she insisted that she didn't feel well? No, that would only prolong her indebtedness to Jaclyn.

Mary decides to buy time by cooking bacon and eggs. She feeds Hercules, and he guards his bowl jealously, eating as though it's his last meal. Mary stops herself from talking to him to calm him for fear of the scathing remarks Jaclyn will make. She has heard enough criticism of Hercules and herself for one day.

As she gets a carton of eggs and bacon rashers from the fridge, Hercules jumps on the kitchen table and then on top of the fridge.

'Strange beast,' Jaclyn says.

'His breed loves to be up high,' Mary says.

She doesn't add that he must be feeling threatened to be that high up while she is home. Sometimes he's up there when she returns from work.

Mary cracks two eggs into a buttered cast iron frying pan. Each one sizzles as it hits the hot pan. She finds comfort in the sound. Despite Isabel's deceit, Mary still remembers the happy times with fondness. Like hot breakfasts on the weekend, a tradition her stepmother started when Mary was about 10 years old. She would always jump out of bed and run into the kitchen at the sound of eggs frying and the smell of salty bacon grilling.

'I'm going into the lounge room,' Jaclyn says. 'The smell of eggs makes me gag.' Her voice is like sandpaper rubbing out a perfectly good moment.

When Jaclyn leaves the room, Hercules stretches out of his curled pose and meows.

No, Herc, she's not gone, she wants to tell him.

The cat jumps down and tackles more of his food.

Mary goes about her breakfast routine normally. The aroma of her food has given her a temporary reprieve. She makes it last. She heats milk for hot chocolate, puts toast in the 30-year-old toaster and places bacon under the grill.

The house is quiet, and she assumes Jaclyn is resting.

Mary serves up her hot breakfast on a thick yellow ceramic plate and glances at the big face of the timber-framed clock. Quarter to six.

It's too early for breakfast on a weekend. The gas stove has heated the kitchen, and she wants to stay here. Who in their right mind would venture into that cold unless they had to?

Hercules sits at her feet as she consumes her breakfast. It tastes good. She is noticing the orangey yellow of the runny yoke as it drips over the piece of toast. The bacon is salty and fresh.

I really don't want to go anywhere with Jaclyn. Why can't I stand up to her?

Mary finishes her breakfast and knows it is time to face her guest again. She gathers all her strength and walks into the lounge room. There is no sign of Jaclyn.

'Jaclyn!' she calls.

Mary walks into the entrance. Not there either. She tiptoes into the front bedroom that belonged to her step-mother, thinking Jaclyn might have gone back to bed. The bed is empty. The blanket she used to cover her last night lies in a heap on one side, spoiling the otherwise pristine nature of the room that is the same as it was when Mary's stepmother died. The blinds are closed with the soft georgette pink curtains held back with ties on each side. The air is stale.

Jaclyn is not in the second bedroom either. Panic grips Mary as she walks through the hall to her own bedroom. Will she find Jaclyn lying on her bed like a cursed princess in a fractured fairytale? What will she do?

She opens the door. She gasps at the sight of open drawers and clothes strewn on the floor. One door of the armoire is open. Skirts, pants and dresses have been flung on the bed.

'Jaclyn,' she mouths, barely audibly. 'Jaclyn.' Her voice is now at a normal level.

The house is silent.

Mary holds the cold antique handle on the closed armoire door and rests her ear against the timber. There's no sound. She tightens her whole body and pulls on the handle in a swift motion.

The motionless form of Jaclyn is standing there, her eyes wide and staring as though she's dead.

Mary pulls back in horror. She shuts the door and runs into the kitchen to check on Hercules.

Her heart races now because she knows this is her chance to escape. She must take Herc with her. Where will she go? She has to get into the car. She will work the rest out later. She needs the cat box, her car keys, her purse. No time to worry about clothes and toiletries. She'll have to buy those.

She runs down the rickety timber stairs at the back of the house to retrieve the cat box from under the house. She doesn't want to leave Herc alone with Jaclyn, but she needs his box, or he'll go crazy in the car. She finds the dusty grey carrier and runs back up the stairs, pushing the fly screen door open. The dark figure of Jaclyn is sitting at the kitchen table. Hercules is on top of the fridge. His tail is thick like a skunk, and his hair is spiked. His pupils are big.

'Mary, you are an odd one. What is all this rushing about at this hour. What's the box for? Surely the cat isn't coming with us, is he?'

'Well, I, um, wanted to clean his box before we left. I have to take him to the vet soon.'

'Why all the running? I thought you were meant to take it easy in the Blue Mountains. Isn't that why people come here? To relax?'

'I guess so.' Mary places the cat box on the table and sits on a chair.

What do I do now?

'So, are you driving, or shall I?' Jaclyn says.

'I will. You're the guest, and I have a full tank of petrol.'

'Great. Let's get going then.'

Chapter 13

Sublime Point is one of Mary's favourite spots. It is only a short drive from the Leura township. She has done it so often it's like the car has a mind of its own. When she passes the golf course, she realises she hasn't been aware of the road for a few minutes. Why didn't she drive to Echo Point where there's bound to be plenty of tourists marvelling at the Three Sisters, even at this hour? Sublime Point can be lonely at any time.

Mary quivers, feeling the bitter air on her face. 'Gosh, it's cold.'

Her stepmother's car doesn't have air conditioning, but she's grateful for Isabel's coat, beanie and scarf. It is amazing how people from other countries don't realise how cold it can get in the mountains of Australia. It is a bitter cold that seeps through to your bones and irritates you until you escape inside and warm yourself near a fire.

This thought leads Mary to think of flowerpot scones. Anything but a walk in the bush today.

She reprimands herself for being so selfish. She glances at Jaclyn, squeezed into the passenger seat. She can feel her face soften and say with her normal tone, 'Jaclyn, you are going to love this spot. I think it would have to be one of the most peaceful and spectacular places in all of Sydney.'

'How many places have you been to?'

'Not many, but living here, why would I need to go anywhere else?'

'I can show you the most amazing places. I will open the world up to you. You've had a very sheltered life, haven't you?'

Mary does not respond and wonders what makes Jaclyn think it is okay to say such judgemental things to people. Perhaps it is her own natural politeness that stops her from protesting that her world is just fine, thank you. She doesn't want to open it up. That only causes problems.

'. . . like my house. It's a wonderful mansion, an exquisite example of Gothic revival architecture.'

Mary realises she has only caught a fraction of what Jaclyn has been saying. The winding road along the cliff has had her in a trance.

What does she want with me?

Mary parks her car in the small car park surrounded by bush. She turns the key in the ignition with trepidation and remains in the driver's seat while Jaclyn gets out of the car. It is eerie being alone in that rugged beauty. Quiet. Standing on the rocky outcrop with only a short wire mesh fence between you and a mighty plunge down the cliff face. Would anyone even hear you scream?

There's a sharp tap on the window. Mary jumps in her seat.

'Well, aren't you going to show me this beautiful spot?' Jaclyn smiles.

Mary puts on gloves to complete her woollen ensemble. As soon as she opens the car door the air bites her nose.

'Aren't you cold, Jaclyn?' she asks, wrapping her arms around herself. 'You don't even have gloves.'

'A little cold never hurt anyone,' Jaclyn says. 'Let's go.'

'After you.'

'I'd rather you walked first. Bit scared of snakes. I think they'd hear you coming better than me.'

Mary wants to say it's too cold for snakes, but that would be futile against Jaclyn's protests. She walks ahead, quickly. Branches and dry leaves crackle beneath her feet. Jaclyn is only a few steps behind. Mary turns around.

'Isn't it peaceful here?' she says.

Jaclyn stops and brushes leaves from her red pump. 'How far to the point?'

'Just a few steps and we're there. It could be the world's shortest bush walk. See?'

Mary turns back to the path indicating the sandstone steps. Suddenly the cold air is invigorating. She gulps it in and runs up the steps.

'Silly girl.'

Jaclyn's irritation is palpable. Mary runs faster. Then there it is, the sweeping view of the Jamison Valley covered in pink light. The Three Sisters have their backs to her, and yet she wonders why this place is never teaming with visitors. At Echo Point, the popular tourist spot, it's like you're looking at a post card. Here, you are part of the scene, floating above the Australian bush.

Mary hears the clack of Jaclyn's stilettos on the sandstone and then her curses when a heel gets stuck in a crevice.

'What's sublime about this?' Jaclyn's tone is snide as she sidles up to Mary.

Something tells Mary not to answer. If Jaclyn cannot see the wonder of this place, she can't say anything to change her mind.

Jaclyn steadies herself on the wire mesh fence as she slips off her stilettos and places them on the ledge. She hitches her short skirt up to her thighs and swings a leg over the fence.

Mary gasps at the sight of Jaclyn standing on the small sandstone outcrop hanging over a sheer drop.

'Jaclyn, what are you doing?'

'Making this visit a little more exciting.'

Mary's stomach rises as though she's imagining herself free-falling.

'I really think you should come back over to this side,' she says.

'Oh, don't be such a scaredy cat. Come over with me. It's such a thrill.'

'I can't watch.' Mary turns her back on the view and heads for the bush track.

'Look, I'm right on the edge . . . of the world,' she hears Jaclyn behind her.

'I'm not looking,' Mary shouts as though she is talking to a child acting out for attention.

'You're not even curious what happens when I lean over.'

'I can't watch you—'

The scream cuts her words short. She spins around.

'Jaclyn?'

There's no sign of her. Mary's heart makes a heavy thud in her chest.

'Oh, God, Jaclyn.'

She runs to the fence.

'Help me,' comes a cry.

'Jaclyn? Where are you?'

'I'm on a ledge. I'm hurt. You're going to have to help me.'

'You stay where you are, I'll get help.'

'I think I can reach the edge of the rock, if you can pull me up.'

Mary sees a hand grip the edge, and then another. Her heart is pumping. Her face is flushed. Sweat is breaking out on her forehead. She removes her coat and her gloves and forces herself to put one leg over the wire fence and then the other. She feels dizzy and sick at the thought of Jaclyn pulling her over the edge.

She'll kill us both. What was she thinking?

Mary plants her feet firmly on the rock. She glimpses the menacing valley below. Her head is light. What did Isabel say about not looking down?

She looks directly at the thin hands with red-painted nails which shift around the rock every few seconds.

'Mary, you have to help me. I can't hold on like this for much longer. I'm on my toes and my legs are going to give out any minute. And I'm very cold.'

Mary kneels near the edge. The rock surface is rough through the gabardine of her trousers. She inhales deeply to calm herself.

'I am going to pull you up,' she says, forcing a confident tone. 'Can you find a foothold as I lift you?'

'Yes.'

'All right.' Mary takes another deep breath as she grips Jaclyn around the wrists. She eases her right hand under the fingers of Jaclyn's left hand.

'Now I'm going to take your other hand. Please stay calm. Don't pull back.'

Or we'll both go over, Mary wants to say but knows the last thing she wants to do is scare Jaclyn.

To give herself strength, she imagines pulling Jaclyn up onto the ledge before she makes a move. Seeing it in her mind gives her hope and focus.

'Bring one of your feet up to a spot where you can push yourself up as I pull.'

'I don't have much strength left.'

'On the count of three I am going to pull you. Use your feet to push yourself up. You have to help me.'

'Okay.'

'One . . . two . . . three.'

Mary holds herself tight, grips Jaclyn's hands with a strength she didn't know she had and starts to pull. She finds the slight-built woman surprisingly heavy, but she focuses, single-mindedly on pulling and pulling.

Mary hears movement and the sound of something dragging. Skin and clothes being grazed on sandstone. Jaclyn groans.

Keep pulling! Mary tells herself.

Suddenly the weight shifts. Jaclyn is lighter and Mary pulls harder with a grunt. Jaclyn's head clears the ledge. Her face is smeared in blood. Mary stays focused.

'Stay with me, Jaclyn! Keep using your feet. That is helping.' Mary pants.

Now when she pulls, she is stronger. With every 'one, two, three' she counts in her head, she is stronger still and pulls for longer. With this rhythm she drags Jaclyn to the waist. Getting her legs over is easy. Jaclyn lies on the ledge breathing heavily.

'I have to get you to a hospital,' Mary pleads.

'I need to rest, and I'll be fine.'

'Your face needs cleaning up.'

Mary's legs start to wobble, and her stomach is gurgling. She imagines slipping and free-falling to the tree canopy and shudders as she lunges for the fence.

'Aren't you going to help me up?' Jaclyn says.

It is a simple plea, but Mary has no more strength to comply. She doesn't look back. She grips the metal piping on the top of the fence and focuses on the wire configuration in a diamond pattern.

'I got you to the ledge. You'll have to find your own strength now to get over the fence.'

Mary pushes up on her hands on the fence and carefully heaves one leg and then the other over to the safety of the rock platform on the other side. She picks up her coat and gloves and starts walking in the direction of the car.

'Mary,' Jaclyn calls.

Mary is ashamed of her own coldness, her selfishness, but she wants to reach the sanctity of her car before the emotion pours out of her.

'Mary,' Jaclyn calls.

'Maryyyyyyyyyyy!' The scream is bloodcurdling.

Hearing her name expressed so violently is eerily familiar, though she doesn't remember Isabel screaming at her like that, or Jodi-Ann. Jaclyn is a big girl. She can take care of herself. Find her way back to Mary's house, pick up the Buick.

'Mary, they'll think you hurt me!'

The words stop Mary dead in her tracks.

She knows Jaclyn is right. If she left her and she died of exposure, it would be her fault. Mary starts running back to the ledge.

'Jaclyn. I'm coming. Everything will be okay.'

When Mary reaches the lookout, she sees Jaclyn lying on her front. She is very still.

'Jaclyn!' This time Mary is screaming.

'Urrrh . . .' Jaclyn moans.

'You're going to be all right. Nothing is broken, You're tired and cold. I've lost the nerve to come back over the fence, so you're going to have to lift yourself up. Slowly.'

'I can't.'

'You're a very strong woman. You can do whatever you put your mind to.'

131

'You're sounding like Mrs Henderson at the orphanage.'

The orphanage? How can that be? Mary puts the thought to one side and silently wills Jaclyn to get up.

'Think about all the things you have to look forward to when you get home.'

Jaclyn lifts her head, pulls herself up into a sitting position and swings around. Mary is stunned by the seemingly normal activity of her traumatised friend.

'That's it, Sunday dinner. You must come.'

'Tomorrow?'

'Yes.'

I never want to see this woman again. She's completely crazy. What can I do?

'Okay,' she says.

Jaclyn smiles, claps her hands and gets to her feet. Mary notices her entire demeanour has changed. Jaclyn climbs over the fence with ease, puts on her stilettos and virtually races Mary to the car.

'Let's go,' she says, standing by the passenger door of the old Beetle. 'I must get home to make the preparations.'

Mary studies the dried blood on Jaclyn's face, her mattered hair, her shredded and ripped shirt and skirt, her grazed arms and legs.

'You need to go to the hospital,' Mary says.

'What for?'

'You're hurt.'

'I'm fine. What do you think, I can't handle a little bush walk?'

What is going on?

They drive back to the house in silence and even before Mary has turned off the engine, Jaclyn is getting out of the car and walking towards her Buick.

'Don't you want to come inside and wash your face?' Mary shouts after her.

Jaclyn stops and turns around. She wears an eerie grin.

'I left my address on a note on your coffee table last night. Be there at 5 pm sharp tomorrow!'

Mary runs towards the house as the Buick skids and accelerates up the street.

Hercules greets her at the door when she opens it. She picks him up, putting her hand around his rotund stomach. His loud motor-like purr is the most wonderful sound. She closes the front door on the world. She can't be alone. She must call Andrew and ask him to come.

Chapter 14

Every few minutes Mary peers out the lace curtains, waiting for a car to pull up. Hercules lifts his head from his curled position on the recliner. He watches Mary pacing up and down the lounge room, then rests his head again and closes his eyes. Suddenly, his ears straighten, and he looks up.

'Is he here, boy?' Mary runs to the window and sees Andrew parking his car on the street.

She closes the screen door behind her and runs down the few front steps from the porch onto the lawn.

Andrew walks around his classic sports car, looking taller and even more handsome in a russet leather jacket, white T-shirt and jeans.

All the emotions rise in Mary, and she bursts into tears. She turns away so Andrew can't see her but soon feels his arms around her. She turns to face him and buries her head in his shoulder. The tears stop, but she lingers. Hercules meows at the door.

Mary lifts her head and moves out of the embrace, 'Oh, Andrew, you don't know what I've been through.'

She's comforted by the weight of Andrew's arm around her waist.

'Let's make a cup of tea, and you can tell me all about it,' he says.

Mary opens the screen, gently poking her foot between the door and the jamb to prevent Hercules from coming out. The cat retreats.

'Be careful of Herc as you come in. He's a bit like Houdini when it comes to escaping from the house.'

'He's a handsome cat,' Andrew says, carefully closing the door behind him.

Hercules greets Andrew in the hall, purring loudly and wrapping his tail around his leg.

'You've made a good impression already. He usually takes a while to warm to people. I've noticed he responds to the word "handsome".'

'Animals like me. I'm fond of them too.'

Andrew kneels and brushes his hand against the cat's cheek. Hercules responds by rubbing his cheek against the edge of his hand and then pushing his head under Andrew's palm. Andrew pats his head and scratches his chin. When Andrew stands, Hercules circles him, meowing.

'He's looking me in the eye. Do cats normally do that?'

'This breed does. He wants you to sit down, so he can sit on your lap.'

'We have to make tea first.'

Andrew follows Mary through the hallway to the kitchen. Hercules gets there first and sits quietly by his bowl. Mary reaches for the canister of cat biscuits.

'Here, give him some of these.'

Andrew pours biscuits into the cat's bowl.

'This house is so retro,' he says, handing back the canister. 'I've never seen a hall that zigzags like that. And this kitchen. It feels like a museum, so perfectly preserved from the '50s and '60s. I didn't know you were a collector.'

'I'm not. It was all Mum's doing. She taught me that if you keep things in good condition, you don't have to buy much.'

Mary slips a faded rose print apron over her head and ties it at her back, then lifts the kettle from the gas stove to fill it with water. She smiles at Andrew. He smiles back.

'Real tea,' he remarks as she puts several teaspoons of leaf tea into a metal teapot.

Their hands brush against each other as Andrew turns the canister around to reveal the letter 'T' in cursive writing in gold plastic. Mary registers the tingle in her body. The kettle mocks them with its whistle.

'Water's boiled,' Mary says quickly to recover her composure. 'Could you get the milk out of the fridge please?'

She pours the water into the teapot and stirs it twice. She is about to cover the pot in a crocheted olive-green tea cosy when she's struck with its ugliness. She steps on the pedal of the kitchen tidy and discards it, aware of a hint of guilt. She knows it is a defiant act, yet it is liberating.

Suddenly, she's focused again. Andrew is standing before her with the milk. He has a kind of dopey look on his face. He must think her ridiculous, like a comical postcard of a '50s style housewife.

'Thanks,' she says, taking the carton. She asks him to take the teapot into the lounge room.

'Watch out for Herc. He tends to get under your feet when he's excited.' She swings around to see Hercules on the kitchen table, an area they both know is off limits to him.

'Hercules, off!' Mary says, thinking she's not the only one pushing boundaries today.

The cat ignores her.

'Come on, Herc,' Andrew says, getting an immediate response as the cat bounds off the table and runs ahead to the lounge room.

Mary laughs.

'He's not used to having another male in the house,' she says. 'Must see you as top cat.'

Mary comes through the swinging door, carrying milk, sugar and a tea strainer, trying to compose herself. She leans over the table to put the items down and glances at

Andrew. He is looking at her intently. Their eyes linger. Mary stares at the table, placing the strainer over Andrew's cup. She can feel his eyes on her as she pours the tea.

Mary sits on the other side of Hercules, glad the cat is forming a barrier between her and Andrew. As she stirs her tea, the silver spoon tinkling in the porcelain cup and then clinking on the saucer soothes her. She sips her tea. It is good. This moment is good. Having Andrew in her house is good. Maybe she can forget the business with Jaclyn. What's the point of going over it?

'Mary, this is as good a time as any for you to tell me what happened today.'

Andrew puts his cup on the saucer and sits back, ready for a long chat.

'Can't we talk about something happy?'

'We can, and we will, but first I want to hear what happened.'

'I'm glad you've met Jaclyn because after what I tell you, you might think I'm mad.'

'Mary, you're one of the sanest people I know. You said something about her turning up out of the blue and a cliff fall.'

When Mary starts to tell him the story, the words pour out. She recounts every detail of the ordeal. It's like she's living it all over again. This time Andrew's here with her. She's safe.

'You could have been killed.' Andrew sits open-mouthed. 'If you'd fallen over the cliff . . . Do you think she was trying to cause an accident? The main thing is you're not hurt.'

'I'm a bit shellshocked, but better now you're here.'

Andrew leans over Hercules and puts his arm around Mary. She picks the cat up and moves across to be closer to Andrew, then puts Hercules on her lap. They sit that way for a few minutes. Suddenly, Andrew pulls back from her. His eyes are full of panic. He pulls a laptop out of his satchel and hands it to Mary, suggesting she set it up on the kitchen table, so they can both look on.

'It's time we did some research on this Jaclyn woman. Do you remember her last name?'

'Shove Suri. I don't know how to spell it.'

Mary types the name spelled a few different ways, but nothing comes up.

'Oh, she said the name of her house is "Seaview Manor". Maybe we can find something on the house.'

Mary discovers several articles about Seaview Manor, mostly historical. She tries the combination of 'Seaview Manor' and several spellings of 'Jaclyn' before finding the right one. She reads them out to Andrew. The house belongs to Edith Green, whose niece, Helen Demitriou, has asked for public help to find her aunt after the police failed to hear her pleas that she was missing and is offering a reward of 'an undisclosed sum'. She says the last time she spoke to Edith was a month ago, and they have missed one of their Sunday drives. She has called the house and visited, and each time Jaclyn Chauve-Souris says her aunt is asleep or has gone walkabout. A police spokesperson said they had put out a missing persons bulletin for the elderly woman, although the woman's housemate had said Edith had wandered before and always returned.

'That's the story I was reading the other day,' Andrew says. 'I showed you the house.'

'Yes, that's Seaview Manor, where Jaclyn told me she lives, and there's the photo of Edith. She's so sad.'

'Sure is. I hope there's an explanation for all this. Maybe the lady is just a wanderer. There was no mention of a reward in the other article. The niece must be getting desperate for information.'

'And listen to this: "When the *Daily Bugle* went to the woman's house at midday on Friday, Jaclyn Chauve-Souris, a psychology student, said Edith Green was sleeping. She claimed her companion . . ." is she trying to say they are lovers?'

'Sounds that way.'

Mary continues reading the article aloud.

She claimed her companion had told her she didn't want to be disturbed by journalists. But

Ms Chauve-Souris did give a brief interview on the doorstep of the historic house.

'Edith has been having problems with her niece over a period of time, and she would prefer their domestic issues were kept out of the media,' Ms Chauve-Souris said.

'This is a stunt by Helen Demitriou to put her elderly aunt in the grave, so she can take over our magnificent home.'

'How can Jaclyn say these things? She wouldn't even know the niece,' Mary says, continuing to read silently.

'I had a bad feeling about her from the start,' Andrew says, shaking his head.

'Do you think it's possible that something sinister has happened to the old lady?'

'Something weird is going on. That's for sure.'

'Helen's given her mobile number here. I think we should ring her and go and see her today. But first I want to do a bit of research on Jaclyn.'

Andrew leaves her in peace to go and get them hot chocolates at the local chocolate shop she's raved so much about. Mary wonders if he's using that as an excuse and all this drama is becoming too much for him. She's only involved because she ignored Isabel's advice and accepted help from a stranger. Now she must find out everything she can on this woman.

Wanting the extra warmth and comfort of the lounge room and Hercules's company, Mary moves to the lounge with the laptop to continue her research. There are countless entries for Jaclyn Chauve-Souris, both in the news and general web searches. The stories about a missing elderly lady, her housemate, are all similar. There is another story about a house fire three years ago. Jaclyn Chauve-Souris escaped but her housemate died, trapped in the attic bedroom.

Mary is still scrolling through references to J Chauve-Souris when she sees a name she recognises. *Fairy Glen Home for Children*. She's applied for records outlining her own time there. How is this possible?

When she opens the page, there are no details. It is a random list of names. She scans the list but doesn't see any others she recognises. It is dated two years after she was supposed to have left the home.

Andrew arrives before she has a chance to dig further, and she decides to keep this final piece of information to herself until she knows more. She tells him about the tragic fire.

'I wasn't going to tell you this, but now I can see it reinforces that you need to stay the hell away from Jaclyn.'

'What is it?'

'She turned up at work looking for you after you'd left on Friday and was sprouting all sorts of nonsense, like you have similar classes at uni and your friendship goes way back. She said it was like you were sisters, sharing clothes, handbags and boyfriends.'

'Why didn't you tell me about this earlier? You didn't believe her, did you?'

'Of course not. I should have called you immediately, but you have to admit you've been pretty protective of her.'

'There's something not right with her.'

Mary has been so focused on telling Andrew about the incident at Sublime Point that she has forgotten to mention the events leading up to it. She describes the way she felt when Jaclyn appeared in the shadows on her patio and seeing her dead eyes when she opened the armoire door.

Andrew's jaw drops. 'You can never see that woman again. You have to protect yourself from her. Get an apprehended violence order or something.'

'At Sublime Point, to get her over the fence to safety I had to agree to go to her dinner party.'

'You're not going?'

Mary looks at Hercules and pats him without saying anything.

'Mary?'

She looks up at Andrew and ponders his stern expression.

'It's tomorrow. It's the only way we are going to get any answers.' Mary doesn't want to tell Andrew she's afraid

Jaclyn will go to the police and accuse her of attempting to hurt her at Sublime Point. 'Will you go with me?'

'This is madness but try and stop me.'

⁕

Andrew drives Mary to Helen's brick cottage in a modest neighbourhood in the south-western suburbs of Sydney.

'Inheriting her aunt's property certainly would improve Helen's financial position,' Andrew says as they walk up the cement footpath to the verandah.

'I have no idea what I am going to tell her,' Mary says.

Andrew slips his hand into Mary's and holds it firmly.

'I'm with you on this,' he says.

She looks in his eyes and knows he means it. She nods a couple of times. It feels good to have him by her side; it's just a shame about the circumstances.

'Perhaps the best approach is to let Helen talk,' Mary says. 'She may fill in some of the missing pieces for us.'

'For sure,' Andrew says. 'We can't assume just because Helen was quoted in an article that she's telling the truth. Maybe she does just want the house.'

Mary stops and takes a couple of deep breaths.

'It's okay,' Andrew says.

Mary walks up to the door and knocks firmly three times. She hears footsteps in the hall and then a woman in her early 40s with a gentle face appears in the doorway.

'Hello. We're Mary and Andrew. I spoke to you on the phone,' Mary says.

'Thank you so much for coming. Please come through to the lounge room and make yourselves comfortable.'

Mary and Andrew sit together on a tan leather lounge.

'Can I get you anything? Coffee, tea, juice, water?'

'I'd love a cup of tea,' Mary says.

She smiles, aware she's asking for what she really wants, not declining the offer to avoid inconveniencing her host as Isabel had always said was the right thing to do. She's pleased by her act of rebellion.

Andrew gives her a perplexed look.

'Could I have a coffee, milk with one,' he says.

'What's amusing?' Andrew says when the woman has left the room.

'Nothing.'

There's a hint of something cheeky in his look that Mary can't work out, but she likes it.

'Helen seems nice,' she says.

'A little weary, like she's been through a lot.'

The approaching sound of rattling china stops this line of conversation.

Helen places an ornate tray on the heavy wooden coffee table, setting out a complete silver service, delicate cups and a sweet slice in front of them.

Andrew reaches for his coffee, while Helen pours tea into Mary's cup. The liquid has a lovely dark rose colour, just the way Mary likes it. Mary adds a dash of milk and takes a sip. It is refreshing.

'Please help yourself to sugar and a piece of lemon and coconut slice. I made it myself.'

Andrew and Mary reach for the slice at the same time and their hands touch. Mary feels an electric charge.

'Oops,' she says smiling.

Andrew is looking at her intently. 'You can knock hands with me any time.'

Helen clips the edge of her own teacup with the leg of the teapot.

'Oh, I can be so clumsy.'

She recovers her composure, pours her tea, then sits in a recliner across from her guests, holding her cup and saucer.

'Mary, thank you for coming. I asked you here because I thought you might have something meaningful to tell me about this Jaclyn Chauve-Souris woman, since you said you know her.' She pronounces the 's' on the end of Jaclyn's surname.

The phone rings. Helen excuses herself to answer it in the hallway, explaining that her husband, Joe, is at the hardware store. He couldn't handle watching her anxiety levels rising from all the 'crazies' asking about the reward.

'Of course, don't mind us,' Mary says.

As they wait, Mary wonders why they've come. How are they going to help this distressed woman? She suggests to Andrew that they leave before they waste Helen's time.

'We need to know what she knows,' Andrew says.

Helen returns after a few minutes.

'Before Mary tells you about the housemate, why don't you tell us what you know about your aunt's disappearance?' Andrew says.

Mary realises he is trying to help them stick to the plan of allowing Helen to do most of the talking.

'I used to speak to Aunty Edith twice a week and we would go to church and for a long drive on a Sunday once a month. But then about four weeks ago I rang and her housemate told me she wasn't there. She was taking a nap. The next time I rang, Aunty Edith had gone to the shops. This was so strange because I always call on Tuesday and Thursday at around 1 pm during my lunch break. Aunty knows that and always seems so pleased to hear from me. Also, she never leaves the house except to go on drives with us.'

'So, you went to pick her up on the Sunday?'

'Usually, we confirm the arrangements for the Sunday in our Thursday phone call, but I knew something was wrong, so we went to the house anyway. I figured I could at least question this woman who seemed to be stopping

147

me from talking to my aunty, or ask Aunty Edith what was wrong, why she had suddenly cut me off.'

Helen describes how she knocked on the door of Seaview Manor, tapping the big iron ring knocker three times. When this was met with silence from inside, she knocked louder. Footsteps broke the impasse. The door creaked as it opened part of the way. A young woman peered around the door, only her black polo shirt showing. It was early for a Sunday morning, but she had a full face of ghostly pale make-up.

Startled by the stranger, Helen leaned back, bumping into Joe, and shuddered with the chill from the house.

'"Can I help you?" Jaclyn asked with a superior air.

'"We've come to pick up Aunty Edith," I said.

'"She's not here."

'"What do you mean she's not here?" I said. "We always take her to church and for a drive on the last Sunday of the month. We've been doing it for years."'

Jaclyn told Helen that Edith had taken the bus into the city for the day. She had been quite forgetful lately.

'"Can I ask what you are doing in Aunty's house?" I asked.

'"I live here."

'"Aunty never mentioned she'd taken in a boarder."

'"More like a companion. She's been very lonely."'

Helen says this revelation shocked them because they have been Edith's support.

'The woman even claimed she had lived there for two months and that Aunty Edith hadn't mentioned me the whole time. Can you believe that?'

'No. Does your aunt enjoy the drives with you?' Mary says, taking a second piece of lemon slice.

'She wouldn't miss them for anything, always waiting outside in her Sunday best, all smiles.'

'Where do you go on your drives?'

'All over the place. To the Blue Mountains, the south coast, the Central Coast. It is exhausting for her, but she has a grin from ear to ear the whole time. It's been rare to see her happy like this. She's had a lot of heartbreak in her life and that has made her bitter.'

'What kinds of things?' Andrew asks.

'She lost her husband in a tragic accident when she was in her 20s. She was pregnant when she heard the news and lost the baby. She never really recovered from that.'

'That must have been terrible for her,' Mary says.

'An elderly spinster aunt died a few years later, leaving her Seaview Manor. Aunty Edith loves that house, she talks about it on our drives. It is so big, but she visits every room and imagines it full of people. It's like her friend.'

'Has she lived by herself for a long time?'

'Always. That's why I was surprised to see Jaclyn, such a young woman. Aunty Edith criticises the young people of today. She says they are selfish and bad-mouthed.'

'Do you think maybe she thought Jaclyn would help her around the house, so she wouldn't be a burden on you?'

'It's possible. Joe and I offered to help her do some painting and renovations in the house, but she knew we were both working full time and wouldn't hear of it. Oh, what's happened to her?'

Helen starts to sob. Mary rises from the lounge and puts a hand on Helen's shoulder.

'This is hard on you. Would you like us to go?'

Helen wipes her eyes with a handkerchief.

'I break down every time I think that woman has done something to my aunty. She gives me the creeps. I don't think Aunty's forgetful. I spoke to her a month ago, and she was perfectly lucid.'

'So that's why you believe Jaclyn is lying?' Andrew says.

'Yes,' Helen whimpers. 'I pleaded with the police to do a search of the house and the grounds, but they seem bewitched by that woman.'

Mary argues with herself, or maybe it is the voice of her late stepmother, saying it's time to back out. Anything she tells this woman about Jaclyn will simply stress her more. But she has to tell her something.

'You know it's always good to talk about hard things over a cup of tea,' Mary says. 'That's something my moth—my stepmother used to say. I'm glad we have this wonderful tea and that you're comfortable, because what I'm about to share is not easy.' Mary drops her head, wondering where she is getting the strength to tell Helen what she knows.

'Anything you can tell me might help.'

Mary recounts the episode at Sublime Point as factually as she can without the emotion.

'Oh my dear, that must have been so hard for you. I think I would have left her there.'

Mary doesn't confess that she nearly did. She's not proud of that moment.

'Unfortunately, there's something worse than that. Several years ago, there was an incident at another house where Jaclyn lived. A fire. A woman died. Fire and Rescue determined arson was the cause, but no charges have been laid.'

'Do you think Jaclyn lit the fire?'

'Jaclyn said she tried to rescue her housemate, but the flames pushed her back. The suspicious thing is that Jaclyn had had a fight with the woman who died and was asked to leave. That was the day of the fire.'

'This confirms everything for me. That woman is up to something. Either she's keeping Aunty Edith locked up, or she has killed her.'

'We can't be sure what's happened without evidence,' Mary says.

'We should leave that to the police,' Andrew says, giving Mary a concerned look.

'We can't rely on them,' Helen says. 'Joe and I are going to Seaview Manor tomorrow to see if we can get inside.'

Mary says she will talk to Jaclyn to see if she can get any information they can take to the police.

'You would do that?' Helen says.

Mary nods.

'So long as you don't end up getting hurt yourself,' Andrew says. 'The same goes for you and your husband too, Helen.'

'We have to do something. I need to know one way or another.' Helen walks to the doorway. 'Before you go, I'd like to show you some photos of Aunty Edith. I want you to know her like I do.' And she's gone.

'When we go to that old house tomorrow, you're not thinking of doing anything stupid are you, Mary, like asking Jaclyn about the old lady?'

'What else can I do?'

Mary knows she must get to the bottom of this, otherwise she might always be looking over her shoulder, wondering what Jaclyn will do next.

Chapter 15

Edith hears knocking. Someone is tapping the iron ring on Seaview Manor's front door. She peers through the curtain of the sitting room and sees her niece, Helen, with her husband, Joe.

'Hey, Helen!' she calls. After a few minutes, Helen and Joe turn back down the driveway. 'Wait, where are you going?' Edith screams. *Why didn't Jaclyn tell them I'm here?* 'Helen, wait!'

Edith hears footsteps on the stairs and a key turning in the door.

She's letting me out at last.

'I don't know what's happening. I was calling out to Helen from the window, but she couldn't hear me. It was like a bad dream where you're screaming but you have no voice.'

'You had no voice? What are you talking about?'

Edith suspects Jaclyn locked her in to stop her from seeing her niece, but why?

'They came to take me out. Why didn't you tell them I was up here? You . . .'

Edith thinks better of angering Jaclyn by accusing her.

Jaclyn shrugs her shoulders. 'They said they were in a hurry, meeting up with someone in the afternoon.'

'Young people are very busy, aren't they? Having to take me on outings is a bit of a drag for them.'

'Have you ever thought of going to live with them?'

'And leave my beloved Seaview Manor? Never. I'll be here till the day I die.'

'I can't stand here chatting. I have an essay to write.'

Edith tries to remember the last drive she took with Helen and Joe. Was it a month ago? Two? Suddenly she feels tired.

༒

There is a haze over the kitchen and dining room as Edith watches Jaclyn fuss around preparing for Sunday dinner.

'Need any help?'

Jaclyn spins around. Her eyes are wide open.

'Leave me alone, old woman. You have never wanted to be involved before. Why start now?'

Edith wants to say so much. For one thing it's her kitchen and Jaclyn has no right to be there.

She watches Jaclyn moving between the kitchen and the formal dining room, looking busy but not actually doing anything. No places are set. Edith inspects the antique sideboard and sees all the plates and silverware on the shelves as she has always stacked them.

'Get out of the way, you crazy old lady.'

'I'm the crazy one?'

'You don't need a housemate. You need a psych nurse.'

At that moment, Edith beholds a vision that tells her she is either dreaming or crazy. Guests in colonial gear suddenly appear in the formal dining room as if they've come from thin air and take their places around the long table that is instantly laid out with mutton stew, pickled pork and bread. The silver service and wine and rum goblets are there. Candles are lit. The room has taken on a particularly sombre hue.

This can't be happening!

The guests are talking among themselves. Jaclyn becomes harried at their appearance but nothing about how they got there seems to surprise her.

Edith sees a final guest, Amelia, the one in the unusual nightgown attire, literally walk through the wall.

That's impossible!

She studies the guests around the table, then Jaclyn. They are decidedly different. The guests seem lighter of spirit, less weighed down than Jaclyn. Their bodies are, like Edith's, almost see-through.

Why is my body transparent?

'Because it is an illusion,' a voice says.

Suddenly, Edith is standing by the angel fountain, the softness of angel wings around her.

'You no longer have a body. You are simply perfect as you always were, a divine spirit.' The love in the angel's voice is comforting.

'You mean I'm . . . I'm dead? I can't be. Everything is as it always has been.'

'Is it?'

'I'm going to wake up at any moment.'

'No, you won't. Do you remember when I showed you your last moments of human life?'

'That wasn't a nightmare or a vision?'

'No, it wasn't. But you still weren't ready for the full story. I had to make it seem like a nightmare, even though you don't sleep.'

'You know I can't remember the last time I slept.'

'Now you can come with me and cross over to the original light.'

'This is a lot to process. For a start, Jaclyn can't get away with this.'

'She has many of her own demons to face. She has a dark road ahead.'

'But she might kill another innocent soul. I am . . . I mean I was an old woman. Maybe next time she will murder someone who still has their life before them, like that friend Mary she keeps talking about.'

'That is not your concern.'

'I can't go with you until this mad woman is brought to justice and my niece inherits my house. Helen! She doesn't even know I'm dead.'

'I cannot take you to heaven without your consent. But I will watch over you and visit you again. Whenever you are ready, or you need comfort, call on me, Yehudiah, and I will be with you.'

Edith feels a rush of a big and powerful love through her being, and, without knowing how her spirit got there, she is back in the dining room, watching the dinner guests eating and conversing, with Jaclyn fussing about them.

She looks more closely at the guests and the entire setup of the dinner and notices it is like a projection. She looks down at her hands and they seem hollow too.

It's true! I'm a ghost. Why didn't I notice this before?

Despite her housemate's actions and occasional words directed at the guests, it appears Jaclyn does not influence the course of the dinner at all. The food, the layout, the clothes, the conversations are the same as the last one. A ghostly repast that is repeated at the same time, five o'clock, every Sunday for eternity.

This is history happening in her very own dining room. Will the dinner continue even when the bricks and mortar are gone? Why didn't they cross over with Yehudiah? Does this dinner keep them in between the worlds forever?

'Thomas, I didn't have the pleasure of speaking to you last time.'

'How do you do, Edith? Are you not eating?'

The rotund man with gravy in his beard dishes stew into a bowl and passes it to Edith. She hesitates, wondering if she will even taste the food if she wasn't part of the original dinner or privy to its wild flavours from almost two centuries ago. She tries to remember when she last ate. She can't remember the meal. Probably something bland like lamb chops and mash potato.

'Go on. I bet you have never tasted anything like it. Peter has a name around town for his mutton stew.'

Edith puts a spoonful of stew to her lips. It is salty, but the meat and sauce combination is rich with flavour, not watery as she would have presumed of food in those days.

'How is this possible?' she says.

'I know. It's good, isn't it?'

'Do you think taste is purely in the mind rather than physical?'

'Our new guest is somewhat of a philosopher I see,' Peter says. 'We could welcome that kind of discussion at our table.'

'Oh, I am a simple, old woman. I wouldn't know anything about philosophy.'

'And yet you ask such deep questions.'

'I have been through a lot that is making me question my existence.'

'You are always welcome here if you can challenge us to question ours.'

Edith chuckles to herself.

If only you knew.

She instantly wills herself to a chair next to the convict couple. She loves her new powers. She can't wait to walk through walls.

'Hi, I'm Edith. You two look happy. How long have you been together?'

The young man, not much more than a boy, smiles at the young woman. 'About three weeks. Sarah is going to the gallows next month and Peter said we could come to dinner to have this precious time together.'

'I begged for clemency for Sarah, but even my influence has not been enough,' Peter says.

Having an explanation for the bruise around the young woman's throat, Edith pulls her own white scarf down to show the guests her neck.

Peter grimaces. 'Aww, Edith. Put the scarf back. That is horrible.'

'Yes, Edith, our guests are eating,' Jaclyn scorns.

Why doesn't Jaclyn squirm? Why doesn't she show any hint of recognition?

Someone so young. How is it possible that she killed me?

That thought reminds Edith of the final scene of her death. Rainbow-coloured light pierces the glass Jaclyn is holding, and an angel appears. The woman's eyes are wide with no sign of remorse or empathy as she drags the glass from one side of Edith's throat to the other. The angel envelops Edith in his light and love as her soul leaves her body minutes before the blood pours out, bleeding it of life, and her evil housemate bends down and catches the red fluid in her mouth.

Edith shudders at the scene in her mind and forces herself to focus on the present moment. 'Amelia, you must notice something strange about me.'

'Not particularly. Your clothes perhaps, but I figured they might be the latest fashion from Paris. I don't get to read much news. Life is very different here to back home.'

'I can only imagine. No, I think my garments were made in China.'

'Oh.' Amelia has a look of shock on her face. Edith supposes it is because her clothes do not look particularly Oriental in nature.

'Do you think this is a dream, or are we really here?'

'Oh, we're here all right. The food wouldn't be this good in a dream.'

None of these beings realise they're ghosts and that they're repeating the same dinner over and over.

Edith thinks it's not fair that they should have to re-live the same moments for eternity.

Jaclyn is staring at the young convict.

'Got your eye on him, have you?' Edith says.

Jaclyn doesn't look at Edith. 'Young blood. That's the best kind,' Jaclyn says.

'Ah, but you've tasted old blood too, haven't you?'

'What are you babbling about?' Jaclyn turns to face Edith and screws up her face. 'Have you given up smoking? Haven't seen you with a cancer stick for a while.'

Edith holds up her hand and realises she doesn't have a cigarette, phantom or otherwise. She no longer craves nicotine. She no longer needs a crutch or a reason to procrastinate or calm her nerves. She is free.

Maybe this is part of crossing over, leaving the past behind. It feels good. But she can't distract herself with that now. The young woman Jaclyn talks about bringing to the house may be her only chance to reveal what happened to her and give Helen Seaview Manor.

'Oh Jaclyn, when is Mary coming?'

'She promised she would come today. She should be here soon.'

Chapter 16

It's mild on the coast, with an afternoon sea breeze that brings a chill to the air but nowhere as cold as in the mountains. The late afternoon is Mary's favourite time of day; so quiet apart from the rumbling of the ocean. Mary stops midway up the steep incline to turn around and look over the magnificent view of the sea and rocks. A big cemetery sprawls around the cliff. She calls out to Andrew, who has kept walking ahead.

'Andrew, look at this!'

'I know. It's amazing. I walk around here quite a bit. You should come with me to the cemetery some time. Some great stories there.'

Mary takes in the scene and breathes deeply, wondering if Jaclyn truly appreciates her surroundings. She sees Andrew waiting for her, and they ascend sandstone steps to the main road. When they reach the top, Mary sees the mansion on the rise.

They cross the road, and Andrew shakes the wrought iron gates attached to stone columns, but time seems to have fused them together. He pushes them again, and the rusty latch gives way. He opens both gates right up and they walk through.

'We could have driven up,' Andrew says.

Mary stops at the gate. The stone path is overgrown with weeds and bordered by a jungle of vegetation on both sides. She turns back to look at the ocean again. She's always lived in the mountains and wonders why the sea holds such appeal for her. She wants to run along the beach rather than face Jaclyn and her dinner party.

At least Andrew's with me.

'Hey, Mary, are you coming?' Andrew shouts. He is already way ahead of her.

As soon as she steps through the gate onto the path, a darkness falls around her as though a cloud has blotted the sun. She has walked from the light into a strange other world, another time, another place, the never-never. Her whole body trembles from an involuntary shudder. She inhales deeply and looks around her for a presence.

'Don't be silly,' she quietly reprimands herself. 'It's a bit run down. That's all. There's nothing here.'

She quickens her pace to catch up to Andrew and walks beside him.

'This place gives me the creeps,' Andrew says.

'I'm glad you think so too. I thought it might just be me.'

She has no logical reason for feeling someone is watching her. She looks in the shadows for Jaclyn, then grabs hold of Andrew's arm.

'It's cold, isn't it?' she says, wondering if he knows she's scared.

Spiky weeds grab her stockinged legs, and a weeping fig leaf drags on her face, making her jump.

Andrew stops. 'You okay?' he says.

'Only a leaf on my face, felt like a feather.'

'Try not to spook yourself before we get to the house.'

'I think it's too late.'

Mary is grateful when the path meets what must have once been a magnificent gravel driveway. The surface is more even at least. They walk up a slight rise to the house, a dilapidated, Gothic-style mansion. Despite its unkempt state, the entrance makes her think of Manderley in *Rebecca*. She is excited and revolted all at once.

It's nothing like the stately mansion Jaclyn described. The classic stone building has the typical pointed arches, but instead of ornate, stained-glass windows, they frame broken ones. Looking up to the first floor, Mary sees a curtain drop as though someone is there and has been watching them.

'Andrew, did you see that?'

'What?'

'Someone up there?'

'It's probably that creepy woman.'

Mary lets go of Andrew's arm and stares at the front door ahead of them. It's heavy wood and too imposing for the sandstone frame, which is dirty and crumbling around it. What is waiting for them inside?

Andrew's right. I'm spooking myself, but there is some-thing sinister about this place.

The autumn light has faded. The shadows cast by the giant fig trees are stretching and joining together. They bring the darkness over Mary like a widow's veil. The temperature suddenly drops a few degrees. She shivers and looks at Andrew, who is already on the landing. Mary still has the sense of something watching her from the dark recesses of the trees, and from the windows. At that moment, she trips on a big stone jutting out of the driveway, one of the hidden snags along the way. She knows they're there. Her stepmother continually protected her from them, but maybe now she must trip a few times to establish the truth of who she is, and what she's made of.

Mary steels herself to walk the next 20 paces to the front door. The steps are uneven. One has completely broken away. She is looking down now to be sure of her footing.

'I hope she has a wood fire burning,' Mary says.

'I think we should brace ourselves for what's inside.' Andrew's usual humour is missing.

'I hope you're wrong.'

Mary lifts a cast iron nose ring of a tarnished brass lion and drops it against the door. The thud goes through her. They stand for a few moments, and Mary half expects Mrs Danvers herself to walk straight off the pages of *Rebecca* and open the door. The thought sends a shiver down her spine. Why does she read so many dark novels? Or better still, how could those writers have described this scene so perfectly, right down to the eerie feeling? She strains to hear any sound from inside. Nothing. She's relieved.

'This place seems deserted,' she says. 'Everything's in darkness.'

Andrew wipes cobwebs off the wooden name plate hanging at an angle on the side of the door.

'Seaview Manor,' Mary says. 'This is definitely the place.'

The sound of something crashing on the floor behind the door makes Mary jump.

'What was that?' she says, holding on to Andrew's arm.

'I think we'd better get out of here.' He takes her hand and pulls her away from the door.

They walk down the steps and take a few paces down the path when the sound of unoiled hinges creaks in Mary's soul.

❦

'Jaclyn, I think Mary is here.' Edith sees Jaclyn in a trance, fussing around the table of her colonial dinner guests. 'Jaclyn!'

Edith wills herself to the sitting room and looks out onto the entrance. She can see a woman and a man walking up to the house.

Great. Mary brought someone with her. Smart girl.

Edith cannot call out to Mary, so she wills a chair to fall over in the foyer downstairs. It makes a crashing sound. Both the man and woman turn to go. She can't make out what they're saying, so she places herself on the ground behind them.

'I think we'd better get out of here,' the man says.

Edith wills the front door to open, creaking on its hinges.

Mary and the man stop and turn around.

'Who's there?' the man says. 'Is that you, Jaclyn? Are you deliberately trying to scare us? Part of your sick game?'

I wish you could hear me. I need your help.

'Let's go, Mary,' the man says.

'Andrew, I said I would come to the dinner party. If Jaclyn's here, I need to face her and tell her I don't want to see her anymore.'

Edith circles the couple. *Yes, Andrew, let her do this.*

She comes up so close to Mary she can feel the warmth of her aura. It's like having the sun on your face on a winter's day. Death is cold. She longs to live again. She acts entirely intuitively and attaches herself easily to Mary's pure soul.

❧

Mary quivers as she peers through the small opening of the heavy door, which is now ajar.

'Hello. Is anyone home?' Mary says.

'What about this?' Andrew swings a rope hanging from a metal bell. The loud ringing makes Mary jump. 'She should hear that,' he says.

'All the ghosts in the cemetery must have heard it,' Mary says.

Andrew muffles a giggle. Mary laughs out loud. She puts a hand to her mouth and wonders if their urge to make light of the situation is a nervous manifestation of fear.

Mary pushes on the door, which gives out a high-pitched 'eeeee' sound.

Andrew takes keys out of his pocket and switches on a small torch on the end of the ring. The tiny spot of light illuminates a run-down foyer.

'I got this when I was a boy scout. It's amazing how many times I've had to use it. Will I go first?'

Mary nods and falls behind Andrew as he opens the door fully and shines the torch up the run-down wooden staircase a few metres in front of them.

'This place doesn't look like it's been lived in for years,' Andrew says.

I guess I did let the place go, a voice says. *But I'm, well I was, old. It's a lot of work for an elderly person.*

'Did you hear that?' Mary says.

'Hear what?'

'Nothing.'

Mary waits in the foyer as Andrew ascends the stairs. There's just enough light peering through the stained glass above the door to see thready cobwebs hanging off the chandelier in a shape mimicking the chandelier. Mary ascends slowly, noticing each step creak beneath her footfall. She holds the banister for support. Her hand becomes gritty from a thick layer of dust. She brushes it off with the other hand.

A draft blows on Mary. Her whole body shivers. She wonders if Jaclyn is hiding in the shadows.

'Mary, where are you going?' The low, slow tones of Jaclyn's voice are unmistakable.

Mary turns and jumps at the sight of Jaclyn, wearing a white long sleeve blouse with a long black skirt and her hair in a bun.

Mrs Danvers in the flesh, Mary thinks.

Jaclyn seems strange. Mary feels she is looking past her. Mary walks closer. Maybe it's the fading light playing tricks with her eyesight. But, alas, Jaclyn appears to be in a trance, just like at Sublime Point.

'Andrew, come and see Jaclyn,' Mary calls.

She sees him running down the stairs.

'Couldn't you hear us, Jaclyn?' Andrew says.

Mary notices that Jaclyn does not acknowledge Andrew or even seem to notice that he's with her.

'What is going on?' Mary whispers to Andrew. 'Is she part of some kind of cult? Is that what this is about? Speaking in tongues and laying hands on people. We have to get out of here.'

'Come, Mary, meet the other guests and warm up by the fire.'

With the cold air biting Mary's ears and nose, she follows Jaclyn before the word 'fire' has left her strange friend's lips. She stops in the doorway of a big, empty room dimly lit by a single light bulb hanging from a high ceiling. She surveys the old, torn red velvet drapes, a fireplace that's been boarded over in the corner and cobwebs everywhere. It's deathly cold. She watches Jaclyn walk over to the big, timber table in the centre of the room and make weird gestures as though she's holding a plate and offering it to someone.

'Another helping of mutton stew, Jeremiah?' Jaclyn says. 'My friend, Mary, has come to see you. Oh, you must meet her. She's such a kind person.'

'Andrew, let's get out of here.' Mary's voice is commanding as she pulls Andrew after her, running through the foyer, out the open door and up the driveway. They stop at the overgrown path. Andrew lights the way with his torch. They jump over fallen branches and twigs and keep running until they have cleared the front gate. They cross the road and run down the steps to the car, jumping in and locking the doors. Andrew turns on the ignition. Tyres screech as the car leaves the curb.

'Mary, promise me you'll never come back here again.'

'I promise.'

I'm afraid before too long you will have to return to my beloved Seaview Manor, an elderly voice says.

'Did you hear that?' Mary says.

'What?'

'Never mind. I think I'm so spooked by this place I'm imagining things.'

Chapter 17

As Mary catalogues and stacks a fresh delivery of the latest edition law textbooks on the shelves, she tries to stop her mind from wandering back to the eerie encounter with Jaclyn at Seaview Manor. Jodi-Ann wanted her to answer enquiries today, but Mary couldn't handle dealing with people and made an excuse that she had a lot of boxes to unpack. Andrew volunteered to be on the desk. Good ol' Andrew. What would she do without him?

You are going to have to deal with this at some stage, an elderly woman's voice says. *You can't hide from your problems forever.*

Mary turns around to see the source of the words. Nobody is there. She is going crazy hearing voices again.

Property law. Focus on cataloguing this book on property law. That's normal.

Putting all her attention on the books in front of her, she stops the monkey mind for a few minutes, but then Tony rings, disturbing the little peace she has found. The nagging sensation in her gut has returned. It's like every weird incident has fed into it. She believes that Tony is her father, but she still knows very little about him. It's best they meet in public.

'There's something I need to tell you before I . . .' Tony says.

'Before you what?'

'I need to talk to you.'

Mary has always wanted to attend the outdoor light festival that occurs every year around this time. She thinks the fluorescent installations might brighten her mood, and Tony agrees to the idea. She was thinking of suggesting it to Andrew as an after-work activity, but she can always go with him another time.

Andrew appears at their cubicle as she's having the thought. He pulls a funny face. Mary bursts out laughing. It feels good to laugh but, as though her body has mixed up the emotions, her laughing turns into sobs.

'Oh, Mary, don't cry. I was trying to make you laugh.'

'You did, but then I couldn't control myself. Everything's so weird. I don't know how much more of this I can take.'

I'm sorry dear, but . . .

'Leave me alone,' Mary says to the air.

'What did I do?' Andrew says with a frown. 'I thought I helped you out today.'

'Sorry, Andrew. I wasn't speaking to you. I was voicing my frustrations at the air.'

'I know you've been through a lot. What about a stroll around the Quay tonight?'

'Another time maybe.'

'Sure.' Andrew's quiet tone and dejected look instantly make Mary want to cancel her arrangement with Tony. At least she could have come clean and told Andrew she was meeting her father.

Why is it so hard for her to do the right thing? Was it because Isabel didn't have rules for situations like this? She must make them up as she goes.

☙❧

As Mary leaves the safety of the library and walks along the cement path towards the street, she feels a chill in her spine. She knows that feeling. Someone is watching her. She looks behind her, but no-one is there.

Strange. It's like that day at the uni.

Mary, be careful of Jaclyn, a voice says. *She's hiding in the shadows.*

Mary spins around but she doesn't see Jaclyn or the owner of the mysterious voice.

I am imagining things again. I wonder if I'm just tired.

Mary is relieved to see Tony on the street. He has his back to her and when she brushes his arm and greets him, his eyes light up. It's the happiest she has seen him. He has combed his long hair and is wearing a baggy suit. A strong cologne barely masks the acrid smell of homelessness.

'Been off the booze for a week and borrowed this suit for our outing,' he says.

'I noticed.'

Mary appreciates the effort Tony is making for her. She knows how hard it must be for him to brighten up physically and emotionally.

As they walk side by side towards Circular Quay, she starts to speak, but the words get caught in her throat.

'What is it dear?'

'This is hard to say.'

'Just tell me.'

'I have so much craziness going on in my life that I don't think I can . . . I don't think I have the strength . . . to have a relationship with you.'

Mary puts her hand over her mouth and dry wretches. There's a pain so deep inside her that wants to be released, but she can't even cry. She wants to let out a low guttural sound but stops herself.

'I know this is hard, and I wish I had the strength to walk away and let you be, but I can't,' Tony says.

'I need to work myself out. This has been a lot. You seem to need more from me than I can give you.'

'I don't want anything except a little time, and I don't have much time left.'

'What do you mean?'

'I'm dying.'

Mary shivers. 'Oh no.'

'I found out that first day I called you, and you hung up on me.'

The words 'you hung up on me' linger in the air, accusing Mary of a callousness she always believed she could never be capable of.

'I didn't know who you were. You scared me.'

'I know. I'm sorry. A father should protect his daughter, not make her afraid.'

'What do you have? Are you getting treatment?'

'No, it's bad. The cancer has spread throughout my body. I've decided to let nature take its course. I may have six months if I'm lucky.'

Tears stream down Mary's face.

How could I be so mean and only think about myself.

'I have made peace with it,' Tony says. 'When you're given a death sentence, suddenly what's important hits you in the face. For years you say you'll do things, but you never do and then you have this deadline and everything becomes clear.'

'I can only imagine what that's like.'

'I'm sorry to lump this on you, Mary, but I'm a desperate man. I hope you'll reconsider your decision.'

'My entire life is so strange at the moment, I don't know which way is up.'

'And I've added to that.'

'But my worries pale compared to yours. I desperately want my life to go back to the way it was, but the reality is it never will. I don't know how, but the least I can do is try to help you through this.'

Suddenly, Mary feels warmth in her chest. It's the same sensation she has when she watches Hercules gobble his food and sleep curled up on his favourite recliner. It's good to take care of another, to be needed. It takes your mind off your troubles.

'I'll be okay. I don't want to be a burden on you.'

In the middle of a crowd of happy people dotted with kids wearing fluorescent necklaces and holding spinning lights, Mary puts an arm around Tony. Her father pulls her in tightly and kisses her cheek.

'You are the one truly great thing I've done with my life,' he says. 'You give my life meaning. You make me more than just an old drunk.'

Mary walks with her arm around her father amid the big crowd excited by the moving pictures on the pylons of the Harbour Bridge. She doesn't feel the need to talk as they head towards the Opera House, its famous shell now a giant outdoor screen. Mary marvels at the Indigenous paintings of kangaroos, snakes and fish and points to them. Tony nods. Soon families, couples and groups jostle the pair and Mary suggests they head back to the chocolate café on the way to the station for a takeaway hot chocolate.

'Could we find a spot out here?' Tony says as Mary hands him the large paper cup. 'There's something I want to tell you about your birth mother.'

A couple leaves a space on the harbour wall. They both see it at once and sit down. Mary pulls a beanie out of her coat pocket and covers her head and icy ears.

You have to help me, a voice says.

Mary ignores the words and tells herself she has been under a lot of stress.

'You wanted to tell me about my birth mother?'

'She could speak to spirits.'

'What, like voices in her head?'

'Yes. When you were four, you used to speak to imaginary friends. Do you still have the gift?'

'Is that what it's called, a gift? I don't even believe in ghosts and spirits.'

'I think Isabel knocked it out of you. She was always saying it wasn't Christian to be speaking to imaginary friends. Come to think of it, she probably knew deep down they weren't imaginary. I wondered if you might have been speaking to your dear departed mother.'

'I don't remember any of this. How did this ability manifest itself with my birth mother?'

'It came on out of the blue soon after we were married. She would wake up at all hours of the night. I thought she just had trouble sleeping, and then she told me that it was the spirits of strangers waking her.'

'Did she say why?'

'They needed her to give messages to their loved ones.'

'And did she?'

'She tried to ignore them but only lost more and more sleep. Eventually, I suggested she try to test the information they were giving her. The mother of our bank manager said her son's wife was cheating on him and he needed to know.'

'What happened?'

'I could not let Mary go up to a stranger and tell him that, so I did some amateur detective work. I was out of work. It was before you were conceived. One day I followed the bank manager home. Then every weekday I staked out the house, hoping the mystery man would go to the house, or I could follow the woman when she met him.'

'Did she?'

'She appeared to be the devoted housewife, spent most of her time in the kitchen. I could see her from the street. She liked to gaze out the window. Maybe she was watching her neighbours. I wondered if she ever saw me. She never left the house and always greeted her husband at the front door when he came home at precisely 5.30 pm. I began to wonder what I was doing invading her privacy like that.'

'I bet it was pretty boring for you, sitting in your car for hours at a time. Didn't people get suspicious?'

'A couple of kids came up to me once, but I told them I was an undercover detective. Swore them to secrecy. They looked afraid and ran off.'

'So, you spent your days sitting outside a house waiting for something to happen.'

'I was thinking of giving the whole thing up, but the bank manager's mother kept waking Mary at 2 am each day with the same message. She had to tell him his wife was cheating on him. From that point on pure faith guided my actions. I had no rational reason to stalk this good couple.

'Then after three weeks of nothing, it all paid off. I saw a young man jump the back fence and enter the house through the back door. He too was greeted enthusiastically by the bank manager's wife. Maybe more enthusiastically than her husband.'

'How did you see all this?'

'I snuck around to the rear of the house and peeped over the fence.'

'Weren't you afraid they would see you?'

'I didn't think. I acted on impulse. I sat there so long with nothing to show for it, and then in an instant there was movement. The adrenaline rushed through my veins. It occurred to me he might be a robber or a pervert. But then I saw them kiss.'

'What did you do?'

'I went back to the car and waited half an hour for this mystery man to leave so I could get a photo. Then an idea came to me. With camera in hand, I rang the front doorbell and ran around the back expecting the mystery caller to come back out the way he came. Bingo! He looked at me scared out of his wits and then ran like the wind. There was no point chasing him. I had him on film.'

'But you didn't photograph them together.'

'No, I didn't. I saw the bank manager's wife sitting on the back step wearing a slip. She was smoking a cigarette. I held the camera above the palings and looked through the view finder ready to take her picture. Suddenly I felt ashamed. I was the pervert. Taking a photo of a woman in her underwear was unheard of. I only hoped my maker could forgive me.'

'But you didn't take the photo?'

'No, but I felt bad that I'd gotten so carried away with the whole thing. It was satisfying to finally have an answer and know your mother wasn't mad.'

'Did my mother tell the bank manager the news?'

'No. I sent the photo of the young man anonymously to him at the bank with a note suggesting he ask his wife about the man leaving their yard in a hurry.'

'Do you know what happened to them?'

'No, but his mother stopped waking Mary in the early hours of the morning. In fact, she never heard from her again.'

'Did you have to play amateur detective on other cases after that?'

'No, because Mary had proof that she wasn't going mad, and it was something she would have to live with. She learned how to control the voices. She told them to communicate with her in the waking hours and to show her how she could help them. She delivered a lot of messages to family and strangers. Some were surprisingly well received. Others called her a lunatic.'

'Thank you for sharing this about my mother, but it seems a wild idea to think I could ever do that. I wouldn't want to. The idea of seeing a ghost freaks me out, let alone talking to one.'

'Maybe you never will. I wanted you to know that it is okay if you do. I know you have your mother's heart and strength, and you will manage it as she did.'

Tony reaches into his trouser pocket and brings out the same pretty cameo he tried to give her at the house. 'Mary, I want you to have this.'

Mary extends her hand to accept the brooch. She studies the ivory carving for a moment in the artificial light, then holds it to her heart. In a quivering voice, she says, 'She's beautiful. Is this my mother's face?'

'No. It is your mother's mother, your grandmother. That is why Mary loved the cameo so much and wore it everywhere. She would have wanted you to have it. I see a strong resemblance in you.' Tony stands up and gestures to pin the brooch to Mary's coat. 'May I?'

Once pinned, Mary covers the cameo with her hand and feels its warm vibration in her palm.

'I love it, and I love that I have something special of my birth mother's.'

The thoughts distract her from the voice in her head, but it's becoming louder.

Mary, you know I am real even if you can't see me, the voice says. *I need your help.*

This is not happening! I am ignoring this. Maybe my mother was crazy after all.

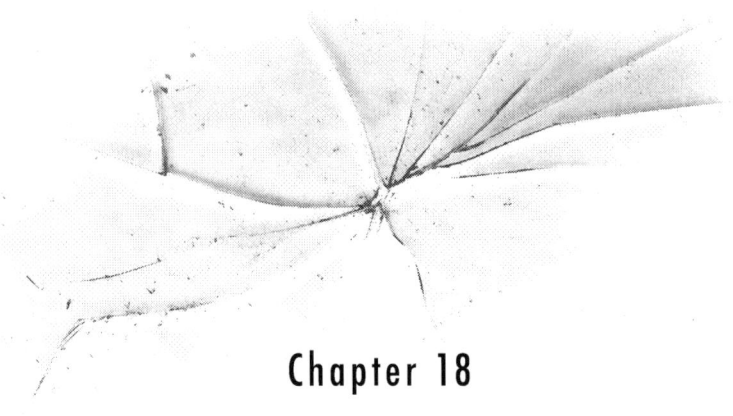

Chapter 18

When Mary made the arrangement with Andrew to go on the ghost tour, she had no idea she would be plagued by weird, dark scenes and voices in her head. Now a ghost tour seems like the worst place to be. Could an experience like this tip you over the edge into insanity? She is sane enough to know that dates with Andrew are rare and it was her idea. If she can stop freaking herself out, it's a chance to spend quality time with him outside the office. She is comforted by the crowd out in force for the light show.

Mary waits at the tour meeting place, the historic Cadman's Cottage. She's early. The façade is lit up in fuchsia. In the daylight hours, the simple two-storey sandstock building from the early 1800s is virtually invisible in its 21st-century setting along the Sydney Harbour foreshore. At night, it dominates the landscape, normally lit with white floodlights. Mary attempts to quell her rising anxiety and remind herself that she is lucky to be visiting this famous structure. But a cold wind blowing off the water sends chills up her neck, followed by a sense of foreboding.

What am I doing here? she thinks.

'Are you here for the tour?' asks a deep English voice. A figure in black startles her.

Mary focuses on the man in a long 19th-century undertaker's cape, a large hat sitting over thick, dark, shoulder-length hair. His face is leathery, but his brown eyes are gentle and kind.

'Yes, I am.' Mary forces a smile.

'Good. We're starting in about 10 minutes.'

Mary breathes more calmly at the sound of a more Australian voice as the man falls slightly out of character and then walks away.

Something brushes against her arm.

'Boo,' a voice grunts.

Mary screams.

'Oh, Mary, it was only a joke.' Andrew looks worried and touches her shoulder.

'I'm not in the mood for jokes. I'm still jumpy from everything that's been going on. Stay close.'

'I sure will.'

Mary thinks she sees a twinkle in Andrew's eye as he gives her the biggest grin she has ever seen.

About 20 people gather outside Cadman's Cottage under a clear, dark night with a crescent moon. The cloaked guide puts on his best horror movie voice, with tales of murder and the victims who linger as apparitions. Each participant is allotted a character part and given props and torches. Two men are lantern bearers. Mary is Amelia Belaise and Andrew is the coffin maker. They have no idea what's in store.

'Elizabeth Cadman, could you follow me?' says the guide, creating a sense of anticipation.

A young woman follows him through wooden doors of the cottage. The rest are left outside. Mary looks up at the first floor. She notices a shadow glide across the window above the door.

'Did you see that?' She pulls on Andrew's arm.

'See what?'

'Someone's up there.'

Mary becomes aware of how tightly she's holding onto Andrew's arm and lets go.

'You can't be seeing ghosts before the tour has even started,' Andrew says.

'I tell you I saw someone up there.'

'That's why they have gone inside ahead of us. It's all part of the fun.'

'Seriously, I think the ghost of Elizabeth Cadman is upstairs.'

The guide appears at the door and signals the group to come inside. Mary marvels at the tiny room closed in by heavy sandstock walls and the damp stench that fills their nostrils. The smell is a combination of wet dirt, mould and sewage. It is overpowering, and yet Mary can only wonder that this is the same smell that John Cadman, a convict who was pardoned and became superintendent of boats in Sydney, and his wife, Elizabeth, would have experienced all those years ago.

'Gosh, get a whiff of that,' Andrew says, holding his nose.

Isabel would not have approved of his impolite reaction. 'Some things you just have to put up with out of respect for others,' she used to say.

The room is lit only by two lanterns and the guide's torch, which he uses to light his face, giving him an eerie Halloween presence.

'People working upstairs at night have reported hearing sweeping from down here. Elizabeth Cadman was a fastidious cleaner.'

'Oh, I don't know how much longer I can tolerate that smell,' Andrew complains.

Like the cellar at Seaview Manor, an old woman says.

Mary jumps at the mention of the creepy house.

'Andrew, did you hear that?' she whispers.

'Hear what?'

'The voice of an old woman?'

'You are seriously spooking yourself.' Andrew bumps her arm with his elbow in a mocking way.

A woman gives a shout and appears from behind a wall. Mary is surprised by her own calm, but the tourist playing Elizabeth Cadman has a scream so fake, it is more funny than scary.

I wish you people would get out of my house, an old woman with an Irish accent says, but no-one in the group is speaking.

Mary knows this voice is not the one she heard earlier.

'You must have heard that, Andrew.'

'What?'

'There's another woman's voice. They must be playing a recording to scare us.'

'All I hear is the tour guide.'

Come on, get out, all of you, the Irish woman says.

'Andrew, I have to get out of here.'

'Why?'

'There are two ghosts here.'

'Really? Can you see them?'

'It's even more creepy. I can feel them and hear them. I'm feeling a bit short of breath.'

Mary walks out of the stuffy cottage, enlivened by the fresh night air and the salty aroma of the harbour. Andrew follows her.

'I know you're going to think I'm crazy but an old woman, who I think must be Elizabeth Cadman, wanted us out of the house.'

'It's okay,' Andrew says, putting an arm around Mary. 'They were setting everything up to get us in the mood. You just took it a little further.'

'You don't believe me, do you? I know there was a second spirit because she had a different voice and mentioned the creepy manor where Jaclyn lives.'

'Now I know you've let your imagination run away with you. You've been through a lot.'

'It's happening. I have my birth mother's curse. I am hearing spirits.'

Mary gasps for air.

'It's okay,' Andrew says. 'Take a few slow, deep breaths.'

Mary inhales and feels her lungs fill with air. It calms her. She sees the concern in Andrew's eyes.

'I know what I heard,' she says.

I am hearing ghosts.

Mary, you did hear me, a woman says. *I need your help.*

Mary feels her whole body weaken and sway backward. Andrew grabs her arm to steady her.

'Mary, what's wrong?'

She feels like she is having an asthma attack, but it is a huge sob.

'What's happening? Are you having a panic attack?'

Andrew's calm expression has been replaced with white horror. Mary shakes her head from side to side.

It's all right, Mary, says the old woman.

Mary hugs Andrew around the neck.

'The voice . . .' she whispers, resting her head on his shoulder.

The group spills out of Cadman's Cottage. There is laughter until they spot Mary and Andrew standing outside on the gravel. The guide approaches them.

'Is everything all right?' he asks in an Australian accent.

'Something weird happened in there,' Andrew says.

'You saw her? What does she look like?'

Mary can't control her tears and buries her head in Andrew's neck.

'Unfortunately, we have to leave the tour,' Andrew says.

'That's a shame. You two had the best parts – the coffin maker who hammers for eternity and Amelia Belaise, who haunts the Windmill Street cottage. If you made contact with Elizabeth, there's a good chance you would feel those spirits too. Look, if you ring tomorrow and mention what's happened, you can book another tour gratis.'

'Thanks,' Andrew says.

The guide takes their props and returns to the group.

'Okay folks, let's move on to Sydney's first morgue.'

A tall woman breaks away from the group and approaches Mary.

'This is your first experience of this, isn't it?' The woman gently places her hand on Mary's arm.

Mary is comforted by the touch and the woman's warm face and friendly eyes.

'How do you know that?' Mary's eyes widen.

'I haven't always had this gift. It happened spontaneously when I was at a sacred Native American site. Suddenly, I was hearing spirits. I know how freaked out you must be.'

Mary gives Andrew a quizzical look.

'It's okay,' the woman reassures them both. 'Could I have a moment with your friend?' she asks Andrew.

Mary nods that it's okay for him to give them space. Something in her trusts this woman.

'He seems like a lovely man, but this message is for you,' the woman continues.

'Okay,' Mary says.

'You have a spirit with you. She told me she needs you to help her. She was murdered.'

'Murdered? Oh no. How are you doing this?'

'Spirits communicate with me.'

'But how am I meant to help her?'

'Follow your heart and you'll know what to do,' the woman says, reaching into her Louis Vuitton handbag.

She pulls something out. It's a shiny pearl-coloured rock. She hands it to Mary.

'Keep this moonstone with you. My cousin charged it with the powerful energy at Uluru, and it's helped me stay in touch with my inner voice.'

'I couldn't take something so special from you.'

'It's time for you to have it now. My cousin will be happy when I tell her. By the way, you knew Elizabeth Cadman was upstairs didn't you, not downstairs like he said?'

Mary nods. The woman smiles and is gone. Andrew appears at her side.

'What was all that about?'

The shock is sinking in after the stranger's revelation that the other old woman talking to her has been murdered. Mary starts to shake.

'Mary, what's happening?' Andrew says.

'I need to go somewhere warm to process all this.'

'I know the perfect place. The chocolate café.'

❦

Edith knows that convincing Mary to help her will be challenging. The young woman seems scared of everything, but there must be a way. When Edith was alive, she let life take her along its ebbs and currents without directing the course. In death, she feels stronger, no longer feeble in her body or weak in her mind. She feels invincible and, no matter what, she will enlist Mary to help her reveal Jaclyn's dark secret and pass the house to Helen. A few years ago, she invited a celebrated lawyer to Seaview Manor to draw up her will, leaving everything to Helen, her late sister's only granddaughter. At least she had the foresight to do that.

Now I must convince Mary to find my body.

Edith lingers in the ether in the vicinity of Mary. She likes the calm energy of the café and considers it a safe space to give Mary more messages. But not just yet. She knows Mary needs time to process the idea that she is hearing the spirit of a murder victim.

༺ঔৈ༻

People sit at outdoor tables and brave the chilly harbour wind. The store sign flaps. Mary and Andrew head inside for a small table looking right onto a glass counter with dozens of desserts that are more like works of art. The deep, rich chocolate aroma floats pleasantly in the air, replacing any memory of Cadman's Cottage's earthy mould scent.

'This place is perfect.' Mary smiles, dropping the stone she's been gripping like her life depended on it into the pocket of her stepmother's coat.

She starts to take the coat off and Andrew is immediately behind her, helping her out of it. He folds it and neatly rests it over the back of her chair.

'Thanks.'

Andrew nods. He takes his seat opposite and hands her the menu.

'This is on me, so have whatever you like.'

Apart from Tony, Mary hasn't met a man who likes chocolate. Not someone who talks about it like she does, anyway.

We're not here for a play date, says an old woman's voice. *You have to tell him I am dead, and I need help.*

'Andrew, did you hear that?'

Andrew screws up his face and puts down the menu.

'Hear what?'

'Please don't look at me as though I'm mad! She's talking to me again.'

'Who?'

'One of the spirits . . .'

'What is the spirit saying?'

Mary is relieved when a waitress interrupts them for their order.

'Can we share the chocolate Belgian waffle and have separate plates?' she asks.

'Sure. And to drink?'

'The praline hot chocolate.'

'Milk hot chocolate for me,' Andrew says.

The waitress takes the menus quietly and is gone.

Mary sees care in Andrew's eyes and believes it is real. He puts his hand across the table and offers it to Mary, but she folds her arms. He gestures to her to take his hand.

'If you hold my hand as you tell me what happened, it will be easier,' he says.

She stretches her right hand across the table. The touch makes her self-conscious. She likes the sensation but instantly feels guilty that she likes it too much.

'Go on,' Andrew says.

Mary sits up in her chair, so she has an excuse to pull her hand back again and place it in her lap.

Yes, Mary, go on, the old woman says.

'Okay, I'm doing it,' Mary says to the air at her left before turning back to Andrew.

'Doing what?' Andrew says.

'Telling you about the voices. There were two distinct voices. One was Irish and she kept saying she was tired and couldn't cope with all of us there. I think that was Elizabeth Cadman. At one point I felt pressure on me, as though she was pushing against me.'

'Really? And the other one?'

'This will sound nuts, but I started hearing her voice when we were at Seaview Manor. She's an older woman with an Australian accent. She seems to be with me now. She wants me to tell you about her.'

Andrew leans in towards the centre of the table, so he can focus on Mary's every word.

That's right, Mary, the voice says. *You must help me.*

'She keeps repeating that I must help her.'

Mary bows her head.

Andrew gets up and pulls his chair around to sit close to her. Mary looks up at him.

'That woman outside Cadman's Cottage was a medium or something. She told me the spirit with me was of a woman who had been murdered.'

'This is a lot to take in,' Andrew says.

Mary starts crying. The waitress appears with the waffle on an oversized plate and places it on the table. Andrew pushes it to one side.

'Is everything okay? Can I get her some water?'

Mary raises herself to sit up straight.

'No. I need something other than water, but thank you,' she says politely, dragging the plate in front of her and cutting the waffle in half to have something to focus on. 'I thought I asked for two plates.'

'Mary, it will be okay,' Andrew says. 'We'll figure this out.'

For a minute she thinks he is talking about sharing the waffle from one plate but realises he is referring to the bigger issue of her perceiving apparitions.

'Why is all this happening to me? My life was simple. It was safe. As Mum said it should be. And then all this. I'm only prepared for a safe life. I don't know anything else.'

Tears flow and Andrew hands her a serviette. Mary is looking for reassurance from him, but he doesn't look at her, just takes a bite of the warm waffle smothered in Belgian chocolate ice cream, swallows and pauses. She is annoyed that he can eat now.

'You know, Mary, the thing about life is that you can never be completely safe, no matter how hard you try to protect yourself.'

'But I was safe before I accepted help from a stranger. How do I go back to my simple life?'

'You don't.' Andrew and the old woman speak the words in cosmic unison. Mary shudders. The waitress appears.

'Who was having the milk hot chocolate?'

'Me,' says Andrew.

'So, the praline hot chocolate is for you.' The young woman smiles at Mary as only waitresses can at will.

The aroma of the chocolate and hazelnut does not offer its usual comfort. It is making her nauseous. She pushes the mug away from her. She notices Andrew make a face, suggesting he's confused by the action.

'Mary, you're staying with me tonight.'

'It's all right. I can drive back to the mountains.'

'No, I insist. I have a sofa bed in the study. It's surprisingly comfortable.'

'Okay. I guess it would be good not to be alone.'

'Then that's settled. Let's enjoy this delicious dessert and forget about ghosts for a while.'

Mary is aware of an excitement brimming beneath the fear of having a ghost attached to her. She knows it is the thrill of spending more time with Andrew. She feels his closeness and breathes in his scent mixed with an agreeable aftershave.

Suddenly she has an appetite for her favourite things. She brings the mug to her face and tastes the smooth chocolate liquid on her tongue. Then she takes a piece of waffle. She sees Andrew do the same. He is now part of one of her most memorable chocolate moments.

☙❧

Mary is standing in a pretty glen and hears the sound of a gentle brook. The sun is on her face and peace is all around her. An old woman with a bun and wearing a white blouse, navy pleated skirt and Mary Jane shoes walks up to her, smiling.

'I don't want to alarm you dear but . . .'

'Am I dead?'

'No, but I am.'

'How can I see you if you're dead?'

'That doesn't matter. I have to tell you who killed me.'

'That's okay. I don't need to know. I will wake up any second now.'

'It was Jaclyn.'

❧

Mary wakes with a start in Andrew's car.

'Are you okay?' Andrew says.

'I had the weirdest dream. An old lady, who looked like Edith Green, told me Jaclyn murdered her.'

'Edith's housemate and your stalker?'

'It's certainly a strange coincidence.'

'Your subconscious is bringing all the information together in a bizarre way, as dreams do.'

'You're right.'

The Jaclyn who killed me is the person you know, the voice says. *She may try to harm you too.*

'Urrgh!' Mary gasps and puts her head in her hands.

'Mary, what's happening?' Andrew runs his hand over Mary's hair as though she is a sick child in need of comfort.

Before Mary can utter a word, the woman says: *You have to tell Helen I've been murdered and that Jaclyn did it.*

How am I going to do that? Mary thinks, wondering if the ghost can read her thoughts.

Start by telling Andrew to take you to the nearest police station now.

'Andrew, you're going to think I am completely crazy. The ghost wants me to go to the nearest police station.'

'There's one near Seaview Manor. I don't know what you'll say to the police. They will think you're stark raving mad. I have to admit I'm having a hard time with this.'

'You're having a hard time. What about me? The one who's hearing the voice? I think I have to follow this through, or the spirit may never leave me alone.'

◈

Mary and Andrew walk into the small police station and go straight up to the counter. A young female constable is bent over the computer. She looks up.

'What can I do for you?'

'Where do I start?' Mary says.

'We need to report a possible murder,' Andrew jumps in.

'Murder? Please come around to the interview room,' the constable says.

She leads them through a side door, down a corridor and into a small, bare room with several chairs and a low square table.

'Can I get you tea, coffee, water?'

'White tea with one sugar please,' says Mary.

'I'm right,' says Andrew.

The constable leaves the room. Mary brings her chair closer to Andrew's and holds his hand. She wonders why she ever listened to the old woman in the first place. She can simply stand up, walk out and leave all this behind her. That is what her stepmother would have told her to do. That is the safest option. But what would Andrew think of her? Would he think her a coward? How could she live with herself if she didn't see this through?

'Andrew, do you know how crazy we're going to sound?'

'I'm sure they get all sorts of weird stuff. You don't have to tell her about the voice you're hearing. Just tell the police officer what you suspect.'

'What if she doesn't believe me?'

'At least we might be able to convince her that they should revisit the property and check the grounds.'

Mary feels relieved that Andrew is starting to believe that this scenario is at least plausible.

The blonde police officer walks in with tea in a white polystyrene cup and a glass of water.

'Thought you might want this.' She smiles at Andrew. 'These interviews make for thirsty work.'

Mary feels a pang of jealousy and looks at Andrew to see if he reacts.

'Thank you,' he says seriously, apparently unaware of the attention.

He holds her hand more tightly. The act reassures her.

The constable sits on one of the black vinyl chairs and takes out a small notebook from her trouser pocket. She picks up a standard issue ballpoint from the table.

'You have information about a homicide?' She directs her question at Andrew. 'What's your name and address?'

Andrew mechanically states his details.

'Actually, my friend Mary White is the one with the information.'

'Oh?' The constable raises an eyebrow to Mary. 'So, what can you tell me, Mary White of?'

'I live in Leura. Um, well . . . ?'

'We think the victim was elderly and her name is Edith Green,' Andrew says. 'She lived at Seaview Manor. You know, the old mansion overlooking the cemetery?'

'Yes, I know the one. In fact, Miss Green's niece was here again this morning, with more claims that her aunt is missing.'

Oh, thank God, says Edith.

Mary smiles and squeezes Andrew's hand. He smiles back but doesn't say anything.

'We have put out a missing persons bulletin,' the constable continues. 'Her niece is concerned about her safety. She didn't say anything about murder. What information can you give me? Did you see something? Did someone tell you something?'

The constable looks Mary straight in the eye. Mary knows this woman has probably spoken to hundreds of people and can tell when someone is lying.

'I'm not sure how to put it,' she says.

'Well?'

'Her friend has been behaving strangely, like she's got a death wish,' Andrew says.

Mary catches Andrew's eye and shakes her head, hoping he will understand she wants him to stop helping.

'Your friend?' the constable asks Mary.

'Yes, Jaclyn Chauve-Souris.'

'Miss Green's housemate?'

'Miss Green's housemate,' Mary states matter-of-factly.

Now we're getting somewhere, Edith says.

'How do you know Miss Chauve-Souris?'

'I met her a little while ago at Sydney Uni. She's a psychology student. I was dropping off books.'

'You said she was behaving strangely?'

'I hardly know her, but she turned up at my house in the Blue Mountains and insisted I take her sightseeing early one morning.'

'When was that and what happened?'

'It was last Saturday. She was showing off and climbed over the fence onto the ledge at Sublime Point at Leura. She fell onto another ledge below and I had to pull her up to safety.'

Mary looks at Andrew. 'I still don't know how I found the strength to save her.'

Andrew squeezes her hand.

'Was she hurt?' The constable is intently taking notes.

'She was grazed on her face and body.'

'Did you report this at the time? Take her to a hospital?'

'She said she was all right, that she didn't need to go to a hospital.'

'And then what happened?' The constable is still writing.

'She drove off.'

'Now, let me see if I've got this right. You let an injured woman drive off after a cliff fall and you didn't report it, and you're saying that *she's* the one behaving strangely?'

'You'd have to know Jaclyn. She's a very forceful person.'

'Miss White, I have met Miss Chauve-Souris. We went to the house to check out the niece's story when she first came to us a few weeks ago, and then again this morning. Seems like a lovely woman. So cooperative and concerned about her elderly housemate's state of mind. Says she goes missing quite frequently but always comes back.'

'You've been inside the house?' Mary asks.

'No, when we saw her today Miss Chauve-Souris was very apologetic. Said she had the cleaners in. She took us down the road for a coffee. Lovely little café. I asked her about the mark on her face and she told me she'd grazed it when she was bushwalking, slipped and hit her face on a sandstone rock.'

'But I was there. I can tell you she fell over a rock ledge.'

'Any witnesses?'

'No.'

'It's her word against yours then. Now unless you have some real information to support your suspicion that a homicide has been committed, you'll have to excuse me.'

You've got to tell her something, Edith pleads. *Tell her you know where the body is.*

'I don't know where the body is,' Mary says into thin air.

'Pardon?' the constable says.

'I think what Mary is trying to say is that she knows she doesn't have hard evidence, just a gut feeling,' Andrew says. 'And we appreciate the law can't be upheld on gut feelings. We're sorry we wasted your time.'

Mary, I can show you where my body is. You must trust me.

'Come on, Mary, the constable is very busy, and we've overstayed our welcome,' Andrew says. 'Before we go, could we get your card, in case we have any further information.'

The police officer reaches into her top pocket and hands Andrew a business card.

'Call any time.' There's a glint in her eye.

Andrew pulls Mary through the corridor and out of the small police station into the cold air.

'Sorry, for rushing you, but it was turning bad,' he says. 'We had to get out. You were starting to look like a crazy person, talking to thin air.'

Mary, you should have said something. Edith sounds desperate. *You should have made her listen.*

Mary puts her face in her hands and cries.

'I felt so helpless. What was I supposed to say, that a ghost told me Jaclyn killed her?'

'We have to come at this from another angle, but first we both need to get some sleep.'

Mary, you can't give up on me. We have to see justice done.

'Andrew is right. I have to rest.'

'Yes,' Andrew says into the air, 'let her rest, and we'll come up with something tomorrow.'

☙

Mary wakes smiling in an unfamiliar room. For a moment she has forgotten everything that has happened in the past few weeks. Now she is with Andrew. Does anything else matter?

She snuggles into the down pillow. Sun streams through a gap in the calico curtains. She looks around the small room, overwhelmed by its colour. The walls are a warm yellow. There's a bright red bookcase full of novels.

'Even his study is wonderful,' she whispers to herself.

The red digital clock on the desk reads 9:00. There's a knock at the door.

'I'm awake,' she says.

Andrew pushes the door open with his hip. He is holding a tray. The first thing she notices is the small clear glass vase with three pink roses. She smells the cooked breakfast before she sees the food on the plate. There's a glass of orange juice and a tiny teapot, a white fine china mug and a little jug of milk.

Mary strains to get up, pulling the doona up to her neck to cover her bra.

'I'll leave this on the side table here, so you can have it when you're ready.'

'This is so nice. You really didn't have to do this.'

'I wanted to. I don't have guests often. Never, in fact, so it's good for me to be able to play host.'

Andrew closes the door behind him.

Mary lies back on the pillow and wonders how she can be so lucky. To think she could have totally missed out on this. If things in her life hadn't become so weird, she may never have known Andrew as a friend.

The aroma of the breakfast delights her nostrils and suddenly she is starving. She sits up, swings her legs out of the sofa bed and leans over the side table. She feels a slight chill and pulls her jumper over her head, then tucks into baked beans, fried eggs and sausages with thick toast. It may be the best meal she has ever tasted. How is it possible that food she has had a hundred times can taste better than she's ever known?

Mary dresses in a blur of happiness. Andrew is here with her. Maybe they can forget this horrible mess and just spend the day together.

She walks into the small sunny lounge room. It's cool but the balcony door is open, letting in a fresh sea breeze. Andrew is lying on the sofa staring at a laptop computer. He sits up as Mary enters.

'Good morning. How was breakfast?'

'Wonderful.'

'Good. You needed some nourishment. Now maybe you're ready to read this.' Andrew slides the laptop on the coffee table in Mary's direction.

'What is it?'

'You left some tabs open from your search on Seaview Manor and the orphanage, and I dug a bit deeper. There was a scandal at the home. It was all over the news in 1995.'

'That was three years after Tony and Isabel brought me home.'

'I think you should sit here and read it.'

'What will you do?'

'I will see if there's a lighthearted movie on at the Ritz this afternoon. You will need a laugh after you read all that.'

'You're scaring me.'

Mary thinks she would rather watch trailers of the latest movie lineup with Andrew than have to read about the dark past of an institution where she lived. How could it help her now?

I agree, Edith says. *I think you should let me show you where my body is hidden in the grounds of Seaview Manor.*

'Suddenly reading this seems like the brighter option,' Mary says.

'What, better than going to a funny movie?' Andrew says.

'No, never mind.'

'You know you don't have to read the articles, but I think you should know what went on in that place. I can go into my bedroom if I am too much of a distraction.'

'I don't know why I'm hesitating. I didn't tell you that I found Jaclyn's name on a list associated with the home.'

'Why would you keep that from me? It might explain why she's so obsessed with you.'

'I thought you might overreact, as you are now.'

'I'm overreacting? You are friends with a psycho, and I'm overreacting. I think you should read the articles. I will leave you to it.'

For the next hour and a half, Mary reads everything she can from the news reports on the 'scandal that rocked the NSW foster care community' involving administrators at the Fairy Glen Home for Children and a number of people later convicted for sexual assault matters concerning children. Posing as foster carers, the perpetrators were paying $50,000 to be prioritised on the list and each had access to up to 10 children aged between three and 10 years old. Police found indecent photos of the children and had testimonies from the older children that they had been sexually abused. The managers claimed they would never have allowed the children into those homes if they had known about the danger.

Oh my God. Could I have been one of those children and I don't remember?

She searches her memories for anything associated with the time before she went to school and only comes up with the bullying scene in the sleeping quarters. That is bad, but she hopes that is the worst that happened to her.

Perhaps I should have counselling in any case. My phobias and lifestyle aren't exactly normal. I'm not normal.

Mary starts to cry. Maybe she is a freak with frumpy clothes and a home that resembles a museum. Whether it is the awful stories she has just read or the realisation that her fears and quirks may be related to her early years in the institution, Mary feels a wave of heaviness spread through her being.

Andrew seems concerned when he joins her again.

'Mary, I'm so sorry. I thought it might help. It is a fascinating story, the way the racket managed to convince the administration that they were helping the children's wellbeing by contributing funding to the home.'

'You were thinking like a researcher, and not how this would affect me. Didn't you think that maybe I would be worried that this horrible thing happened to me?'

'No, I didn't. I assumed you had been spared.'

'But you can't know that. And now I can't get the possibility out of my head.'

It is rare for Mary to experience the blues, but she knows a movie, even with Andrew, won't alleviate the feeling. She needs chocolate, tea and Hercules. The thought of Hercules immediately makes her feel lighter.

'I'm sorry. I don't mean to be ungrateful. Could you take me back to my car so I can go home. I need some quiet time to take this all in.'

Chapter 19

Mary rings Jodi-Ann's mobile at 7 am sharp when her boss is normally at the gym, and is thankful to go through to voicemail. She leaves a message to say she has had some traumatic news that has caused her considerable stress and needs to take a personal leave day. She reassures her boss that she is aware that, because it's Monday, she will need a medical certificate even if she only takes one day of leave. Mary hopes this will prevent Jodi-Ann from calling her back, because she doesn't want to have to go through the third degree talking about the exact nature of her situation. Jodi-Ann will try to glean as much information as she can, as she does with Mary's colleagues who complain that she is being nosey rather than looking after the interests of the library. Mary obtained the job four years earlier with the help of Isabel's friend, who was a cousin of the woman who is the rightful owner the position. Isabel told Mary working for a government institution would give her job security and that the library was close to a railway station. Mary was grateful for the role because she hadn't worked much since graduating from high school. Her usual boss was always kind to her, but then she went on long service leave and Jodi-Ann arrived to fill in. Mary can normally find something to like in everyone, but not Jodi-Ann.

Mary feels lighter after leaving the voice message. She lines up at the medical centre just before opening time and doesn't have to wait long. The doctor is sympathetic, writing her a certificate and telling her to take it easy for the rest of the day. She treats herself to a café breakfast and remembers being there with Tony – at her favourite table. She wonders where he is, where he slept over the weekend and how much pain he's in. She told him she'd help him through his final days, but what's she doing? Eating smashed avocado with a poached egg on rye sourdough for the first time and drinking a strawberry milkshake.

'No flowerpot scone today? No hot chocolate? Mary, you've gone rogue. How is the avo toast?' the waitress says.

Mary takes a bite.

'It's fresh and light. Is this what healthy tastes like?'

The waitress laughs.

It begins to drizzle when she arrives home, and it is bitterly cold, so gardening is not an option. Soaking in a warm tub seems the more appealing therapy. When the bath is full, Hercules stretches his full length to reach the edge and gently taps the bubbles with his paw. It's funny what entertains animals. But, like most of these improvised games, he soon tires of it and returns to the warmth of the lounge room, where he curls up on his preferred recliner. Mary sinks into the hot bath, feeling the cool bubbles and then the sting of the hot water until she is acclimatised and comforted by the heat. The room is quiet and still. The water is soothing. Then the thoughts begin, and they loop. Did she live with an abuser? Is the truth lingering in the recesses of her mind? If her innocence was destroyed at such a young age, what good would it do her to know? Why is all this coming up now? It happened so long ago. Why can't she just go back to her simple life? Before Tony showed up, before she met Jaclyn, before the incident at Sublime Point, before the ghost tour, before Edith's spirit began talking to her.

This is all so confusing.

Not as confusing as being dead, Edith says from nowhere.

I can't handle this. How can any one person handle this? How can I hear disembodied voices?

That's so impersonal, Edith says.

Mary doesn't reply. Suddenly the bath is no longer a comfort for her. She dresses in her most stretchy pants and sloppiest jumper, searching her mind for a way to quell the noise in her head. Everything in the house is organised; that is, except for Isabel's room. She can finally work out what to do with her stepmother's belongings.

Maybe I can help, Edith says.

Mary ignores the voice, thinking if she doesn't respond, Edith might think she's lost her ability to communicate with the dead. Getting to work in Isabel's room, she wonders why she can hear a stranger and not the woman who raised her. Apart from vacuuming and dusting the room, and cleaning the sheets and bedspread after Jaclyn was in the house, Mary has not touched anything in her stepmother's room.

Three years is a long time. It's not that she hasn't wondered how long is long enough to keep the room a shrine to the woman she knew as her mother. At first, she couldn't go in there at all. The thought of picking up the paddle brush that Isabel used to brush Mary's hair every night or looking into the matching hand-held mirror seemed like sacrilege. That bedroom at the front of the house is the main bedroom. And this is Mary's house now. But she has always come up with an excuse for why she can't make it her room. The view into the ravine is nicer from her bedroom. Her mother's room is too big. She can't sleep in the room that has such a strong presence of her mother.

Now she is wondering what would happen if she took everything out and repainted the room? How would it feel? What kind of furniture would she buy?

Her thoughts are interrupted by the phone ringing. Dare she answer it in case it's Jodi-Ann? She has other people in her life now. It could be Tony or Andrew. She picks up the heavy receiver.

'Hi Mary.' Andrew's voice is comforting. 'I wanted to see if you're all right. You were pretty upset when we parted yesterday.'

'Yeah, I'm okay. I thought it was Jodi-Ann ringing and I would have to tell her my life story.'

'She has been ranting about not being able to find good help these days. Just kidding. But she was here checking up on me to see I was taking on your work and wasn't slacking off.'

'I'm sorry I left you with extra work.'

'Don't be, but it is hard to get the momentum going when you're not here. You're so organised and focused.'

'Really? Sometimes I wonder how much value I add.'

'Don't be silly. You're a fantastic worker.'

Mary doesn't say anything, just sniffles softly.

'Mary?'

'My head is so sore from thinking. It's all too much.'

'It's going to be okay. What are you doing to take care of yourself?'

Mary tells Andrew about her plans to make chicken soup and pack up Isabel's things so she can redecorate the room later.

'I can't believe I kept her things these past three years.'

As she says the words, Mary can feel a lightness in her being. How is it that removing old things and someone else's possessions can make your home and your soul feel less burdened?

'Once you start decluttering it can become addictive because it feels good. Be careful not to do too much too soon, because it can cause sudden and big changes in your life. My mum sorted every room of her house and discarded a lot of possessions over the course of one week and within a month she was living in a new house and had a new job that she hadn't planned for.'

'Okay, I will only make a start on Isabel's room for now. Besides I have to go back to work tomorrow.'

'I hope we're okay. I didn't mean to stress you with those articles about the children's home.'

'It has put me into a spin. I can't stop thinking about it.'

'I'm so very, very sorry.'

'I know,' Mary says, reaching for something truthful.

She doesn't want Andrew to feel bad, but Isabel was wrong telling her she needed to push her own feelings down to make others feel good about themselves.

'Showing me those articles was very shocking,' Mary continues. 'It may take a while to get over it.'

'I understand. Let me know what I can do to make it up to you.'

'For now, I just need to be on my own.'

'Fair enough. Don't come in tomorrow if you're not up to it. I can cover for you.'

Back in Isabel's bedroom, Mary pulls out all the drawers of the 1950s dresser and tips the contents of each one on the bed until there is a pile of underwear, belts, socks, pantihose, tops, shorts, jewellery and various nicknacks. Nothing that Mary wants to keep. When she upends the bottom drawer, yellowed newspapers fall out on top of hand-knitted jumpers. Why would Isabel have kept old newspapers?

Unfolding the papers reveals front-page stories about the Fairy Glen Home for Children scandal. They are similar to the archived online articles, but reading them in the paper from the time makes it more immediate and real.

At least 10 children are thought to have been involved . . . Police believe they have all known suspects in custody . . . The defendants will stand trial . . . Head of the home at the centre of the child abuse scandal found dead . . .

In the last article, Mary recognises the name Henderson as the same name Jaclyn mentioned at Sublime Point.

Sonya Henderson was found dead in her home at 10 am yesterday. Police have not given details of how she died but say there are no suspicious circumstances. Mrs Henderson, Head of the Fairy Glen Home for Children, was due to give evidence tomorrow at the trial of four people appearing on 15 charges, each relating to the abuse of minors who were in Mrs Henderson's care when they were fostered by the defendants' families.

Oh dear! Mary thinks. *What a terrible tragedy! So many lives destroyed. No wonder Mum kept such a tight rein on me. She was scared the world would hurt me, if it hadn't already, and she wanted to keep me safe.*

But despite her best intentions, Mary knows it wasn't right that Isabel had kept her psychologically bound to this house and her place of work, and discouraged her from venturing anywhere else. Looking at her stepmother's room and then through the house, Mary feels angry, with Isabel but also herself. She is an adult now and has allowed herself to live Isabel's life, so tightly bound by her stepmother's controlling behaviour and rules, well beyond the grave. Despite Andrew's warning about doing too much decluttering too quickly, she wants to throw everything out, starting with the old newspapers. But first she scoops Hercules out of his recliner and sits down with him in her arms, burying her head in his fur.

He struggles and slips out of her arms backwards onto the floor. She bows her head and cries, and as though he realises he's needed, Hercules jumps back on her lap and licks her hand.

Chapter 20

M ary rarely ventures into the old library next door, but today she has research she must do for her job. She knows she has done enough investigation into her own past to last her a lifetime. She wishes she could give back the time she spent reading the articles about the child abuse case at Fairy Glen and everything she learned about it. She tries to focus on her appreciation for these wonderful surroundings, like the rows and rows of shelves on the walls that seem to go up to a mythical ceiling. Where the modern library is alive with its café and bookshop, this building is a holy place where librarians use gloves to turn pages of precious antique books, and people rarely speak. Mary can smell hundreds of years here. Time is stored between pages instead of in a capsule, and the timber railings give off their own fumes. Mary has never climbed one of the ladders that take the librarian to a top shelf on one of the many levels, but now she wants to. She wants to grab the rarest, oldest, most difficult-to-reach book and lose herself in it. She wants to be anywhere but where she is in her head right now. Lost, where nothing makes sense. Her past. Her present. How can she even imagine a future?

᠊ᢀ᠊

Mary sits at a round metal table under an umbrella, sipping on a tall glass of lemonade.

Her stomach is in knots, and she can't think about eating. She looks around for any sign of Jaclyn. They agreed to meet here at 1 pm. It is now 1.15 pm.

'So, you decided to buy me that coffee?' Jaclyn says, approaching from behind.

Jaclyn puts a hand on Mary's right arm and swings around to give her an air kiss on her left cheek. Mary jumps at the touch.

'Oh Jaclyn, you came,' she says, feigning a smile.

Jaclyn sits opposite, her long black hair falling straight over her shoulders, her dark eyes framed by thick black eyeliner and grey eyeshadow. Her pupils seem normal. There's no hint of the strange trance Mary has witnessed in the past two encounters. She relaxes.

'I am sorry I'm late. I got talking to my lecturer after class. She's such an old school Jungian.'

'You'll have to forgive me. I don't know what that means.'

'We'll take care of that,' Jaclyn says, looking past Mary to the waiter wiping a nearby table. 'Hi, could I get a long black?'

'I'm glad we could meet up.' Mary feels the lump in her throat and sucks lemonade through the straw to disguise an involuntary swallow.

'Yes, it's about time. It's been a while since I helped you out with those books. I thought you weren't going to come through.'

'We've had lunch here since then, and there was that sightseeing trip in the Blue Mountains and the little matter of saving your life.' Mary can't help herself.

Jaclyn's eyes widen. 'What are you talking about?'

'You came to the Blue Mountains and had an accident at Sublime Point.'

'Have you lost your mind? I haven't been to the Blue Mountains since I was a little girl.'

'Oh! You don't remember coming to my house.'

'Your house? In the Blue Mountains?'

'Yes.'

'Oo ah, Mary. Either you have an active imagination, or you are hallucinating. I know a good shrink I could refer you to.'

Oh my God, she is crazy! 'Maybe it was a very vivid dream,' Mary says. 'Can I tell you about it?'

'Why would I want to hear about a dream where I had an accident? Pretty dreary. Maybe if I won the lottery, that's a dream I'd want to hear about. Come on, Mary, you must admit I have my work cut out with you. Now that you're confusing your dreams with reality, I might even be able to practise my psych theory on you.'

Mary wants to run away and never see this creepy woman again. How could she have thought coffee with her was a good idea? She wishes Andrew were here, though she knows she has to work this out alone.

'So, Jaclyn, what have you been up to?' she begins.

'Uni has been pretty full on. I'm seeing two of the lecturers at once, so that's a challenge.'

'Seeing them romantically?'

Jaclyn draws back and grimaces. 'Seeing them romantically? Oh, you're cute. We're hooking up. There's nothing romantic about it.'

Heat rises in Mary's face.

'Look, you're blushing. Have you ever had such good sex it blows your mind?'

Mary is silent.

'Wait a minute. You're a virgin! I knew it. We have so much work to do.'

Mary is now glad Andrew isn't here to listen to this. How embarrassing! What can she do to get out of this? She stops the thought because she knows she must get information about Edith.

'How's your housemate?' Mary looks Jaclyn straight in the eye. The power of her look must be strong because Jaclyn turns away.

'She's gone on a short holiday with her niece.'

'Oh. When did she leave?'

'I haven't seen her since Sunday night a week or two ago.'

I don't think she can see or hear me outside Seaview Manor, Edith says.

That's the night Andrew and I went to the house, and I heard your voice for the first time.

That's right.

'Do you remember when my friend Andrew and I came to your house that Sunday night?' Mary asks, not knowing where this new-found courage is coming from.

'How can I remember something that never happened? Are you playing with my head, Mary? Because if you are, I can play with the best of them.'

'No, just getting a reality check. Must have been another vivid dream.'

The only difference is Andrew was there, and he can vouch that it happened!

That's right, Edith says.

Mary looks behind her, thinking she feels a presence.

'Is something wrong?' Jaclyn asks.

'Thought I saw someone I knew.'

'Now about your makeover. Don't be too shocked about this, but we have to start with your weight. What's that you're drinking?'

'Lemonade.'

'Right, from now on you will drink only sparkling natural mineral water. What else did you have for lunch?'

'Nothing.'

'That's good. You'll lose it fast. Remember it's energy in, energy out. If you don't use the energy, it will build up as fat around your waist, as it already has. As for your clothes . . .'

'What about my clothes?'

'They're hideous. You're in your late 20s, right?'

'Twenty-seven.'

'And you look like a middle-aged frump.'

'Jaclyn, that's not very nice.'

'It's called being cruel to be kind.'

'What do you think I should wear? Suits like you? They're not me.'

'And this granny jumper is?'

'Well, I'm comfortable.'

'Let's look at this another way. You're going to stay a virgin if you dress like that.'

'Jaclyn, you can't talk to me like this.'

'Friends have to be honest with one another.'

I can't be honest with you, or I'd tell you you're a fruitcake.

Jaclyn talks like this to everyone, Edith says. *She thinks she is the world's expert on fashion and style. But look at her. She's pale, thin and sickly. Looks like she belongs at the castle of Count Dracula.*

'You're right,' Mary says to Edith, forgetting she's talking out loud.

'Of course, I'm right,' Jaclyn says. 'Now why don't you take the rest of the afternoon off and come shopping with me. I suppose you have a credit card?'

'No, my mother said credit cards were tools of the devil. I pay cash for everything.'

'We'll have to go to an ATM then.'

'I was wondering if I could ask you about the orphanage you mentioned. You stayed there when you were a young girl. The Fairy Glen Home for Children. What do you remember about it?'

'I think you're mistaken. I was never in any orphanage. I had two loving parents who brought me up in a beautiful home. You must have me mixed up with someone else.'

'It's strange that I saw a J Chauve-Souris on a list of names associated with the Fairy Glen Home for Children. Was it someone else, or did something happen there that you don't want to remember, like the accident at Sublime Point?'

'I honestly don't know what you're talking about.'

Mary knows she is about to poke the bear, but maybe Jaclyn can get the help she needs if she can address the trauma she's faced.

'Jaclyn, it's okay if you want to deny being at the home, but I was reading some interesting articles on what went on there.'

'Don't go there, I'm warning you.'

'So, you know about the child abuse?'

'Stop!' Jaclyn is holding her palms over both ears.

'I think you might need counselling.'

'I'm not hearing anything you're saying.' Jaclyn is shouting, her eyes wild, and people at other tables are staring at them.

Jaclyn still has her hands up to her ears. Mary doesn't know if she can hear her, but she knows she has to leave before Jaclyn becomes violent.

'Sorry to have to rush off, but my boss is going to be asking a lot of questions if I don't go back now,' Mary says as calmly as possible. 'Thank you for the lovely suggestion of the shopping trip. We'll do it another time.'

'You better make that a promise, Mary White.' Now Jaclyn has her hands down, and she seems satisfied.

Mary leaves the table and hurries inside to the counter to pay for the lemonade and coffee. 'My friend out there is waiting for her long black. I'll pay for both drinks now.'

Mary dashes by Jaclyn and tells her the coffee is on its way and that she has paid for it. 'Have to go back to work now. See ya.'

Jaclyn's 'But' is faint as Mary runs up to the traffic lights, which turn to 'walk' as soon as she arrives. She keeps running.

That's it. I've had it with all this craziness, Mary says silently, intending the words for Edith.

Mary, you must work something out, for me and for Helen, Edith says. *You're our only hope.*

I never want to lay eyes on that woman again. Ever. You heard her. She's completely nuts.

Of course, she's crazy. She killed me, didn't she? But she's put it out of her mind the way she's forgotten about the fall. Maybe she has some condition where she can blank out trauma.

Suddenly Mary feels different, as though her thoughts are only her own. Edith's presence has gone. She looks across the road and sees Jaclyn alone at the little round table, pulling at her hair. She wonders if Jaclyn did in fact experience something so horrible that she shut out all memory of it and turned it into an obsession with fixing others. What was she trying to fix with Edith?

Instead of going back to work, Mary turns left to take a short stroll in the Royal Botanic Garden. It is cool and overcast. There's a sense of foreboding rather than lightness of spirit among the century-old figs and countless palm varieties.

Taking three deep breaths to inhale the clean air exhaled by the trees, she closes her eyes and tries to hear the squeaks of the few bats awake in the daylight hours.

'So, this is where you are,' Jaclyn says, walking up beside the giant water gum.

Oh no. This sanctuary is no longer safe either.

'You're naughty, Mary, and I thought you were such a nice girl. Work, my ass.'

Come on, Mary, Edith says. *Now is your chance to ask her about her childhood.*

'I can't,' Mary says.

She starts running along the cement path.

'Mary, you can run, but you can't hide,' Jaclyn calls.

Jaclyn's haunting cackle chases Mary all the way to the library's glass entrance. Her sprint has left her exhausted, but a quick glance behind tells her there's no sign of Jaclyn. Safely inside, she doubles over, hands on her knees, drawing in air. Several of the library staff ask if she's all right. 'I'm fine, thanks,' she says, although she isn't. Her chest hurts. 'Bit unfit, that's all.' She stands erect, gives them a weak smile and takes the lift to the second level.

At her workstation, she dumps her handbag and drops into her swivel chair, slumping over the desk.

'What's wrong?' Andrew asks. His voice is reassuring.

She looks up and sees his brown eyes, pools of hope and security. But this safety will be short-lived because she will have to go home sometime, and Jaclyn will be waiting, watching and directing her every move. How ironic that just as she is learning who she is, she has become less free than she's ever been. Someone once said 'you can choose not to be scared', but how does that work? She *is* scared, really scared. And no-one can get inside her head and understand her fear. Apart from this mad woman. She is inside her head. How can she be free of her?

Mary shrugs and turns away to avoid Andrew's eyes. 'I did something stupid.'

'What did you do?'

'I invited Jaclyn for coffee.'

'In broad daylight, I hope.'

'We were in plain view of the street. I had no idea how sick she is. There was no way I could have told her about the history of Fairy Glen. She would have ripped my head off. I don't know what to do.'

Mary starts to tear up. Andrew offers her a tissue with a gesture to wipe her eyes.

Their boss sweeps in like a gust of unwelcome wind.

'Mary, have you finished cataloguing those new scientific journals?' Jodi-Ann snorts.

'Um no. I took a few calls from government departments wanting to know about booking our meeting rooms.'

'Those should be handled within a few minutes, max. What were you doing with the rest of your time?'

'Jodi-Ann, I can vouch for Mary,' Andrew says. 'She hasn't stopped since she got back. You know how high those reports and journals were piled on her desk.'

'Mary, since when have you been using your colleagues to speak on your behalf?' Their boss is staring her down. 'Cat got your tongue?'

'Um, no. I have been working very hard.'

'You know my motto. You don't need to work hard if you work smarter.'

'Yes, ma'am.'

'Now get on with that cataloguing. I want it done by the end of the day.'

'But . . .' Mary pauses.

'You have nothing else to say?'

'No.' Mary looks at the ground.

'Very well then, back to work. Oh, and put that medical certificate on my desk as soon as possible. You do have one for me, don't you?'

'Yes, ma'am.'

Jodi-Ann turns to walk away and then twists around.

'Mary, have you been crying?'

'It's nothing.' Mary looks at Andrew, and he nods in reassurance.

'Good,' Jodi-Ann grunts. 'Wouldn't want to think I'm encouraging soft employees. It's bad enough you had all that leave for your personal issue. Hope that's been dealt with.'

'Yes, it has.'

'Oh, what a manager has to put up with,' Jodi-Ann says to no-one in particular as she breezes off in the direction of another poor, unsuspecting staffer.

'Boy she is riding your ass more than normal. What has gotten into her?' Andrew rolls his chair across to her desk.

'I have taken two personal days in a couple of weeks, and I never take leave, not even holidays. Maybe she is feeling like she's losing control of me.'

'I say put in some annual leave. You deserve it, especially in the middle of everything that is going on.'

Mary sits in her ergonomic office chair and swivels around to her small desk, which is still covered in papers, reports and journals. Jodi-Ann has done nothing if not focus her. She has had a figurative slap in the face, but she needed it, for reasons her boss could never under-stand. She needed to snap out of her obsession with Jaclyn, Edith and Helen and concentrate on the real world. The mundane world of work . . . boring phone calls . . . endless data entry. That pays her bills, keeps her stomach full and her house maintained. Not a fruitless hunt for the answer to a mystery which has dragged her in by a means she doesn't understand.

She sorts the science journals from the medical ones and wonders about the amazing minds who are discovering cures for disease and helping the blind see. She will never do anything even remotely wonderful for humanity.

'You shouldn't worry about anything Jodi-Ann says.' Andrew's words seem to come out of the blue.

'She's done me a favour. Brought me down to earth. I was getting so caught up in this bizarre world of ghosts, murder and scandal that I forgot what was real. This is real.' Mary picks up a student's postgraduate thesis bound at Officeworks. 'Cataloguing the work of great minds, who've written up their research for the benefit of others.'

'Maybe you could write a book when you solve this case.'

'I'm not solving anything. I'm done.'

'No more ghost tours?'

'Not in this lifetime.'

'What about dinner after work?'

'That would be something normal. I have to eat.'

'You have to tell me about what happened with Jaclyn.'

'At dinner. Better get back to it or I'll be sleeping here.'

Chapter 21

Edith feels relieved to be at her front door again. Apart from her monthly outings with Helen and Joe, she never left the house. Even her groceries were home delivered. While having the adventure with Mary and being so focused on her mission to expose Jaclyn, she's forgotten how good it is to be in Seaview Manor. She imagines the grounds as they once were, with cherry blossoms and dozens of varieties of roses in the large garden rimmed by tall Australian gums.

What a perfect place for children's parties. Helen's children.

Edith knows she has lost Mary's help temporarily, and it's now up to her to dig up more information on Jaclyn. She floats beside Jaclyn as she runs up the stairs, along the hall dotted with paintings of Edith's family going back several generations and into a large bedroom with a dusty, dark timber four-poster bed. Edith hides in the doorway out of sight of Jaclyn, who has her back to her. Jaclyn pulls an old suitcase from under the bed. She opens the case to reveal a porcelain doll. It looks like a young girl frozen in time from the 19th century. Jaclyn sits on the bed and cradles the doll, its long brown hair falling over her arms. Edith wonders if she should stay in the hall. She can see through the walls anyway, but there is no need. Jaclyn is giving all her attention to the doll. Until this moment Edith had treated Jaclyn's ability to see and hear her as nothing strange. Now, observing her in this state, she knows there is something very odd about her.

'Oh, my darling, Jaclyn. I love you so much,' she says.

Jaclyn? Edith is curious.

'I'm sorry I died when you were so little. It wasn't your fault. But you felt so alone in those foster homes, didn't you?'

'It was terrible,' Jaclyn says in a high-pitched voice.

Oh no! Edith thinks.

Jaclyn holds the doll with its head on her shoulder and pats it on its back.

'There, there. I'm here now. You never have to be afraid.'

'Oh, Mummy.'

Jaclyn sobs and cries out.

Edith wants to reach out to her. She can feel her pain in the ether. It is unbearable.

She is about to sit on the bed and try to comfort Jaclyn but stops.

This is your killer, Edith reminds herself. *There is no excuse for what she's done.*

Edith's thoughts are pierced by the sound of porcelain smashing. Jaclyn has the doll by the feet and is thrashing its head against one of the bed posts.

'Die, you devil. Die. Jaclyn, you're wicked beyond redemption. You should die. Die. Die.'

The thrashing continues in rhythm with the word 'die' until the doll's head has caved in. Edith reminds herself that it is only a material object that Jaclyn is thrashing, but the sudden anger she is expressing towards herself is shocking.

Jaclyn cradles the doll again and sits on the bed, patting the doll on the back.

'Now. Now. What have those nasty foster parents done to you? They beat you hard. Oh, my baby. I'm so sorry I left you. You deserved better.'

'They took me back to the or-fu-nige,' Jaclyn says in a young child's voice, mispronouncing the word 'orphanage'. 'And some people picked up that girl, Mary, the one with the long curly brown hair, and took her home.'

That's why she's obsessed with Mary.

'And how did that make you feel?' asks Edith.

'Sad,' Jaclyn replies in her regular voice, hugging the doll tightly. 'I was all alone in the world. I had absolutely no-one to love me. But everyone loved Mary. She was so sweet and pretty.'

Jaclyn begins singing the nursery rhyme Ring-a-Ring o' Rosie. She grabs the doll by the feet and starts bashing its damaged head against the bed post again.

'Die, Mary, die.'

I must do something before she harms Mary.

Edith goes into her own bedroom, which is still the shambles it was on the day of her murder. *There must be something here that will incriminate Jaclyn.* She looks around the room. All she sees is overturned furniture and smashed glass. The glass has blood all over it. Some of it would be Jaclyn's, but a lot would be hers. The police would have to be suspicious about that, and then they would have to search the yard for her body. She needs Mary.

Edith concentrates on creating a rumbling sound in the room as though there is an earthquake. The room shakes. She hopes it's enough to wake Jaclyn out of whatever trance she's in and make her investigate.

Jaclyn is soon in the doorway.

'Edith, what's going on? Look at this mess. Has there been an earthquake?'

The rumbling and shaking stop.

'An earthquake didn't cause this mess.' Edith walks over the broken shards around the dresser, which lies on its side. She doesn't make the usual crunching sound of weight on glass. 'But I think you know what did.' She studies Jaclyn to see if any acknowledgement of what she's really seeing registers in her expression.

'You silly old woman,' Jaclyn scorns. 'How could I know what's happened in here other than thinking it was an earthquake.'

'Did any other part of the house shake?' Edith smiles.

'Maybe it was a centralised quake.'

'And I'm a young woman of infinite beauty.'

'Ha ha ha.'

The cackling of Jaclyn's laugh pierces the ether and sends a chill through Edith's soul. The hurt reaches her in a place she is barely aware of.

'You may laugh, but I was beautiful once. Believe it or not, you'll be old and wizened one day; that is, if you live that long.'

'Now you're just being cruel,' Jaclyn says.

'There's more where that came from if you don't tell me what happened in this room, or will I tell you?'

'I don't have to listen to this.'

Jaclyn runs out of the room and up the hall to the sitting room. Edith is already there, sitting on the tapestry recliner.

'How did you do that?' Jaclyn's eyes are wide.

'You tell me!' Edith is enjoying the game.

'Don't be ridiculous. Why are you asking me questions I couldn't possibly know the answers to? I'm really sick of you, old lady. Why don't you go into an old people's home where you belong?'

'Where I belong? I belong in an infinitely beautiful and peaceful place where there is eternal light and love, a place you couldn't even imagine.'

'Buzz off then.'

'I have to do a few things first.'

'What things?'

'I need the world to know the truth about what happened to me, what you did to me.'

'Old lady, I've told you you're mad, but I guess you're so insane you don't comprehend what I'm saying.'

'I could say the same to you.'

'You're playing with my head. I see right through you.'

'You should. I'm not really here. I'm only in your mind.'

'I've had enough of this. Can't you leave me in peace? I've had a big day, and I want to sit in the recliner and rest.'

Edith has been treating the whole situation with a certain levity, but Jaclyn knows how to push her buttons.

'You've had a big day? What the hell would you know about having to endure anything? You're so spaced out half the time you don't even know what you're going through.' Anger builds within Edith with each word. She feels the sudden warm pressure of her angel's wings wrapped around her and relaxes.

Jaclyn sits on the recliner as if to sit on Edith and jumps back up when there is no flesh or bones beneath her.

'What the?'

Edith smiles through squinting eyes. It is good to win without even trying.

'Jaclyn, what I've been trying to tell you is that I am a ghost.'

'That's impossible.'

'Is it?'

'Stop messing with my head and tell me what's going on?'

'It would be easier if you could remember yourself.'

'I can't handle this. I'm going downstairs. Don't follow me.'

Edith waits in the kitchen by the giant stainless-steel fridge she bought a year ago when the old ice box could no longer be repaired. She looks around the galley kitchen with original timber slab benches, shelves and cupboards. The fuel stove and gas top next to it. She misses cooking in this kitchen the way her ancestors did.

I guess I will see them wherever I'm going.

Jaclyn approaches the open doorway looking behind her. She turns around and jumps.

'Edith, you almost scared me to death. What is your problem?'

'I am dead. And you killed me.'

Edith pauses to let the words sink in. Jaclyn has a blank look as though she has entered a trance.

'Jaclyn, did you hear me? I told you that you murdered me.'

Jaclyn is not responding. She walks to the fridge and pulls out a huge complete pavlova. She places it on the wooden bench opposite, pulls out the rickety drawer beneath and brings out a huge kitchen knife. Edith shivers at the sight of a knife in Jaclyn's hand.

She can't hurt you now, she hears in the ether. There is something so soothing in the delivery of the words that she knows it is her angel.

It's more than what she did to me, she thinks for the angel's benefit. *I have a sense of what she might do in the future. I must stop her from hurting Mary.*

Yes, Edith, your task is more complex than you first realised, but I had to let you come to that conclusion.

Edith is overcome with emotion. A soft energy envelops her which is immediately soothing. Then she feels the love, all-encompassing, pass through every part of her being. It lifts her up. She feels whole. She questions this feeling of bliss, and it begins to fade. The angel's feathers are gone too. Suddenly she wants them back.

I promise I won't doubt anymore. I want that love again.

It is there in you, Edith hears in the ether. *Soon you will know nothing but love. For now, earthly matters occupy you.*

Once again Edith has glimpsed the real miracle of existence. If only she had a body to shed the decades of tears that have built up in her subconscious. She imagines herself as a girl sitting on the grass with her back against the gum tree, crying and crying because the brats at school teased her and said she was a rich snob. That 12-year-old self helps her express some of this repressed despair. She is ready now to do whatever it takes to have eternal love.

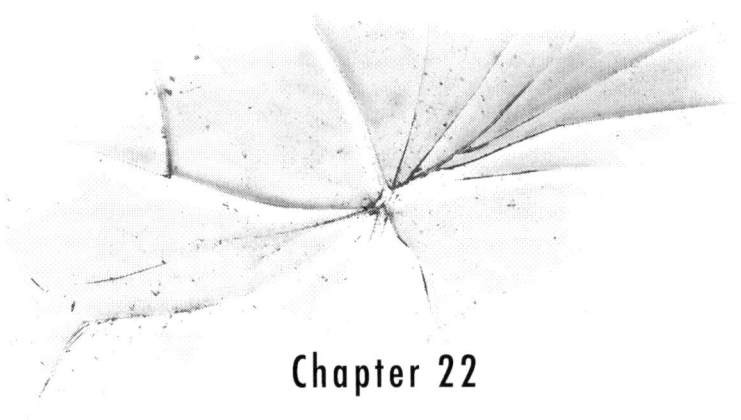

Chapter 22

Walking onto the concourse of Central Station, Mary notices an elderly man with scraggy clothes pouring coins from a tin into his frayed pocket. He picks up a cardboard sign. Now, as on every other occasion when she sees a homeless person, she is compelled to read the nature of his plight.

The sign reads: 'I'm dying. Help make my final days a little more comfortable.'

Mary automatically digs into her bag for her purse and pulls out a couple of gold coins. She notices the overpowering urine stench as she draws closer to the man.

'Here, take this!' she says.

He looks up.

'Dad?'

Tears well up in his eyes.

'Mary, that's the first time you've called me "Dad". You've made my day.'

'Why are you begging?'

'I got kicked out of the hostel because I couldn't pay. The pain was so bad, I went on a bender. Used all my pension.'

'And you're living on the streets?'

'On the trains.'

'What?'

'It's dry and warm. And it's nice to feel I'm constantly moving. For a minute I forget how I've wasted my life. I share the train with happy families and young people and old couples who've grown to look like each other.'

Words rise in Mary's throat, choking her. She tries to stop them, but it's too late. 'You have to come home with me.'

'I couldn't impose.'

'You can have a long hot shower, shave and put on some men's clothes my mother, I mean stepmother, kept. They may even be yours.'

'Isabel never threw out anything, did she?' Tony says.

'No, she kept it all neatly stored. I'm still wearing near-new clothes she kept but hardly wore.'

'You wear her clothes?'

'I live on a meagre wage, and clothes are expensive. Anyway, we were talking about you and your new start. Once you're cleaned up, I'll make us some steak and veggies. Hercules will be happy about that. He loves steak.'

'Who's Hercules?'

'My cat. I think he'll like you.'

Tony puts a rough dirty hand in his pocket to pull out some coins.

'I may be homeless, but I still pay my way,' he says.

They walk over to the transport card machine and queue with businessmen and women. Tony's appearance is in rude contrast to their perfect make-up and smart office attire.

One young woman turns around and screws up her face. Mary gives her an embarrassed smile. No words can explain why she is with this smelly, homeless man. Her father. Thousands of homeless people are someone's father, mother, brother, sister, uncle, aunty. But their unsightly appearance and lack of hygiene hangs over them like a veil of anonymity and justification for judgement.

Mary understands, but that doesn't stop her embarrassment. The other homeless are lost causes to her, but this is one man she might be able to help. A swelling of warmth starts from her chest and spreads around her body.

She is relieved when her father takes his ticket from the machine, and they can walk away from the crowd. She convinces him to go with her to the fast-food counter on the country platform, and he lets her buy him a meat pie and a white coffee. He has eaten half of the pie before they get to the barriers on the platform for the express Blue Mountains train.

It is dark and the air is crisp. Mary is grateful for her stepmother's overcoat. She sees the holes in her father's jacket and imagines the air seeping through and chilling his bones.

They sit on a wooden slatted seat. A woman motions to sit with them and then turns and walks briskly past. Tony breathes in the warm steam from his coffee and takes a sip.

'Not as good as the coffee at the café in Leura, but warm,' he says.

Mary bites into her railway pie. It's good. The pastry is crusty, but not too hard. The meat is chunky in a tasty sauce. It is the perfect remedy for her hunger. She sips her hot chocolate. It is milky but hot. It warms her and closes her senses to the stench enveloping her.

The railway tracks, lit by station light, seem firmly positioned, forming a clear guide for the train. Her father gobbles the rest of his pie. How did his life go so far off the tracks? Mary puts her hand out for his empty cup and scrunched-up paper bag and puts all the rubbish in a bin on the platform. When she sits down again, Tony holds a dirty hand out to her. Mary fights her repulsion and puts her hand in his. Soon their hands warm with the contact.

A train pulls alongside the platform and dozens of people spill out. Mary and Tony wait till they have dispersed to approach the open door of the intercity train. They select seats in the small vestibule near the door and swing two of the seats over to create four together. Mary sits the wrong way, facing her father. They take two seats each, knowing it is unlikely anyone will want to sit with them. The stench from her father, an unholy combination of urine, sweat and alcohol, is overwhelming. Even Mary isn't sure how she will endure the two-hour journey.

People walk by them, some holding their noses, and leave the unlikely pair the section to themselves. Finally, the train pulls out. She finds its rhythm soothing.

⊙⸙⊚

When Mary and Tony walk up the path to her front door, she is comforted by the welcoming light on her front porch. She leaves it on all day now. She scans the length of the timber porch and is grateful there are no nasty surprises. The screen door opens easily. She leaves it unlocked now to avoid the key jamming. A large envelope is propped up against the main door. She never orders anything online, so at first she wonders what it could be.

State Archive. Oh, my goodness. My file from the children's home.

Mary wants to open it then and there, but she knows her father must take priority over her own curiosity. If Isabel taught her anything, it is that patience is a virtue.

Tony does nothing quickly and now he is repeatedly scraping his shoes on the worn straw mat, and then some more, as though he is trying to wipe off years of dirt, or is it years of shame? Cold air is blowing into the hallway. She just wants to get him inside, close the door and turn on every heating source, forgetting about the cost. But with each swipe of his foot, she recognises the love and respect this man has for her. That is something else that is part of her essence, respect. It isn't just something Isabel thought she was drumming into her. Now she sees that respect, like patience, is a real part of who she is. It has been part of her all along because she inherited it from her father, a man with no worldly possessions or status who has not lost his consideration of others.

I was looking for likes and dislikes and talents to show me who I was, but my core values have been there the entire time.

'I appreciate what you're doing, but it's only carpet,' Mary says.

'Your mother and Isabel were meticulous about cleanliness.'

'As am I, but I am starting to see there are more important things, like connecting with people, including your own flesh and blood.'

Tony looks up from his feet and smiles at Mary. She sighs and nervously keeps checking for Hercules, asking Tony to hurry before her feline tries to get out. They walk in a zigzag through the hall and Tony studies the sketches of the Three Sisters and various gorges from the area.

'Mary and I put those up when we first moved in. I can't believe you've kept them.'

'I love these pictures. They are so much a part of the house, but I assumed Isabel was responsible for all the decor. She was always telling me about the importance of keeping everything in the house authentic.'

Tony walks ahead towards the kitchen and is met with a cry from Hercules, and a tail wrapped around his leg.

'Oh, hello,' he says, leaning down to pat the cat.

Hercules sniffs his hand curiously, then cries and looks Mary in the eye.

'Yes, I know, it's dinner time. Dad, why don't you go into the lounge room. You'll be more comfortable in there.'

'Isabel and I lived in the kitchen,' Tony says. 'The lounge room was off limits unless we were entertaining guests.'

Mary frowns. 'You sound like my moth— stepmother.'

'Isabel insisted that we had to preserve the lounge room and not enjoy it. I'm not sure who we were preserving it for because we rarely had visitors. I think she had a deep-seated fear of people.'

'It was the same while I lived with her, but it's different now that she's gone. I live in the lounge room. Go in there, and I'll put on the gas heater. It should warm you up in no time.'

Tony unlaces his scuffed black boots at the lounge room door and steps out of them, revealing dirty bare feet with long unsightly toenails.

Something breaks inside her. She walks past him into the lounge room and lights the gas in the heater that is set within the fireplace. Its heat radiates and warms her legs. Hercules is there next to her. In winter, warmth is almost as important to him as food. Tony is still standing in the doorway, hesitant.

'I'll just get everything dirty,' he says.

He might be the dirtiest person she has ever seen. Not an inch of him is spared. But at that instant she sees past the soiled material and skin and sees a broken man in need of love.

'Why don't you stand here.'

Tony gingerly walks over the cream carpet to stand in front of the heater, looking behind him at the pile for traces of dirt. But there is none. He seems disappointed. Would tracks at least be evidence of himself and a way to reclaim this house he once owned?

Hercules looks up at him and meows.

'I think he thinks you might feed him since I seem to be ignoring him. Would you like a cup of tea or coffee?'

'I'm okay, love. Thank you.'

Hercules rubs his face against Tony's leg and cries. Tony smiles, showing his missing and broken teeth. Mary's desire to care for him deepens. 'I'll run a bath for you.'

In the spacious bathroom, she regulates the water running into her white clawfoot tub, pours in vanilla-scented bubble bath, adding an extra squirt for good measure, and places a fresh cake of chunky lemongrass soap on its gold tray. From the cabinet near the window, she pulls out a thick navy bath sheet and matching flannel, hangs them over the heated brass towel rack and positions the navy mat on the floor beside the tub. She wants her father to feel only comfort when he steps out of the water.

The small radiator with the pull cord above the door is already replacing the cool air with warmth. When the bath is half full, Mary tests the water with her elbow. It is hot, and just right to melt away weeks, maybe months of dirt and odour. Mary doesn't want to think about the effect on the body of not washing for months. Instead, her focus is on the wonder of hot water and soap and its power to erase the past and cleanse the soul.

She pops her head into the lounge room. Tony is still standing in front of the fireplace, his face red from the heat, and Hercules curled up at his feet.

'Everything okay?' she asks.

'Perfect.'

'Your bath will be ready soon.'

Tony nods. Mary goes into the spare room and collects some men's clothes and underwear from a drawer in the large armoire. She always wondered who these clothes belonged to but now guesses they were part of a prior life of the man standing in her lounge room. How differently that Tony's life would have been if his Mary hadn't died.

She arranges the brown trousers, shirt and jumper over the warm rails next to the towel and pops the underwear and thick socks on top. The clothes are a little musty, but this effect of years of lack of use is nothing compared to the stench which hangs over her father. Taking the retro metal razor which has been in the mirrored cabinet over the sink for as long as she can remember, she removes the rusted blade and replaces it with one out of a tiny envelope that appears surprisingly new. Then she puts the razor and a black comb on a little round table in the corner under the window, which is covered with frilly, white chiffon curtains.

The bathroom is heated now. She feels warm and relaxed, knowing her father is safe in her home and will soon be clean and comfortable.

When Mary returns to the lounge room to tell Tony his bath is ready, she sees him kneeling next to the heater, with Hercules lying beside him extending his head as Tony scratches his jawline.

'He likes that,' she says.

Tony looks up. 'He's a gorgeous animal. Such a lovely temperament.'

Hercules rises and struts over to Mary, meowing.

'And he has a one-track mind. I'll feed him while you have your bath, and then we can talk while I make us dinner.'

'Sounds good.'

Tony and Hercules follow Mary to the bathroom, and the cat weaves in and out of their legs.

Tony picks up the clean shirt. 'I can't believe you still have my clothes,' he says.

'And your old razor.' Mary points to the table. 'You never know when you might need things again.'

'Raow,' says Hercules.

Mary and Tony laugh.

'Even the cat agrees,' he says.

Mary pulls back the floral shower curtain.

'There's shampoo in the shower to wash your hair after your bath. I guess it would be simpler to just have a shower, but I figured it would be soothing for you to soak in the tub.'

'That's very thoughtful, Mary, thank you. It looks very good. I only hope I don't fall asleep in there.'

'Take your time. Come on, Herc.' The cat obeys immediately, and Mary closes the door.

She lingers outside the door for a minute, not sure why. Hercules, who is almost at the kitchen door, turns back and cries. She waits for a sound inside the bathroom, some assurance that her father is all right. Hearing the spray of the shower, she realises the lovely bath will be wasted. She should have asked him what he wanted.

Hercules's cries become more and more insistent, and he eyeballs her to make sure she's paying attention to him.

'Okay, boy, you've been very patient, not to mention hospitable to Dad. I think you deserve extra kangaroo mince tonight.'

'Raow.'

Hercules turns into the kitchen with a determination that shows he knows Mary is going to keep her word this time. She honours his trust, turns on the light, pulls the cord on the heater and goes to the fridge for his fresh mince. The cat jumps onto the sink ready for the evening ritual of Mary dishing the food into his bowl with his special plastic spoon, while he nudges her and tries to sneak some meat. When she places the bowl next to his water on the floor, Hercules jumps down in a flash and eats so fast it is as though he is inhaling it.

Now that the others are taken care of, the large envelope on the kitchen table beckons her. She sits to receive its contents, though she wonders if there will be only administrative details and nothing of any value. She pulls out a thick manila folder and reads the first page detailing why she was left there and the dates she lived in the home. It coincides with what Tony has told her. She scans incident reports concerning her and the other girls. Several girls reported that she hit them. Mary thumbs through the pages to see if there are any accounts of the kind of bullying she has seen in her flashbacks. She can't seem to find any. There are colour photos of her with other girls smiling. They seem to belie the fragments from her own memory. Then she sees it. A photo of her with a dark-haired girl who looks like a young Jaclyn. Mary has one arm around the girl and in the other she is holding an antique doll, dressed in a tartan dress with long brown curly hair – the same doll she saw in Jaclyn's car.

That was my doll.

Mary has a vision of the dark-haired girl snatching the doll from her hands and running off. She is standing alone in front of her single bed with the white hospital-style blanket tucked into its metal frame. She feels alone and lost without her doll that she held so tightly.

It seems from the photo that we were friends, but Jaclyn was only interested in me because she wanted the doll.

Mary reads in the papers that another girl, whose name has been crossed out, took her doll on several occasions but always returned it. Mary was sent the doll anonymously when she was three years old.

So why does Jaclyn have it now? Oh, why am I worried about this? It is only a doll, and the fact is I got to go home with a family. Jaclyn was left there, and who knows what awful things might have happened to her.

Mary gathers all the papers and photos together in the folder and puts it on the kitchen bench. It feels good to file the past away again. What good does it do to dredge it all up?

Her train of thought is interrupted by the phone ringing in the lounge room. It has an eerie, hollow tone and she almost doesn't want to answer it. Stepping from the kitchen to the lounge room is like going from a cooler room into an oven.

'Hello,' she says.

'I'm so glad you're home and you're okay.'

'Andrew?'

'Please lock all your windows and doors.'

'Why? What's going on?' Mary sits on the lounge. Hercules jumps on her lap, licking the sides of his mouth.

'Jaclyn was here. She cornered me as I was leaving work. Said she needed to talk to you. When I said you'd already left, she said she knew where you lived.'

'Dad's here with me.'

'You're alone with a man you hardly know?'

'He's harmless.'

'Mary, I'm coming over.'

'You don't have to do that. We're okay.'

'I think you're in danger. Jaclyn's acting like the crazy person she is. She said you pushed her off that cliff at Sublime Point.'

'She said that?'

'She said she didn't blame you, just wanted to talk things over. I'm worried what she might do.'

'I told you everything that happened. I pulled Jaclyn to safety. You don't think that I could have pushed her, do you?'

'Look, if I were in a desperate situation, I'd defend myself too.'

'Andrew, it wasn't like that.'

'You don't have to explain.'

'But if you think I'm capable of harming another human being, then you don't know me.'

'It's all right.'

'No, it's not all right. You are taking the word of a crazy woman over mine. I thought we were friends. Look, I think I can hear my dad. Gotta go. Goodbye, Andrew.'

Mary carefully places the receiver on its brass cradle. She feels tears on her cheeks and wipes them with her jumper sleeve. Hercules gives a little whimper.

'It's okay boy. I've just had a fight with Andrew. Maybe I should call him back.'

The lounge room door opens, and a strange man enters. He is clean-shaven, his long hair is wet and he is wearing clothes that hang on him slightly. The odour and the dirt have completely gone, and her father looks 10 years younger.

'How do you feel?' Mary says.

'Refreshed.'

'That's great. Come and sit in the kitchen with Hercules and me. It will soon warm up more when I put the stove on. I've been a bit upset by a phone call, but I'll put the vegetables on now.'

'How about I help you?'

Hercules follows Mary and her father into the kitchen but reaching the cooler air, he turns around and goes back into the lounge room.

Tony laughs. 'Cats know what's best for their comfort.'

'Hercules is a character.'

Her father opens the old fridge, pulling out the vegetable drawer to retrieve carrots and pumpkin and grabbing a bag of peas from the freezer. The potatoes are in the same place her stepmother always kept them, at the bottom of the pantry. Mary smiles, thinking he is easy in the house that had once been his home. There is plenty of room. He should stay with her.

'These are the same vegetables Isabel would cook to go with our steak. In fact, I think it was the last meal I had here.' His eyes well up.

'Oh, Dad, I'm sorry to remind you of the old times. I didn't mean to.'

'It's okay. I'm just happy to be here with you, finally.'

With a paring knife from the cutlery drawer, Tony starts peeling vegetables. 'Tell me about the phone call. Is everything all right?'

Mary brings steak from the fridge and lights the gas stove. She tells her father about Jaclyn's strange behaviour and Andrew's warning that she might be on her way there. She turns a steak, and it sears. The sound unsettles her.

'I've seen people on the street with mental health issues. They're unpredictable. You must stay away from this woman.'

'I haven't told you the worst part. We suspect she killed her elderly housemate.'

Without saying a word, Tony gets up and leaves the room. Mary hears the key in the deadlock in the front door and activity in the other rooms akin to pushing on windows. She pushes a bolt across the back door to secure it. They are safe, and she's not alone.

'Everything is secure now.' Tony seems satisfied.

The kitchen is warm, and the aroma of cooked steak is strong. As Mary serves the meal, she cuts a slice off her steak and bends down to Hercules, who has suddenly appeared. He takes the meat gently from her fingers, then she washes her hands.

'Dad, I wanted to ask you about that day you and Isabel picked me up from the children's home.'

'Sure. Ask me anything.' Tony leans down to pat Hercules, who rolls his tongue around his lips, then rubs the edge of his mouth with his paw.

'Did I have an antique doll?'

'Yes, I forgot to mention that you gave the screaming girl your doll to calm her down.'

'I gave her the doll?'

'It was such a sweet moment to witness you giving something of yours to someone less fortunate.'

'Do you remember anything else from that moment?'

'I think you sang something, and the girl joined in. I know, it was Ring-a-Ring o' Rosie.'

'You're not going to believe this. That little girl is my stalker.'

'No way. What could she want with you now? She could have only happy memories of you.'

'I don't know, but the doll may hold a clue. I first saw it in her car, and there was a photo of us with it in the file that just came. Seeing the photo prompted a vision of her snatching the doll from me. I'm glad I was the one who gave it to her.'

'It's like I said, I couldn't believe such a young girl could be so compassionate. It made me so proud of you and deepened my joy in being able to bring you home.'

Compassion. Something else she can claim as her own!

'You know, if she hadn't seen me at Sydney Uni, I don't think I would be in this mess. I don't even know if she has put two and two together that the doll was mine or that we were in the home together. She must have recognised a likeness or something.'

'It is hard to know what sets an unhinged person off.'

'There is something else.'

'Yes?'

'What do you know about the scandal at Fairy Glen Home for Children?'

'So, you've heard about that? I contacted them when the story broke. They assured me the perpetrators didn't start fostering until after you had come home with us. It was such a relief.'

'I found some articles about it in a drawer that Isabel must have kept.'

'We weren't speaking at that stage, so I don't know anything about what she knew. I guess they told her the same things they told me.'

'It explains why she had such strict rules about everything and kept me living in fear so I wouldn't venture out.'

'She was trying to protect you.'

'Yes, I understand that now, but the truth is it doesn't matter how much we set out to protect ourselves, we are never 100 per cent safe, are we?'

'That is true. I am glad I'm here tonight. Make what small amends I can for not being the father you deserved.'

'I am so glad you're here with me. And don't apologise or denigrate yourself anymore. Let's start over here and now.'

'Sounds good to me.'

Mary stands up and hugs Tony. She can hear muffled whimpering.

'Dad, it's okay.'

'I'm just so happy.'

Tony is first to break the hug and starts clearing the plates. Mary feels her heart swell and a warm sensation fill her body. Loud banging on the front door fills her with dread and for a minute she is more angry than afraid because she has been robbed of a beautiful moment. Hercules jumps down and moves towards the door with his ears back.

'Mary,' a woman screams. 'Mary, I know you're home.'

'Is that her?' Tony asks.

Mary nods. 'I will talk to her through the screen door. I'm not letting her in.'

'Don't open the door. Let's call the police. You told me she's possibly a killer, and she sounds aggressive.'

'Let's leave the police out of it. Jaclyn is crazy. We have to manage her carefully.'

Mary walks up the hall with Hercules running closely behind. She opens the door and Jaclyn pushes her way past her. *The screen door!* Hercules hisses at the sight of Jaclyn. His tail has flared up like a bottlebrush.

'How do you live with this damn cat under your feet all the time?' Jaclyn heads for the lounge room as though she is a regular visitor.

'Jaclyn, this is not a good time.' Mary wants to close the main door to keep the cold out but at the same time doesn't want Jaclyn to think she's welcome.

'Herc. Herc,' Mary calls.

She reluctantly shuts the front door and follows Jaclyn into the lounge room.

'Jaclyn, what are you doing here?'

'Introducing myself to your father. I see your dated dress sense runs in the family.'

'Charming girl,' says Tony.

'Herc! Come here, boy.'

'Mary, stop worrying about that damn cat,' Jaclyn says. 'Is your life not already enough of the spinster cliché?'

'Would you like me to get him?' says Tony, giving Mary a queer look from behind Jaclyn's back.

'He'll be right.' Mary folds her arms around herself. 'Jaclyn, we were about to have dinner.' Mary is aware of her white lie, but she's desperate.

'Don't mind me. I can sit here in the warmth. It's cosy in a rustic kind of way.'

Mary steels herself to give Jaclyn a piece of her mind.

'Maybe I need to be clearer. I want you to leave, Jaclyn!' She glances at her father for support.

'You heard the lady. She wants you to go.'

'But I came all this way to talk to you about something very sensitive.'

'We'll have to do it another time.'

'Maybe the police would like to hear what I have to say about that incident at Sublime Point.'

Mary raises her eyebrows. 'What do you mean?'

'Oh, I think you know what I'm talking about. Attempted murder, when you tried to push me off the ledge.'

'That's it,' Tony's voice booms out of him. 'My Mary wouldn't hurt a flea. You, on the other hand, appear to be unhinged. I can see it in your crazy eyes, and I know something about crazy eyes, having lived on the street.'

'Oh, Dad, too much truth!'

Jaclyn lunges at Tony, grabbing his neck with both hands.

'How dare you speak to me like that, old man?' she says squeezing his neck like she has only one thing on her mind.

'Jaclyn, stop!' Mary screams.

Mary tries to pull Jaclyn off her father, but her strength is no match for that of a mad woman, which seems supersized despite her slight frame. She looks around for something to subdue Jaclyn. She picks up the phone, pulls it out of the wall, grabs it by the cradle and aims for Jaclyn's shoulder, but the heavy base connects with her skull instead. Mary hears a crack and in a split-second Jaclyn has released Tony and is slumped on the floor. Mary drops the phone in shock and is about to check Jaclyn's vitals when she hears her father gasping for air.

She puts a comforting arm around his shoulder. 'Dad, come and sit on the couch and catch your breath.'

'I thought that was the end for me, Mary, and I didn't want it to be. I kept thinking I wanted more time with you.'

'I know, and I was determined not to let her hurt you.' Mary hugs her father more tightly than she's ever hugged anyone. Tony releases first.

'Do you think she's dead?' he says.

Mary looks at Jaclyn and feels nothing. She is surprised by her reaction. 'You know, Dad, I think Jaclyn is one of those people who are like cats with nine lives. You don't get rid of her that easily.'

They sit on the lounge in silence. Mary looks at Jaclyn's limp body; she seems lifeless. What will she do if she has indeed killed her? She's already raised suspicions with the police about the incident at Sublime Point.

Jaclyn starts to stir, groaning and holding her head. 'What happened?' She lifts herself off the floor into a sitting position.

'Dad, let me do the talking,' Mary whispers in his ear. 'Discreetly as you can, get rid of the telephone while I distract her.'

Jaclyn's eyes are wide and darting this way and that, filled with fear. 'What's going on, Mary? What are you whispering about? Who is that man? And how did I get here?'

Mary calms herself. She knows what to do and say.

'Jaclyn, we were so worried about you. You blacked out. It was so scary. You hit your head on the edge of the mantle, and we thought we'd lost you. It seems like you're suffering amnesia too. This is my father, Tony.'

'Where am I?'

'You're in my house at Leura.'

'I can't remember anything since leaving Seaview Manor this afternoon. Mary, I have amnesia. Mary? At least I know you, right? My good friend.'

'I think you need to lie down on the spare bed and rest for a little while, and then we'll drive you back to your house. It's probably better if you're in familiar surroundings.'

'Yes, I'll be fine with a little rest.'

Mary helps Jaclyn off the carpet and guides her to the guest bedroom.

'Isn't this quaint?' Jaclyn remarks. 'I didn't think anyone had these patchwork quilts anymore.'

Mary doesn't react. She is only thinking about getting Jaclyn out of the way so her father can get rid of the phone and any other evidence of their struggle. She pulls up the quilt so Jaclyn can lie under it.

'Mary, don't look so worried. I'll be fine with some rest.'

'Yes, everything is going to be fine.' Mary's words are intended as reassurance for herself.

She walks into the kitchen to see Tony stuffing Isabel's beloved antique-style phone into the bin.

'Is she all right?'

'She'll sleep it off.'

'We should keep an eye on her. People suffering a concussion shouldn't sleep.'

'What else could I do?'

'I know.'

'Raow.'

Mary looks up. Hercules is on top of the fridge.

'He won't come down,' Tony says. 'No matter how much I coax him.'

Mary leans up to scratch the cat on the cheek. 'He doesn't like Jaclyn.'

'I don't blame him. She's deranged, capable of anything. Animals are sensitive to that kind of energy. We have to drive her home and then get as far away from there as we can.'

'We can't talk anymore. She might hear us. I need to talk to Andrew.'

❦

Mary pulls into a service centre on the freeway. She wants to be somewhere public when she stops and leaves her father alone with Jaclyn. For now, her passenger still doesn't seem to know what's happened and is calm in the back seat, but Mary doesn't want to take any chances.

'I'm going to fill up. Anybody want anything?'

'Could I have a strawberries and cream Chupa Chup and a lemonade ice block?' Jaclyn says in a child-like voice.

Mary turns around to look at her and make sure she hasn't transformed into a seven-year-old.

'Okay,' Mary says. 'And you, Dad?'

'One of those sausage rolls, love,' Tony says. He puts a hand on Mary's shoulder. The gesture reassures her because she knows he's telling her he's been in strange situations before and this one will pass.

'And a hot cup of coffee,' Mary says.

'I want to come,' Jaclyn says, retaining her childish manner.

'I won't be long. You wait here with Dad.'

'I don't have a real dad, only a horrible foster father who beats me and . . .'

Physical abuse of a child is bad enough, but Mary is relieved when Jaclyn doesn't complete the sentence.

'I meant my dad. You'll be safe with him. I won't be long.'

Mary twists off the petrol cap quickly and slams the petrol nozzle against the shaft, eager to get the fuel into the car and be back on the road as quickly as possible before Jaclyn regresses further in age and starts throwing tantrums.

She pays the attendant and asks if she can use a phone. He sends her to the back. She pulls a crumpled piece of paper out of her coat pocket and dials the number on it.

'Hello,' says a familiar voice.

Hearing Andrew on the end of the line makes everything better, calmer.

'Hi Andrew.'

'Is that you, Mary? You must have ESP. I tried to ring you tonight, but the phone was constantly engaged.'

'There's a reason for that, but I can't explain now. Jaclyn and Tony are in the car.'

'What's going on?'

'Plenty, and I really need your help. I know you said you would never go to Seaview Manor again, but I need you. Can you meet us there in an hour?'

'Of course. Should I bring anything?'

'Your phone. We may need to call the police. Something is really wrong with Jaclyn.'

'Are you sure you don't want me to meet you closer to where you are?'

'We're at the big service centre on the M4. It's a bit of a hike for you. No, I think I can get us there okay. She's pretty calm, though a bit child-like.' Mary stops herself from telling Andrew about the incident with her father. He is already worried enough. 'Oh, and bring a good torch!'

'You're being all mysterious, but somehow I think you know what you're doing.'

'In some strange way, I think I do. See you soon.'

'I'd rather we were meeting in the Botanic Gardens than at Creepy Manor.'

Mary smiles. There will be time for that when things are normal again. *Oh, for things to be normal.* She longs for the time when she can enjoy Andrew's company and not be afraid, not of some crazy woman nor of her feelings for her colleague.

She finds Jaclyn's sweet treats easily and is careful to keep the hot sausage roll and coffee separate from the ice block. The last thing she wants is a tantrum over dripping lemonade. But when she returns to the Volkswagen Beetle, Jaclyn is curled up on the back seat asleep in the foetal position. Mary drops the ice block in the round bin next to the petrol pump and hands the coffee and sausage roll to her father through the wound-down window.

She walks around to her side of the car wondering what's in store for them next. She settles into the well-worn sheepskin cover, happy something is familiar in the midst of this madness. 'How long has she been sleeping?' she asks. Her father looks anxious.

'She seemed to nod off as soon as you went to pay. You were gone a while. I was starting to worry.'

'I called Andrew, the one I told you about. He's going to meet us at the house.'

'I'm glad you're not in this alone. I'm still not sure what's going on exactly, but I know you can't be playing with this kind of fire by yourself.'

'Thanks to you and Andrew, I'm not alone.'

There is silence in the car for the rest of the trip. Mary doesn't even turn on the radio. She normally likes to drive with music playing, but now she wants to concentrate on her own thoughts. She needs to work out what she's going to do when she gets to Seaview Manor.

෧෧

Mary shudders as she drives her passengers through the open wrought iron gates and over the gravel entrance to Seaview Manor. It is eerily misty. The fig trees hang over their path creating dark menacing shadows through the dull moonlight.

Ahead, Mary sees a single light and then the outline of Andrew's car. As they get closer to the driveway's turning circle, she can make out Andrew.

Everything is going to be all right. What can happen when I've got two men with me?

She turns off the engine and opens the door, impatient to see Andrew. He's there, holding the door, before she steps onto the ground.

Mary shivers again. It is not only the cold air; there's something creepy about the place. Mist covers a sliver of moon, giving it a ghostly aura.

'Gosh it's cold here,' she says.

'Yep, about 10 degrees colder than anywhere else tonight I reckon,' Andrew says.

Apart from the waves crashing on the cliffs and the rustling of leaves on the trees, everything is still. Mary wishes it were daylight. Why does light make everything less menacing and darkness, by its very nature, instil fear? She tries to tell herself nothing is different from when the sun is shining, except now, she sees less and shadows appear as monsters, like in that scene in the Disney *Snow White* movie. Her rational mind knows that, so why doesn't her heart, which is beating rapidly and wondering what is going to jump out at her? She's been here before. She knows this place, but it feels even stranger, more ominous.

Mary starts at the sound of a car door slamming. She feels a presence behind her. A hand touches her shoulder, and she jumps.

'Didn't mean to scare you, Mary,' comes Tony's voice from behind.

Mary puts her hand up to her heart, as though the motion will stop it from racing. Tony rubs his hands together, then holds his right hand out to Andrew.

'Andrew, I'd like you to meet my father,' Mary says.

'Hi, Mr White, nice to meet you,' Andrew says.

'Likewise. Call me Tony,' Mary's father says, looking at the ground. 'Mary, what are we going to do about our passenger?'

'Andrew, could you carry Jaclyn upstairs to bed?'

'I'll need you to guide the way with the torch,' Andrew says, handing Mary the implement.

'She's on the back seat. Be careful not to wake her.'

Their footsteps on dried leaves seem ridiculously loud as they approach the dark house and turn the brass knob.

Chapter 23

Edith is floating among the corridors and rooms of Seaview Manor when she senses movement. Several people. What are they doing in her house?

Edith is confused but not scared by the presence of intruders. They can't hurt her, but they could damage the furniture and the house's interior before Helen moves in. Edith slams the door of the parlour, then of one of the bedrooms. That will let them know someone else is here.

It doesn't stop the thudding up the stairs. There must be two, maybe three people. Could they be friends of Jaclyn's?

Jaclyn, tell those people to get out of my house! she shouts. Edith feels Mary shiver as she brushes past her. *Mary, what are you doing here?*

'Andrew, Edith's here,' Mary says.

'Edith?' a man asks. 'Who is Edith?'

'Just someone who's been banging doors. It's a wonder she didn't wake Jaclyn. Can you take the torch and help Andrew get Jaclyn safely into bed?'

'Will you be all right here in the dark?'

'Nothing will happen to me while Jaclyn is asleep.'

Edith feels the energy change as the men move away.

'Edith, are you still here?'

'Yes, I'm here. What's going on?'

'We've brought Jaclyn back. It's a long story.'

'Now that you're here I can take you to my body. It's near the glasshouse at the back of the property.'

'I think we should wait for Dad and Andrew.'

'There may not be enough time for that. Jaclyn rarely sleeps unless she's in some kind of trance, and she won't be in it for long.'

'I don't have a torch,' Mary says.

'I'll guide you. Feel your way.'

'Edith, I don't think this is a good idea.'

'We don't have time to spare. It's the only way.'

'No, it is not. If I am going to find your body, I need you to help Tony and Andrew in case Jaclyn wakes up. She will listen to you.'

'I like this commanding version of you. Where has she been hiding?'

'Not hiding, just asleep for a very long time. The real Mary is finally waking up.'

❦

Edith senses both men are trying to step lightly, but the floorboards creak anyway.

'The things we do for love,' Andrew whispers. 'It's funny, I don't even know if Mary feels the same way. Maybe this is what they call unconditional love.'

Jaclyn stirs.

'Um, Tony, we may have a problem!'

'Ahhhh,' Jaclyn screams.

Edith detects some commotion and sees Jaclyn's feet on the floor.

'Let go of me, you perverts!' Jaclyn shouts.

'We're just bringing you home.'

Jaclyn struggles free. 'Where is Mary?' she screeches.

'Dear, why don't you calm down,' the older man says. 'Mary will come soon enough.'

'Don't move any closer, old man,' Jaclyn's voice is now deep.

'Tony, she's got a knife!' Andrew cries out. 'Ow. She got me. Watch out.'

'Ohhhh,' shouts Jaclyn.

'Aaaah!' a man screams. Edith thinks it must be Tony.

'Are you okay?' Andrew says.

'She stabbed me in the side, but don't worry about me now. She's gone after Mary. You have to stop her.'

'Here, have my phone. I've put the torch on. There may be a patch of reception somewhere in the house.'

'I'll be all right. You find Mary before it's too late.'

⊚⊱⊚

Mary follows a faint trail in the dull moonlight, not knowing where it is taking her. A door slamming in the vicinity sends dread through her. She presumes it is the front door and the action is the result of Jaclyn's fury. Instinctively, she hides behind a tree.

'Maryyyyy!' The sound of Jaclyn's screaming voice sends a chill through Mary's body. The voice seems to be calling her from some dark, ethereal realm.

Is this hell?

Mary stops, breathes deeply and shakes out the fear overwhelming her.

There must be a shed or a treehouse, somewhere I can hide.

⊚⊱⊚

Edith decides to stay with Mary's father while Andrew finds Mary. Tony seems to be looking for something. He is talking aloud as though he is trying to connect to guides or spirits in the house. Luckily for him, she is there, but he doesn't seem to have Mary's ability to communicate with this side of the veil.

'I need a phone. In these old houses, the living area is usually upstairs. Here goes.'

He takes the stairs carefully and is panting. 'If I can get help, I can save Mary from that mad woman.'

Edith wills the light switches to be turned on, showing the way up the stairs to her sitting room.

'There's the phone,' he says.

'Police.

'Old house near the sea. Come! Quick! Crazy woman . . . got a knife. She's going to kill . . . my daughter. Urghh. She stabbed me . . .

'I . . . urghh . . . hurt . . . bad.'

They are the last words Edith hears.

'Angels, can you help him? Surely, it's not his time to die here tonight. I have to help Mary and Andrew.'

Edith senses vibrations in the kitchen. She guesses it is Andrew. There is a lot of grunting and sighing.

'Where do women put tea towels?'

I wonder why he needs tea towels? To stop the bleeding! At least I can be useful. Edith shines a light on the third drawer.

'Great.'

He will need something to keep it there. His belt.

Edith shines a light on his waist and there is the energy of a lot of frenzied commotion.

Andrew groans loudly and suddenly he has left the house.

❦

'Maaaary!'

The sound of her name is so guttural that it's as if a monstrous beast is hunting her down.

'You are all planning to kill me.' The shouting is getting closer. 'I knew this day would come but you won't succeed. I will kill you first. You better believe me.'

Mary runs faster. It is difficult to see. The available light is obscured by heavy cloud. Wind wraps around her like a furry creature trapping her. But she is determined to beat it. She wants to live.

❦

Edith returns to the sitting room where she left Tony. She must show him Jaclyn's doll. His energy is weak as though he has lost consciousness. She is surprised when he speaks.

'Mary!' He seems lighter and slightly energised. He is filled with a warm glow. Love. 'It's so good to see you,' Tony says.

Edith becomes aware of a spirit. A beautiful young woman in a soft floral dress. Now she can see Tony too, his spirit hovering over his body.

'Tony, you need to wake up and help our girl,' the female spirit says.

'Yes, he needs to show this doll to Jaclyn,' Edith says. Remembering that she can bring material objects to her as she wishes, she produces the antique doll with its ceramic head broken, the eyes bashed in.

Tony ignores the doll and focuses on the spirit of the woman he calls Mary.

'It is important that you wake up,' Mary says. 'Gather all the strength you possibly can.'

Tony starts to sob. 'I can't believe this. You're here! I've missed you so much.'

'We will be reunited soon enough, but now you need to focus on saving our daughter.'

The spirit of the woman disappears.

'Where have you gone?' Tony says. 'Come back.' He stirs but loses consciousness again.

❧

Mary stumbles into corrugated metal. It's a door to a shed. It creaks when she pushes it open. Frozen by the unexpected noise, she keeps still and listens but can't hear a sound. Cautiously, she steps inside, careful not to become entangled in the debris on the floor and daring not to turn on a light for fear the glow might attract Jaclyn. She tries not to think about spiders and bugs crawling around her in the darkness.

Sitting there, her heart beating wildly, she's like a kid again, hiding from imaginary monsters in a cubby buried at the back of a magical garden. But this time she's afraid for her life, not just pretending to be.

What now? I can't sit here like a trapped animal.

Suddenly, the makeshift corrugated iron door creaks and peels back. Mary catches her breath, hoping she is buried deep enough into the darkness not to be revealed by whatever moonlight creeps in. Something slimy touches the nape of her neck and her whole body shakes. She sees the silhouette of a person in the doorway. She holds every part of herself tight. She can do nothing but wait.

Jaclyn seems to be looking in her direction, but her focus seems to be on rows of jars stuck by the lids to the ceiling.

'What's in there? Spiders?'

She trips on something as she moves in more closely.

'Ouch. Stupid rake. Wait a minute. I can hear breathing. Mary. Mary. Mary. What are we going to do with you?'

Mary sees something glint in the moonlight. A blade. Jaclyn is holding it up and runs her finger along the edge.

'I tried to be your friend. I tried to help you become a better version of yourself because frankly you really need one of my makeovers. I knew you didn't appreciate what I was trying to do. But plotting with your friends to kill me? I know that man isn't your father. You told me your father died when you were four. See, I do remember things.

What do you get out of it? In psychological terms, I don't understand your motive, Mary. Unless it's Seaview Manor you want.'

For a moment Jaclyn doesn't say anything, and Mary wonders if she should use the element of surprise and launch herself at her.

'Mary, I think you need professional help. Planning to kill someone isn't natural. You must know that. You pretend to be all mousy, and "Oh, I wouldn't hurt a flea", but deep down you're a cold-blooded killer and I need to protect innocent people, including myself, from you.'

Mary wonders why Jaclyn is standing at the entrance and not coming in to inspect more closely. She takes an involuntary gasp and holds her hand over her mouth to stop any sound. Encounters with Jaclyn flash before her eyes. There were signs. She got herself into this mess. She must get herself out of it.

☙❧

Edith thinks Mary must be near her body by now and wills herself to be there. It isn't Mary but Andrew she sees fumbling in the night with his torch, mumbling to himself about not knowing if he has the balls to save anyone. How can someone with a desk job fight off a crazy woman? Could he even use the big carving knife he picked up in the kitchen? Edith wishes she could tell him that human beings have more strength than they realise, both in terms of courage and physical prowess. But it is whether they are acting from love or anger, or something worse on the negative spectrum, that determines the outcome.

Yes, keep going. You are getting warm, Edith says, hoping that saying the words will cause him to keep moving, even though he stops every few seconds, writhing in pain.

My body is not far. You are nearly there. Keep going. Follow that path.

Andrew veers off, stepping onto a narrow path. A slight rustling in the trees makes him jump. He shines the torch into the branches of a banksia. A flying fox hangs there, eating. Edith doesn't have to say anything else. It is as if something is drawing him closer to her body.

'Oh, what is that smell? What a way to forget your pain. Replace it with a combination of prawn shells, rotting eggs and sulphur gas.'

Andrew keeps walking, shining his torch ahead. The path winds around and finishes at the glasshouse.

'Maybe Mary is hiding in there,' he says aloud.

A rat scurries across his path, coming from under a tarpaulin covering a mound next to the glass structure. He uses the knife to lift the corner of the tarp and shines the torch beneath. Several black, furry rats shoot out at him, and he jumps back.

You found it.

'I can't go on.' He collapses a few metres away from the mound.

☙❧

As Jaclyn rants about Mary's plans to kill her, still standing in the doorway to the shed, Mary wills herself to come up with an idea to distract her. She puts her hands inside the deep pockets of her coat. In the right pocket she feels something cold, a smooth rock. *The moonstone!* 'It's helped me stay in touch with my inner voice,' she remembers the tall woman at Cadman's Cottage saying.

She folds her hand around the stone, leaving it in her pocket. She wonders whether, if she threw it at the window, it would make a loud enough sound to appear that it was coming from outside. It seems glass-like, and glass on glass makes a smashing sound that might be just enough to shock Jaclyn even if the force wasn't enough to smash the window. It could sound like someone was throwing stones at them.

For a moment, Jaclyn turns her back to the shed, and Mary hurls the stone at the window. The crack is louder than she expected and even makes her start. She maintains her still position, thinking Jaclyn may look inside, but she runs off instead.

Not wanting to stay too long in case Jaclyn returns, Mary feels along the bench for anything she can use as a tool or a weapon. She finds a bag. She opens the zipper and pushes her hand through the opening, pulling her face in a grimace as she waits for a spider to bite her. With her hand, she traces the shape of a hammer, a spanner and something round on the end.

A torch!

She finds a switch on the side. The light coming off it is very faint. She is surprised there is any battery power left. She shines the light around the shed. Cobwebs hang from the ceiling, from the benches, off rakes and yard brooms. The long row of glass jars stuck to the ceiling are full of different kinds of nails. Crates and boxes on the floor are full of tins, tools and junk. A large hairy spider swings down over the window to create part of its glistening web. She jumps back but doesn't scream. She is still holding herself in and not verbalising her fears. She grabs the hammer and runs into the night.

Heavy drops of rain hit Mary's face, and the wind howls around her, pulling her to meet her fate. Maybe she would have been better in the shed with the spiders. At least she was dry inside. Out here, it's dark and wet and she has no idea how to get to the glasshouse where Edith said her body is, so she heads back the way she came, in the direction of the manor. Why didn't they leave Jaclyn on the door-step and get the hell out of there? A sense of foreboding comes from outside her, in the elements. She thinks of her sanctuary in the mountains, tucked up dry and warm in her bed with Hercules.

But Jaclyn is loose. Her father and Andrew might be in danger. Drawing on every ounce of courage she has, she points the faint torchlight in front of her and keeps going. She can barely see. The rain is cold. It stings like it is attacking her. She wants to go home. This is the worst night of her life.

Thank goodness for her stepmother's wool coat, or was it her real mother's? She's grateful. It doesn't matter to whom now. The coat is a small mercy.

'I have to keep it together,' she says aloud, half expecting the wind to reply in confirmation.

As she walks among the overgrown hedges and tall gums, Mary listens for sounds. A thorny bush catches the back of her hand and holds on for a few seconds. The pain is searing. Even the vegetation is admonishing her. Her torchlight reveals the offending plant, a barren rose bush. Behind it is a pathway that hopefully will take her back to the house, her car and safety. Running now, she checks her coat pocket for her car key. It's there, although she can't remember what she did with her shoulder bag. She must have been subconsciously planning a quick getaway when she put the key in her pocket.

Testing the weight of the old hammer in her weaker hand, her left, she doesn't know what she'll do with it except to use it to form a barrier between her and her attacker. Mary no longer thinks of Jaclyn as Jaclyn. She can't think of her with any humanity, or she might start to feel sorry for her and weaken her defences. If she's going to survive the night, she must stay strong. But does she have it in her to kill Jaclyn if she must?

Chapter 24

The rain stops. Suddenly the landscape in front of Mary lightens. The path is clearer now. She looks up at the sky. The clouds have thinned, but the sliver of the moon is still covered in a misty haze.

Breathing deeply and concentrating on each step, she listens for sounds. The wind rustles the leaves in the trees lining her path. It is gentler now and almost has a soothing rhythm in time with her breathing. The only other sound is her feet on gravel. She is getting closer to the house.

Her trusty Beetle beckons her in the distance.

Almost there!

She hears a man scream.

Andrew!

He starts screaming her name repeatedly as though he is trying to guide her to him, or is he warning her that Jaclyn is there and to stay away? He is in trouble, and she must help him. He would do the same for her. He is here, isn't he, when they both swore never to come to this place again?

She follows the sound along a narrow path from the back of the house. The path winds around enormous trees and then opens up in a clearing, and she sees the glasshouse Edith mentioned. It is near where the body is meant to be. Andrew has stopped screaming. Jaclyn is nowhere about. It is deathly quiet. Even the wind has subsided. Then she catches the scent of something fowl. With the hammer in her hand, she inches closer to the glasshouse and sees Andrew lying still on the ground near an unusual mound.

'Andrew!'

As she runs to him, he lifts his head and points behind her. She hears a twig snap and turns around. A dark figure with a knife is running towards her.

She can't see her face, but she knows Jaclyn by her slim figure. Mary's shoulders lift involuntarily in revulsion, but surprisingly she is not afraid. She objectively observes that if Jaclyn ran that knife through her, she could be dead instantly. If Jaclyn keeps running and Mary were to step aside, would the momentum see her pursuer fall over?

Jaclyn is running faster towards her. Mary stands in front of the mound.

'Ahhhh,' Jaclyn screams as Mary watches her metres away with the knife in her hand.

'One. Two. Three,' she counts to herself and jumps to the side, opening her hands by some reflex and dropping the hammer and torch on the ground.

Jaclyn runs past her into the mound and trips. Jaclyn starts to get up, but Mary knows she has to restrain her. As Mary moves towards her, Jaclyn kneels on the mound. Whatever is under the tarpaulin gives way beneath her, and she slips into the prostrate position. Mary dives on her and something squelches beneath them. The smell is overwhelming. She holds Jaclyn's arms behind her back and has no idea what she will do now. She sits on her as it starts to rain. Fine drops at first and then faster, heavier ones.

'Get off me you idiot,' Jaclyn says. 'You're crushing me, and we'll both be overcome by that stench.'

'I will sit here until the police arrive.'

Something subsides under them.

That's my body you're both crushing, Edith says.

The body!

Jaclyn wriggles under Mary. 'Edith, why don't you make yourself useful and get Mary off me.'

Mary concentrates on figuring out her next move. She shifts her weight and feels more squelching.

'What is under the tarpaulin, Jaclyn?' she says. 'Is something decomposing? A body?'

'The best way to find out is to look,' Jaclyn says.

Perhaps she should lift Jaclyn off the mound because if it is a body, they could be destroying evidence. Worse, they could become infected.

'C'mon, Mary, you're a nice girl, not someone who restrains another human being,' Jaclyn says.

'What's under there? And what did you do to Andrew?'

'I can't talk while you've got me pinned down like this.'

Mary slowly rolls off Jaclyn while keeping hold of her hands behind her back. She pulls her up, holding her wrists with one hand and her shoulder with the other. Her incredible strength has returned as it did that day at Sublime Point. She feels a sharp pain in her foot where Jaclyn has stabbed her with her stiletto and loses her grip of Jaclyn's arms. Suddenly Jaclyn is running.

'Andrew!' Mary screams. 'What has she done to you?'

'She stabbed me in the leg. I stopped the blood, but I am in a lot of pain and I feel really weak. I don't think I can make it to the house. I need an ambulance.'

'I'm so sorry I dragged you into this.'

Mary takes off her coat and places it over him.

'I will get help even if I have to hail a passing motorist.'

'Go and see what is happening with your dad. Jaclyn stabbed him too.'

Mary can't resist lifting the tarpaulin. She retrieves the torch she dropped. Its light catches stringy grey hair around a human head attached to a decomposed body.

The vermin have indulged in the grey flesh. The smell no longer bothers Mary. She can put up with that. But the sight of a human body discarded like trash makes her tremble.

◦⟊◦

Mary knows her car must be close now, and is relieved she will soon be able to raise the alarm. She senses movement before she sees the shadow. A jolt from the side pushes her to the ground. Pain shoots up her thigh where she hit the hard earth with force. Someone is holding her down. She has no weapon, nothing to protect her. And she is pinned like a fly.

'Let me go!' she says in a muffled tone, lifting her head from the grassy edge.

'Mary, I can't let you go because I need to talk to you.'

'Jaclyn, we can talk inside the house. I'm cold and wet.'

'I can see what you're doing, Mary. You're trying to distract me with your needs, but what about mine?'

The rain begins again. The ground feels hard beneath her, her right leg is aching. It's like no other pain she's ever known. Her face is squashed against wet grass on the edge of the path by Jaclyn sitting on top of her, keeping her in place. Mary wants to cry for relief and release, but she can't. She recalls the morning at Sublime Point. What did she do then?

How did I find my strength? I feel so weak now.

You did what you knew you had to do. You always know what you have to do.

It is a thought in her mind, but it doesn't seem to come from her. Now her thoughts are racing. She can't still them to find the one that will give her the answer.

I need to stay calm.

'Well?' Jaclyn pulls Mary's head up by the hair with a violent jerk and twists her neck.

Mary's heart races. 'I don't know what you want from me.'

'I want you to tell me why you and your friends are trying to kill me.'

'Ow, you're hurting me.'

Jaclyn releases her grip and pushes Mary's face into the grass. 'Lot of good your plan did. I got your boyfriend and the old guy.'

Jaclyn, you're a monster. Mary wants to scream the words at the top of her lungs. She wriggles to free herself from under Jaclyn but feels two sharp angles, like bony knees, dig into her back.

Fighting is not the answer. I need to keep her talking, buy time.

'Jaclyn, you have to believe me. I don't want to hurt you. I . . . I . . . like you.'

'Apart from my friends who come to Sunday dinner, you were my only real friend. You betrayed me.'

'I'm . . . sorry.'

The words catch in Mary's throat. Instinct tells her she has to show humility. Forget everything that has happened up until now and concentrate on appeasing Jaclyn and convincing her to release her.

'Remember the first day we met?' Mary says in as normal a voice as she can muster.

'You were walking on the grass at Sydney Uni and a security guard was about to admonish you. I calmed the situation down.'

'I didn't know that.'

'Yeah, and I drove you to the library with all those heavy books.'

Mary rests her left cheek on the ground to release some of the neck strain. 'I was really grateful to you. I had no idea how I'd get so many books back to the library.'

Mary searches her mind for any clue to subdue her captor. She remembers the story Tony told her about how she gave Jaclyn her doll to console her and sang a nursery rhyme. Maybe the song will help again. She makes her voice as soft and sweet as she can and starts to sing Ring-a-Ring o' Rosie.

Suddenly Mary feels the sharp pressure on her back ease and then the weight keeping her down is gone. She doesn't want to make any sudden or threatening movements, so she calmly rolls onto her back and sits up. Jaclyn is standing a couple of metres away looking at something in the distance. Mary can't see what she's looking at or why she starts walking in the direction of the manor but is compelled to follow.

Mary takes big gulps of air and breathes through her nose to calm herself as her heartbeat outraces her feet in pursuit of Jaclyn. There is enough moonlight now to shine a path to the manor, but Jaclyn is getting away. She ignores the rain spitting on her face and pushes on. Suddenly, the manor opens up before them. Mary sees her father sitting on the step, bent over. Jaclyn is standing in front of him, completely still. Mary creeps up close to them. Tony is rocking back and forth, cradling an object in his arms. Jaclyn stands there mesmerised. Tony looks up and sees Mary. He gives her a nod that says, 'Everything is fine' and 'Keep your distance' all at once. He looks back at the thing in his arms.

'Oh, Jaclyn, you sweet child.' He lifts the damaged head of what appears to be a porcelain doll like the one she saw in Jaclyn's car. Tony starts singing Ring-a-Ring o' Rosie.

'Grandpa,' says a tiny child-like voice. 'I nuv you, Grandpa.'

Jaclyn runs up to Tony and puts her arms around him, bending over and hugging him from behind.

Tony keeps rocking the doll, focusing only on it. 'You are so beautiful, Jaclyn. You are so innocent and pure. We love you.'

'Oh, Grandpa.'

'Things happened to you that no young child should have to endure. They hurt you didn't they, your nasty foster parents? But they can't hurt you anymore.'

'Stop, don't talk about that, Grandpa. Just hold me.'

Tony holds the doll to his chest as Jaclyn pulls in closer.

Mary's chest tightens. She can only imagine what terrible things happened to Jaclyn. She is moved by the scene. Her eyes well up with tears. She wants to hug Jaclyn and comfort her, but as she walks towards the pair, she sees car lights coming up the drive on the other side of the manor. She looks at Jaclyn to see if she has noticed them, but she is still embracing Tony as though in a trance. Mary starts running in the direction of the approaching vehicle with red and blue flashing lights. Police!

Mary waves at the paddy wagon but instead of stopping near her, it continues around the drive and parks well away from them. Two male officers get out holding guns in front of them.

'Everyone, put down any weapons and place your hands in the air.'

Mary looks to Tony for reassurance. 'Do what they say, love.' She puts her hands in the air. Tony puts the doll down and puts his hands up. Jaclyn grabs the doll and seems oblivious to the police.

'Ma'am, I will ask you again. Put the object down and place your hands in the air!'

Jaclyn continues to hold the doll and starts singing Ring-a-Ring o' Rosie. The police approach her. She doesn't pay attention until one of the officers takes the doll and handcuffs her. She seems to wake from her trance and starts to struggle.

'Why are you restraining me? I'm the one they abducted and tried to rape. And ask Mary over there about the time she pushed me from the cliff. Don't be fooled by the Miss Innocence act she's got going.'

'You do not have to say or do anything, but anything you say or do may be used in evidence. Do you understand that?'

'They are the ones you should be arresting.'

'Do you understand?'

'Yes.'

The officer who cuffed Jaclyn walks her to the police wagon and locks her in the back.

Mary sighs. The other officer tells her and Tony they can put their hands down and asks them to give their statements separately.

On the wind, Mary thinks she hears her name.

'God, Andrew, he's still alone in the dark – hurt!'

'The ambulance is on its way, ma'am. Can you take me to the injured man?'

'Yes.'

The police officer sweeps the area with a huge torch while Mary runs in front of him. They run along the path. The strong torchlight is as bright as daylight and makes it easy to see.

'Andrew?' booms the voice of the young police officer.

'Here!'

Mary sees Andrew waving as though he's on a raft lost at sea, afraid his rescuers won't see him.

She runs ahead of the police officer and drops to her knees in the mud to put her arms around his neck and kiss his cheek.

'Mary.'

'The ambulance will be here soon.'

'I'm so weak now. Can't get up.'

'He needs to get to a hospital,' Mary pleads.

'What happened, mate?' the police officer asks.

'I've been . . .' Andrew loses consciousness.

'Andrew! Andrew!' Mary tries to prop him up against her. She can feel rain spitting on her.

'Can you call your partner to get the ambulance here faster?' Mary hears the panic in her voice and tries to calm herself.

The officer speaks into his two-way radio. 'Hey, Charlie, we've got one down here. Need paramedics.'

'And that mound there, under the tarp, is a body,' Mary says. 'We believe it's the missing elderly woman, Edith Green.'

'A body?'

'Yes, you can probably smell it.'

'Now that you mention it.'

'There's supposedly a body. I'll check it out. I think we're going to need backup.'

Mary watches the policeman take big steps, his bright light sweeping the area then stopping at a mound. Andrew stirs as she notices the young officer lift the tarpaulin, lurch back and drop the sheet. He starts running back past her.

'Can you wait here with Andrew until I get assistance?' the police officer says.

'Of course.'

Mary's legs are tired from kneeling. She eases her legs out from under her one at a time, so she's now sitting in the mud. Her mind shows her a glimpse of her deep bath, steaming water and vanilla bubbles and she longs to be in it. The police are here, so Jaclyn is not going to hurt them anymore. The enemy now is time. Andrew needs to get to a hospital and they both need to get out of the cold and the rain. She lifts her wet overcoat off Andrew, sits next to him and puts it over them both.

Their combined body heat soon starts to warm her despite their clammy clothes.

I hope they've given Dad a blanket. I hope he's going to be okay.

'Mary?'

'Andrew, I'm here. The police have come. Everything's going to be all right.'

'If I don't make it, I have to tell you something.'

'What is it?'

'I . . . I love you, Mary.'

Andrew slumps back into unconsciousness.

'Andrew, I love you too. You must pull through this. We have to say all those things we've left unsaid. I refuse to lose you now.' Mary tries to ignore the rain and wills all her conscious thoughts to concentrate on increasing the warmth in their bodies. She pulls in closer to Andrew.

∽✿∾

Edith is with Tony as he opens his eyes after passing out. The spirit of his first wife is there too. They tell him he has to hang on for his daughter's sake. He puts his hand to where the pain is and finds a wound sticky with blood.

'Take it easy, sir, the paramedics will be here soon,' says a man in uniform, who appears to Edith to be more like an angel than an agent of law enforcement.

Tony is awake and forces himself to sit up.

'Easy there, fella.' The constable puts a hand behind him as Tony pushes himself up from the ground.

'Here, let me put this jacket around you. You must be freezing.'

'Thank you,' Tony says, nestling into the lining of the padded jacket around his shoulders. 'I never thought I would experience such kindness from the police. I'm used to you blokes ganging up on me and telling me to move on from whatever railway station I'm sleeping on.'

❧

'When we get out of here, we're gonna do amazing things,' Mary says, feeling for a pulse on Andrew's neck as she has been doing periodically.

'We could take a trip somewhere, a road trip. I've had this thing about the south coast. It looks good in the ads. Never been. I've never really been anywhere, you know. That's all going to change. We will challenge ourselves and do things completely out of our comfort zone because I can't imagine anything will ever be as hard as what we have gone through tonight.'

Suddenly the darkness is pierced by spots of light.

'Andrew, they're coming. Help is coming!'

Mary can just make out three people walking up to them. The familiar police officer is directing a colleague to the body. A warm-faced male paramedic offers her a blanket.

'How's he doing?'

'He's been unconscious for the past 20 minutes or so, but he still has a pulse.'

Mary automatically touches Andrew's neck to feel for his pulse. It's slow. She lets out a big breath.

'Miss, I'll take over from here. Let him lie down and I can check him.'

'Is someone helping my father? I think he's badly injured too.'

'Yes, my partner is with him.'

Mary steps out of the way and pulls the thin blanket around her more tightly as she watches the young paramedic peel off a blood-soaked cloth from Andrew's leg. Involuntarily, Mary looks away and the two police officers catch her attention. They are both shining torches on Edith's body.

Edith, it's all true! Mary can't stop the heaviness in her chest or the tears rolling down her cheeks.

Yes, dear, it's what I've been telling you all along, comes Edith's voice from behind. *But it's going to be all right now.*

But what if Dad and Andrew die too? Will all this be worth it?

Your mother will stay with them until they are stable.

My mother?

Mary spins around in the direction of the voice, but she can't see anything except darkness among the trees.

Yes, darling Mary, you've grown up to be such a good woman, the woman's voice says. *I'm so proud of you.*

This whole thing has made me feel like I'm going crazy, but this, this is too much.

Mary sits on the soggy ground and puts her head in her hands. She sobs.

There, there, Mary, says the voice. *Don't cry.*

I can't help it. This has been such a horrible experience and the thought of losing Andrew and Dad . . .

Try to keep it together a bit longer. Your father and Andrew need you to be strong for them.

I don't know if I can.

An arm draws Mary into a hug. She looks up, but there's no-one there.

I'll be here sending you love, just as I have been since you were a baby.

You've been with me the whole time? Lately, I would feel this calm come over me at times of stress. Was that you?

Yes, and others. You have many supporters on this side. We all want you to spread your goodness in the world. Meeting Jaclyn was no accident, you know.

Mary is overtaken with emotion, but this time tears stream down her cheeks in silence.

I didn't know you existed.

It's okay, your other mother is with us, looking over you too. There is no malice where we are. Only love.

Mary can feel warmth in the area of her chest cavity. She sees a shimmer in her peripheral vision and wonders if that is her birth mother.

How can there be beauty in darkness? This is my darkest hour and yet so sublimely sweet.

'Mary!'

The sound of Andrew's voice brings her back to reality. She jumps up.

'You're awake!' she says.

'Oh Mary,' Andrew strains to hold out his hand to Mary while the paramedic wraps a bandage around his thigh. 'I've had so many terrible dreams, one after the other. It was horrible. In one I was being chased by a skeleton holding a knife around a house in the dark.'

'The nightmare is over now. It won't be long before you're in a warm bed. The paramedics are doing everything they can to get you out of here.'

'It's so good to see your face.'

'I love you,' Mary says.

'Pardon?' Andrew's brow is knit in a stern expression.

'Oh, God, it just came out. After everything we've been through, I don't want to hide my feelings anymore. Didn't you tell me . . .'

'What?'

'You probably don't remember. You must have been delirious.'

Andrew squeezes Mary's hand and smiles.

'You should see the look on your face. I remember exactly what I said. I love you too.'

Mary lifts a fist and punches the air.

'You had me there,' she laughs.

'It was a bad joke. In fact, from now on let's not hide our feelings or joke about them. Thanks for standing by me. I'm sure I wouldn't still be here if it wasn't for you.'

Andrew starts to shiver, and Mary instinctively puts her arms around him.

'He's really cold,' she says.

The paramedic walks away and talks on his radio, then takes long strides back to them.

'My partner's getting the older gentleman into the ambulance, and then he'll come here with the stretcher.'

୬ঌ

Edith watches the busy scene unfold near the entrance to her beloved Seaview Manor. Several police cars. Jaclyn handcuffed in the back of one. An ambulance. Flashing lights. Andrew being lifted into the back of the ambulance alongside Tony, both conscious but weak. Mary talking to a young constable.

Surely, they could let Mary get some rest.

Despite the activity and flashing lights, Edith is overwhelmed by a sense of peace. Her rotting flesh and bones have been discovered, and it won't be long before the truth of what happened to her will be revealed, and Helen will inherit the house.

Helen! If only I could see her again.

As she has the thought, she feels something soft around her shoulders and becomes aware of a small, familiar car coming up the drive.

'She's here!'

The downy softness pulls back as Edith waits for Helen and Joe. When Helen arrives, a paramedic is shutting the doors on the back of the ambulance and getting into the passenger seat. They wait for Helen to drive up behind the second police car on the round entrance before heading along the drive towards the street.

'Helen!' Edith calls as she floats towards her.

Helen rushes to the police officer talking to Mary.

'I think that's all we need for now,' the constable says. 'Will you be right to get home on your own?'

'I got through this night, didn't I? I want to go to the hospital and make sure Dad and Andrew are all right. Herc will have to do without me for one night.'

'Herc?'

'My cat.'

'Yeah, cats are fine on their own overnight.'

Chapter 25

'Officer, I'm Helen Demitriou, Edith Green's niece. I got a phone call that you may have discovered my great aunt's body.'

'I'm very sorry, ma'am. Yes, we think so.'

Edith holds her soul tight as she feels Helen gasp and bend over at the waist.

You need to be strong for her now, Edith, her angel says.

She feels the angel's softness wrap around her and wishes she could transfer this comfort to Helen. She wills it and Helen stands up, tears streaming down her face.

'Aunty Edith was like a mother to me . . .'

'Oh Helen, I'm so sorry,' Mary says.

'Thank you, Mary.'

'It's terrible that your worst fears turned out to be true.'

'It all feels so surreal. I'm sorry you had to get involved, but I'll be forever grateful that you did.'

'I wish I could have met Edith in person. I bet she was a feisty, determined woman.'

'She was one of a kind. I miss her so much.'

Edith feels great pride knowing these two women thought so highly of her and admires them for how they have endured the ordeal. Mary is suddenly gone. Edith says her goodbye to Mary silently, hoping her hero will feel her gratitude at some deep level. She is indebted to her for helping bring the truth of her fate into the open and for finally bringing her peace.

Edith musters her emotional energy in the hope it will have a physical manifestation one last time for Helen. She wills her warm love around Helen like a blanket and is amazed by the vision of Helen pulling her own arms around herself in a big hug, using the pretext of wanting to warm herself in the chilly air.

Helen is answering questions about when she last saw Edith and where her dental records would be kept. She asks when the body will be released for burial.

Edith senses the softness of down-like feathers around her, signalling it's time to go with her guardian to light and peace. She tells Yehudiah she needs a minute with her niece.

Helen, you are such a good woman. You are like a daughter to me, and I want you to be happy at Seaview

Manor. There's enough money for you to fix it up and have the life you deserve. Maybe once your money worries are over, you'll be able to have some little ones.

Helen looks in the direction of Edith and smiles as though she's looking right at her.

Does she see me? Edith asks her angel.

'Yes, she has opened her mind and her heart so she can say goodbye.'

I love you, Helen, Edith says.

'I love you, Aunty.'

'Pardon?' says the constable.

'I feel my aunty around me, and I want her to know how I feel. Wow!'

Helen laughs and then cries.

It's all right, dear, Edith says.

'I know everything will be all right,' Helen says.

'It will get better,' says the constable.

Helen smiles and Edith knows her niece's words were meant for her.

❦

Edith can feel her spirit rising high above the scene, her experience of physical reality becoming fainter, as though she is already entering another realm.

'Edith, it's time,' comes the soothing voice of her angel.

'I can still come and visit, can't I?'

'Yes, but it will be very different because you will have completely left the physical realm. You'll only be able to communicate with those who can reach our dimension.'

'There are other stranded souls who need to come with us. Do you know the ones I mean?'

'The dinner guests?'

'Yes.'

'They refuse to see me.'

'Can't you try again? The new realm has to be better than this perpetual nothingness. I'll call Peter. Peter McNamara, master of Seaview Manor, it is important that you come here.'

Peter walks through the front wall of the mansion.

'Who disturbs my rest?'

'Me, Edith.'

'This better be important, Edith.'

'Oh, it is. May I introduce Yehudiah?'

Peter points at the police cars. 'What are they?'

'It's not important,' Edith says.

'He doesn't see me,' the angel says.

'Peter, could you follow me?' Edith says.

'I'd rather be resting.'

'It will only take a few seconds.'

Edith tells Peter telepathically to meet her at the back of the fountain. They're both there instantly. The angel at the centre of the fountain is glowing in white light.

'Beautiful,' Edith says to Yehudiah. 'Peter, look at the angel in the fountain.'

'I've always loved her. It feels like ages since I've gazed upon her.'

'It has been longer than you know. Now look to the right of the fountain. What do you see?'

Edith smiles at the magnificent angel glowing brightly in a pinky golden light and wearing the purest of white robes, his massive wings testament that he is not of this world.

Peter gasps.

'It can't be. My eyes are playing tricks on me. They are mimicking the statue.'

'No, they are not. This is Yehudiah. Can't you feel his extraordinary love?'

'I can feel something, yes. Peace, calm. Yehudiah, I need proof that you are real.'

Suddenly, Edith sees Peter enveloped in the angel's wings and disappear. Just as quickly, she feels him next to her at the edge of the fountain.

'What happened?' she asks.

'I saw my death. I died peacefully in my bed. But I am alive. It doesn't make sense.'

'It does to me. You loved the house so much you couldn't leave it, even to be reunited with your wife.'

'My wife? Elizabeth?'

At the sound of the name, a woman in her 40s appears next to the angel. She is dressed in a white blouse with a high collar and long brown skirt.

'Peter!'

'Elizabeth!'

The two spirits merge as one and disappear.

'What about the others?' Edith says.

'Look!' the angel replies.

Edith sees four spirits emerging from the house moving towards Yehudiah. They are walking slowly as if in a trance.

The angel opens his wings fully and extends a hand to Edith.

'Edith, it is time to leave Seaview Manor.'

Edith sees a woman she instantly knows to be her mother, a man who is her father and her grandparents beside the angel.

'I am ready now.'

As Edith steps towards the angel, everything loses form and becomes all-encompassing energy of light, love and bliss.

Chapter 26

Mary walks briskly up the hospital corridor and stops at reception. She tries to remember the last time she was in a hospital. It would have been to visit her stepmother on the day she succumbed to breast cancer. She shivers.

Dad can't go yet. He's a tough old guy and we've only just started to get to know one another. He has to come home, where he belongs.

Mary presses a bell and is about to sit on a chair in the quiet room when a male nurse comes through a concealed door and says her name.

'You can come through now. Don't expect a lot. He's in an induced coma to help his body cope with the trauma. We gave him a blood transfusion, but he was very weak. Here he is.'

'Thank you.'

Mary sits in a chair facing the strange man lying in the bed. He doesn't resemble her father. He looks pale but peaceful.

Oh Dad, how could she do this to you? Don't leave me yet. We have so much time to make up for.

Mary rests her head on the side of the shallow mattress and falls asleep.

❧

'Mary?'

Mary feels a hand on her shoulder. She opens her eyes and lifts her head. Her father is looking right at her. She pinches herself.

'Am I dreaming?' she says.

Mary puts her hand up to Tony's rough, wrinkled face.

'No, dear. You're in the hospital.' Tony smiles.

Mary sees natural light through the window and looks at her watch. The hands on the round face of roman numerals show half past six.

'You're awake,' Mary says.

'I had been dreaming that you were being chased by a hairy beast and I was chasing the beast to stop it from getting to you. I woke up when it stopped and turned to face me, ugly thing, holding a kitchen knife. I was so relieved to wake up and see you lying there resting your head on my bed like an angel. For a second, I wondered if we were in heaven.'

'Oh Dad,' Mary gets up and puts her arms around Tony's neck, pressing her face against his. 'We got through it. We're going to be okay. God, what about Andrew?'

A thud of dread crushes her chest.

'I'm sure he's okay. He's a strong lad. You should ask the nurses if you can see him.'

Mary hugs Tony again as a nurse approaches, and she leaves ICU. In the bare corridor she is suddenly overwhelmed with emotion. What if Andrew didn't make it? She sits in the middle of the grey lino and bawls her eyes out.

When a young nurse asks her what's wrong, she doesn't answer at first.

'Here, let me help you up, and we'll get a doctor to have a look at you.' The nurse smiles.

'I'm fine, really,' Mary says. 'I think it's just the shock of a terrible night.' She pushes herself off the floor as the nurse holds her upper arm and elbow.

'Oh, you were at Seaview Manor.'

'That's right. I'm all right now. I just need to see that Andrew is okay.'

'I've come from Andrew Garcia's ward. He's eating breakfast. I'll take you to him.'

Mary wants to drop to her knees and give thanks from the sheer relief, but she is aware of how foolish that would appear. She has already created enough of a spectacle.

She spots Andrew sitting up, his hospital table over his bed full of plastic bowls and cups. His hair is glistening. He is wearing a light blue hospital gown, scoffing down rice bubbles. Andrew sees Mary and gives her a big grin. She responds and the glee is literally pouring out of her – heart, eyes, smile – as if she is lit from inside. Andrew is so handsome – beautiful skin, bright eyes, perfect teeth. He takes her breath away. The fumes of hospital cleaning chemicals are filling her nostrils, but it is love that is overwhelming her. She wants to run to him.

There's no rush. We've got the rest of our lives.

She walks tall, aware of her long strides towards the bed. Andrew's eyes don't leave hers. She feels them piercing her soul. Joyfully, she holds his gaze. Andrew swings the table away from him and holds his arms out. Mary moves her whole body into his for a full heart-to-heart hug, suddenly aware she will dirty his gown but wanting the touch more. She cries into the cotton fabric.

'I'm okay,' Andrew says. 'We're okay. We made it.'

'How is it possible? How did any of it happen?'

'I don't know. But I don't think we'll ever go through anything like it again.'

Andrew's eyes dance as he bursts into laughter. Mary laughs out loud too.

'Keep it down, would you? I'm trying to sleep,' comes the voice of an old man opposite.

Still looking at Andrew, Mary pulls a face that is meant to say 'Well, excuse us for living.'

'You better ring our lovely boss and tell her what's happened,' Andrew says.

'She'll think it's a lie.'

'Until she sees a copy of the police report and my medical certificate.'

'We really need to get new jobs.'

'We do.'

'It's so good you're all right.'

'Mary, I need to know something . . .'

'What?'

'Will you marry me?'

'Yes!' she shouts. 'A million times yes.'

Andrew doesn't say anything, but his smiling eyes and big grin are all the signs Mary needs.

'I think this is the part where you kiss your bride-to-be,' the old man grunts.

Mary leans in and presses her lips against Andrew's plump mouth. The contact is thrilling. She lifts her lips off, opens her mouth and kisses him again. This time there is a surging through her entire body. She is completely in the moment. The world consists entirely of two pairs of lips, and she wants it to stay that way for as long as possible. This is her first kiss. Her first kiss at the age of 27.

Chapter 27

Mary watches Jaclyn through the bars pouring an imaginary teapot and speaking as though she has someone in there with her.

'Do you have sugar?' Jaclyn asks her imaginary companion. 'Well, if you don't want tea, at least have some shortbread. I baked it myself. Come down here. You can't hang up there all day.'

'She's not well, is she?' Mary says to a police officer standing beside her outside the cell.

'Who are you talking to in here?' he asks Jaclyn.

Jaclyn looks past the constable and straight through Mary as though she's a ghost. Mary shrinks back.

'Who's there?' Jaclyn says, then points her nose up to the ceiling. 'Hey, you have to come down and help me.'

'There's someone here to see you,' the police officer says.

'I heard a strange noise. Someone's here,' Jaclyn says, still looking up.

The officer turns to Mary. 'It's no good. I thought seeing you might bring something back, but she's gone. I don't know where, but she's not here!'

'Jaclyn, it's me, Mary.'

Jaclyn jumps back. 'Hey, you've got to come down now. Help me.'

'You're right, officer, I can't do anything.'

Mary follows the young policeman down the corridor.

'What will happen now?' she asks.

'As you can see it's impossible to talk to her. She'll probably need to be assessed by a psychiatrist to see if she's mentally fit to handle the legal process.'

'I'm just glad that awful night is over and I can move on.'

'What do you do for a living?'

'I'm a library assistant, but I'm going to take a holiday and think about what else I can do with my life. I've kept myself locked away for so long, it's time to get out into the world. Maybe become a horticulturalist or give tours of the Botanic Gardens. That's where I had my first date with Andrew!'

'Something good has come out of this then?'

'Yes, I suppose it has.'

The police officer is called away just as he is thanking Mary for coming down to the station.

She walks through the automated glass doors, aware that she is leaving the old Mary White behind and crossing the threshold into a new self, a new way of being.

'Hercules!'

He'll be hungry and frantic.

She turns around to go back inside the police station and use the public telephone in the foyer to ring the hospital and talk to Andrew. But she can't go back. That life ended when the glass doors closed behind her.

❦

The sound of long claws scraping on the glass panel on the front door alternated with desperate meows greets Mary as she walks up the path. She quickens her step. The lawn is overgrown, and several faded supermarket brochures are scattered among the long grass. This doesn't look anything like her neat yard. She opens the door. Hercules pushes past her and then runs back into the house, crying and wrapping his tail around her legs. She puts a plastic bag with groceries down to pick him up and he nudges her face with his cheek, purring more loudly than she's ever heard.

'Did you miss me, boy?'

Clutching him under one arm while closing the front door with the other, she picks up the bag and walks through the hall. She lowers the cat to the floor. He leads her to the kitchen and waits by his wet food bowl, meowing. Hercules goes berserk, pushing his nose into the bowl as Mary spoons the last of the stubborn tuna from the tin.

Outside, Mary surveys her back garden, which she has neglected in all the drama. Moss on the fountain! Weeds around the roses! A strange vine growing over a portion of the miniature carnations! How can this have happened so quickly?

The garden has lost its perfection. And yet there is something wild in this uncontrolled chaos that is beautiful. She will let her father live out his final days and months in the house. For her, it's time to leave this part of her life behind and move in with Andrew. Where would they be happy? Their wild adventure took place in the mountains and by the sea, so where does that leave? The desert?

Mary smiles. As a child she wanted to visit Uluru. It has been a long time since she's thought about that wish, or any other that was hers and not her stepmother's.

What else does she want to do? She holds the old railing and concentrates on not stepping through a broken stair.

I would like to go to the Hunter Valley for cheese and wine tasting . . . climb Mt Kosciuszko . . . buy a new car . . . and learn about the latest books, movies and music.

'I don't want to live in the past anymore,' Mary says aloud as she reaches the top step.

Hercules echoes with his 'let me out' cry on the other side of the door. Mary opens the door and allows her cat to run through to freedom. Suddenly, Hercules stops on the landing as if waiting for a reprimand and then bounds down the steps to the adventures of the forbidden garden.

It's okay. He'll come back for food and loving.

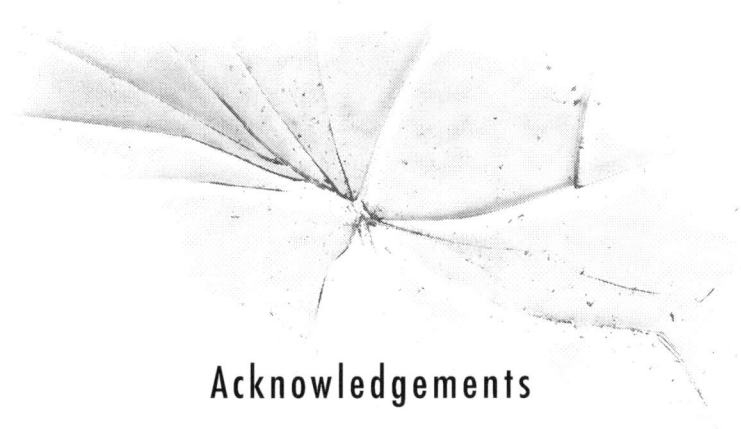

Acknowledgements

This work would not be what it is without the help and support of several people. To my mother, Wendy Laharnar, thank you for believing in this story and encouraging me to publish it, as well as your practical support with several rounds of edits that helped sculpt and refine both characters and plot. To Jessica Perini, I am grateful for your expertise and advice on plot pace, character tension and story structure, which forced me to pull it apart and put it back together and not give away too much too early.

To my daughter, Gabriela Malki, I am buoyed by your love and unwavering support of me and my writing. To Catherine Clifford and Cindy Sciberras, I am truly thankful for your friendship and faith that I had it in me to be a published author. To Emma Yeung, your encouragement on this journey has helped me see it through to publication. Thank you to Jenny LeComte Moritz for appreciating my writing in all its forms – even the early drafts, and to Tony LeComte Moritz for reading a stranger's two bound manuscripts from cover to cover without prompting and saying *The Fractured Woman* was your favourite.

To everyone who read a draft and offered encouraging words including Pamela Thomas, Katie Rogers, Sheryl Storek and Elisha Seiver, I couldn't continue without knowing I have readers who enjoy this story. To Jennifer Edwards and Linda Fletcher, for encouraging me on the self-publishing journey and connecting me with people you know who've done it.

To the judges of The Richell Prize for Emerging Writers, thank you for seeing the potential in the story and the writing to longlist it in 2020.

To the 'team' that worked on the production of the book, you have taken it beyond my wildest expectations. Claire Smith, I am in awe of the hauntingly beautiful cover you created. I love it. Stuart Hipwell, the logo design inspired by Bounty surpassed my expectations and captured his spirit while adding a sense of joy and playfulness. You are a master. Simon Paterson, the combination of your phenomenal typesetting expertise and work on the internal design has created an enjoyable reading experience, and Julie Ganner, your eagle eye helped keep the standard high. David Madden, you showed me my inner diva and helped me emerge from writer to author with your gorgeous photography.

For an emerging writer, and a self-published one at that, every little bit of faith, support, practical assistance and advice helps finish the book and get it into the hands of readers. I am forever grateful.

Natalie Laharnar has been writing fiction for three decades while working in corporate jobs that focus on writing. She was longlisted for The Richell Prize for Emerging Writers in 2020 for *The Fractured Woman*, her debut novel. She lives in Sydney, Australia.

Connect with the author on LinkedIn
linkedin.com/in/natalielaharnar

Manufactured by Amazon.com.au
Sydney, New South Wales, Australia